Perfect Love

Anthony, naked at last, came to her. He slid his warm palms along either side of her lovely face, lifting the long tresses, freeing her body for him.

Lauren felt the covering veil spilling back over her shoulders, was intensely aware of the heat of his body, the texture of his skin, the readiness of his thrusting flesh.

"My love," he groaned, his lips bending to hers. "My own perfect love . . ."

Her mouth yielded to his searching kiss, melting under the honey probe of his tongue. . . .

Her body, too long denied, beat against his. She couldn't remain still, was powerless to keep from urging him to take her, fill her, quell the burning need that tormented her hot, trembling flesh. . . .

Dear Reader:

We trust you will enjoy this Richard Gallen
romance. We plan to bring you more of the best in
both contemporary and historical romantic fiction
with four exciting new titles each month.

We'd like your help.

We value your suggestions and opinions. They will
help us to publish the kind of romances you want
to read. Please send us your comments, or just let
us know which Richard Gallen romances you have
especially enjoyed. Write to the address below.
We're looking forward to hearing from you!

Happy reading!

The Editors of
Richard Gallen Books
8-10 West 36th St.
New York, N.Y. 10018

Royal Suite

MARSHA ALEXANDER

Q

PUBLISHED BY RICHARD GALLEN BOOKS
Distributed by POCKET BOOKS

Books by Marsha Alexander

All Mine to Give
Royal Suite

 A RICHARD GALLEN BOOKS *Original* publication

Distributed by
POCKET BOOKS, a Simon & Schuster division of
GULF & WESTERN CORPORATION
1230 Avenue of the Americas, New York, N.Y. 10020

ISBN: 0-671-45141-3

First Pocket Books printing September, 1982

10 9 8 7 6 5 4 3 2 1

For my brothers
David and Stephen
Durchin
With love and respect

Prologue

The sun was blazing in a crystal-clear sky, bright enough to make polarized glasses a necessity rather than a fashion accent.

Lacking a pair, Anthony DeGiacomo squinted through the rearview mirror of the slightly battered Ford Fairlane and waited for a lull in traffic.

Lauren Wells, watching him, had to smile. Like everything he did, Anthony's attention to the job at hand was concentrated and serious. "You look like a pilot ready to taxi one of those jumbo jets down the runway. Relax, my love. You're not responsible for the safety and well-being of a couple of hundred lives."

"Nope. Just for the most important one, my best girl."

"Your only girl, you mean," she teased, hoping he was aware of the black-and-white that was still visible up ahead. "Come on, Anthony, do we really have to go all the way back to your apartment? It's too cold for a bathing suit, anyway. It'll be nippy on the beach."

"Cold? You call this cold? Listen, you, this is the first

decent day we've had since last summer. The beach will probably be packed with sun worshippers. Those surfers will be out there—"

"Shivering in their rubber suits," she finished, leaning back in her seat while the handsome man behind the wheel made a highly illegal but perfectly executed tight U-turn on Santa Monica Boulevard. "We could just mess around down at Zuma, you know." Zuma was their favorite beach for strolling, but for soaking up the sun and swimming they preferred Venice. "You're pushing the season, you realize. My one full day off this week, and I'll probably end up catching my death of cold."

Anthony grinned. "I just can't wait to see you in a bikini again." He took a left on Vermont.

"Oh, no, not me! Freeze if you want, but I'm just going along for the ride. At least one of us has to stay sane."

Lauren patted the coronet of silvery braids on her perfectly shaped head and slid across the seat until she was right next to his jean and sweatshirted body. "Not that I feel particularly sane on this lovely, lovely day." She put a hand on his leg and inhaled the fragrance of his freshly laundered work clothes, his clean, vital, disturbingly sensual body. It was a miracle to her, this never ending passion he aroused by just being there, the sweet excitement that was generated between them when they were close. She had to remind herself that she was an eminently responsible woman in control of her life when she was away from him. But in his presence, or even just hearing Anthony's voice on the telephone, that fine control melted away and she was ruled by her hormones, a rapid-pulsed teenager all over again.

"I am sane. Away from you." She looked down at his hand that covered hers, feeling its warmth spread from her hand to her arm, into her chest and through her heart. God, she loved this man! She would trade her prized sanity to be with him this way forever, just the two of them. But tomorrow would find them apart again, on their separate treadmills. She didn't actually have to be at work until late in the afternoon, but Anthony would doubtlessly be hunched over his typewriter or his piano as dawn was breaking, forgetting her as he struggled to breathe life into the pop opera he was creating. And perhaps he was the sane one, after all. He was working hard for their future. His self-discipline was necessary, especially now that his big break was at hand. Trained as a classical musician and already critically acclaimed as a classical composer, Anthony now sought a larger audience for his works. He wanted to do what Kurt Weill had done, not only in *The Threepenny Opera* but in the musical comedies he'd written after coming to America: combine serious music and meaningful drama in a popular form. *Evita* and *Jesus Christ Superstar,* the rock operas written by the British team of Webber and Rice, had excited him and pointed him in this direction.

A promising first act had come to the attention of a London based production company that had optioned his work. The advance had been small, but their interest was enthusiastic. The completed opera, to be delivered by the end of spring, could ensure his fame. If his score was approved, casting and rehearsals would begin, with a fall opening in mind.

No, she couldn't be selfish. She had to be grateful for the little time he could take from his work to be with her. Rather than be resentful, she had to make the most of each precious moment.

Anthony glanced down at her as the light turned red, running his dark eyes over her beautiful face with its classic planes, wonderful green-blue eyes and firmly pointed, determined but very feminine chin. Even in the plain tailored blouse and simply cut, matching cream-colored trousers, her long and shapely feet encased in ordinary sandals, she was a stunning, unforgettable woman. That rare kind of woman who had no need of frills to be outstanding. If she were a character in his opera, he would describe Lauren as she looked at that moment—elegant and otherworldly, even in his inelegant car, in her this-world clothing. And when she came to him with her great mass of rippling hair freed from the braid, her seemingly slender body rich with golden curves, her clear eyes narrowed in passion, she was beyond description, as unearthly and irresistible as a sea siren, as potently seductive as a succubus. "Sane or not, I'll keep you," he added, his thickening voice a barometer of the desire her nearness always aroused in him.

She looked back at him through the heavy fringe of her lashes. "The beach seems so far away. . . ."

"It does, doesn't it?" He realized with a start that the irritating horn blast from behind was meant for him. He drove through the now green light and chuckled. "Oh, well. We can always grab a little sun by the pool. After." At the sprawling apartment complex, he parked in front of the entrance closest to his furnished cubicle.

Hand in hand they went inside.

The dream was a good one—the sensuous touch of her young husband's body against her flesh, the gasp of delight, the pounding of her strong heart in response to the ecstatic delight of ardent lovemaking. . . .

As if to capture this remembered embrace, so swallowed by years and other deeds, Alexandra Regis lifted an arm and triggered the pain that had subsided so briefly. The dream burst apart and her eyelids fluttered open.

A faint amber sheen caught her eye, its muted radiance a rippling pool of honeyed light. She tracked it with a feeble spark of the brilliant curiosity that had epitomized her entire existence, a curiosity that was less willing to die than her tired, desperately ill body.

She saw that the amber light was nothing more than the cool water in the porcelain basin by her bedside, reflecting gold from the mellow glow of the exquisite Tiffany lamp shade. Every few minutes the soothingly efficient private nurse would dip a soft cloth into the basin and sponge Alexandra's gaunt face.

The white-uniformed woman then appeared out of the

4

dark shadows, as if summoned by Alexandra's thoughts. The cloth disturbed the reflection, retreated, and was patted gently against the papery forehead.

Alexandra closed her eyes and submitted to the refreshing bath. For a little while, she had been swept to another time, when her skin was soft and pliant, her face beautiful and firm, her body lush and eager. Now she was old and in mourning, grieving for a youth she had wasted with matters of finance and the accumulation of goods. She sighed deeply, felt the pain swell as if to balance the fleeting pleasure of the cool water against her brow.

"Here now, time for your medication. That will ease the pain." The syrupy light glanced off the tip of a needle.

With a grimace of deep distaste, Alexandra waved away the syringe. "No, not yet, Elana. I don't need it yet." She challenged her impending death with the resources built from a lifetime of determination. "Medication! Dope, you mean. Not even the dying are spared from euphemisms, are we? I'm losing my body, child, not my mind." She smiled weakly. "But that's not quite true either, is it? The body takes the mind with it when it goes."

"Easy now, Mrs. Regis. Try to nap a little." Alexandra was both a trial and a pleasure to the nurse, who was used to patients that approached the end by going into the helpless retreat of infantile docility. They failed to stir her emotions as much as this immensely successful woman, who squared off with death and insisted on waging a noble battle with the inevitable.

"Nap? A snack before a feast? An appetizer before the main course? Time enough for sleep, Elana. Sleep enough for all time. Thank you, no, I'd rather not nap just yet." She caught her eyelids as they began to lower and snapped them open. It was tempting to fall back into her dreams, to allow herself to be young again, to be Brett's passionate bride. But there was something she had to do. "It's too dark in here. Throw open the curtains, child!" she ordered huskily. The tone of command in her own voice motivated

5

Alexandra to rouse herself fully, leaving the past in its dusty tomb of time. After all, hers had been a life of doing, not one of musing over past pleasures.

The heavy Italian broccato *drapes were drawn. The hazy sunlight of a mild Los Angeles winter afternoon filtered into the opulent bedroom. "Another smoggy day," the nurse commented. The mere thought of leaving the mansion's purified air caused her to cough.*

"Perhaps. But beautiful. So damned beautiful."

Embarrassed by her increasing sentimentality, Alexandra turned away from the window. "My papers, please, Elana. Now that there's some decent light in this tomb." Her eyes swept over the magnificent bedroom suite, aware that the luxurious artifacts surrounding her made it the tomb of a queen.

Biting back a reproach, the nurse obediently wheeled over the desk trolly, adjusting it so that its flat surface slid neatly over Alexandra's blanket.

The elderly woman motioned the nurse to her own desk in the outer room with an impatient wave of her fingers. She needed to think, and to think best she needed to be alone.

She squinted at her watch and realized she had less than an hour until Norm Lowenthal and his crew would arrive. It was exciting, but terrifying, what she proposed to do. The business world—her world—would be aghast. They would assume Alexandra Regis had lost her wits in the final hours of her life. Even Norm, her old friend and trusted attorney, had advised against this radical change in her will.

"Few people in your position are completely at ease with those to whom they must pass the reigns of command, Alexandra," he had reminded her at their last meeting. "Kings have died in torment at leaving their own sons at the helm. It's only natural that you, with no heirs of the flesh, feel deflated over passing the scepter to an executive board you dislike and distrust. But at least they are professionals and

know the hotel business thoroughly. Isn't there an answer other than the one you have in mind? To leave all this to a complete novice . . . little more than a girl, really . . . and one you've never even met!"

Alexandra had smiled at the concern in her attorney's voice.

Yes, this Lauren Wells was a novice. And yes, she was little more than a girl, when viewed from the vast, telescopic distance of old age.

"Really, Alexandra, you can't be serious?"

The old woman had managed a dry, tired laugh. "Have you ever known me to be frivolous? Now listen carefully. Here's what I want you to do. . . ."

The Lazy Bull had a good reputation, not only for its excellent char-broiled steaks and honest drinks, but also for its comfortably plush atmosphere and friendly service. Charlie Anderman and Larry Fay, the Bull's owners, had set the tone of the Echo Park establishment, but Lauren knew that she was the force behind its successful, trouble-free maintenance.

Charlie and Larry, in appreciation, had made her general manager and deferred to her good judgement without question. They were exceptionally generous toward their key employees, and, in Lauren's case, their generosity spilled over to her family. They looked the other way when her stepfather, Parker Fields, drank too much and created an occasional scene at the bar, or when Shelly Noble, her stepsister, argued too vocally with a boyfriend or used the Bull as a watering hole at which to pick up new men.

There was an unspoken understanding between Lauren and the Bull's owners. Somehow they had sensed that Parker and Shelly were part of the package that came with Lauren—much in the way another employer might accept annoying phone calls from a valued employee's spouse or a spotty attendance record caused by one's sickly child.

Lauren herself took the tremendous sense of responsibility she felt toward Parker and Shelly more or less for granted. It was an old and polished role. As a child, she had been her mother's ally, the two of them working together to keep the family on an even keel. It filled her with pride to know she was so much like her mother—strong, sensible, quick to cover for Parker or Shelly or finish a task one of them had begun.

In the same way, Parker and Shelly were alike in their weaknesses. Shelly floundered, tended to be self-indulgent and daydream through life. Parker could never quite hold things together for himself. Even before his wife's death, he drank a little too much and dreamed impossible dreams.

"It all balances out, darling," Lauren's mother had once told her. "A family is like a single organism. You and I . . . we're the head and the spine. Dad and Shelly, well . . .they're the heart and the funnybone and the adrenaline. Everybody has to do whatever it is he does best and take up the slack in areas that someone else can't handle. Together we create a good balance and a tight family unit, with everyone doing as much as he can."

Lauren reflected on her mother's words often, and usually they made great sense to her. After all, she had obviously come into this world graced with the ability to be supportive.

But there were other moments when she felt a cold stab of resentment, when she was tired of carrying Parker and Shelly, no matter how much she loved them. She would become weary of their continual draining of her emotions. She had better use for the countless hours she spent talking Parker out of a binge and repeating the same advice to Shelly—advice that was solicited and then ignored. And she had better use for the money she paid to keep Shelly's son in a private school and to help Shelly or Parker with other debts. Even Anthony didn't understand why she felt it her duty to assume these problems. He refused to see that if she didn't help, no one would. She was the only cushion

Parker and Shelly had against an uncaring world; she was a survivor and survivors had to lend a hand. Her mother had lived by this philosophy, and she was her mother's daughter. How could she do less?

It was hardest when she calculated exactly how much she could have contributed to the wedding fund, the money she and Anthony had agreed to save before setting a wedding date. Then she would wonder at her mother's words, and Anthony's impatience with her generosity would haunt her. But the same question nagged at her and the answer was always the same—if she wasn't there when they needed her, what would happen to them? They were all the family she had. If they drowned, so would she.

Parker and Shelly were both sitting at the end of the bar when Lauren started her shift. "Well, it's nice to see the two of you together," she said with a trace of reprimand in her tone.

Her father and sister almost never came to the Lazy Bull on the same night, which never failed to amaze Lauren, because both spent considerable time at the restaurant since she became its manager.

"I take it you've made up?" She kissed Parker on the cheek and gave Shelly an affectionate hug. She had reason to feel pleased; any reconciliation had to be the result of the hours she had spent convincing Parker to be less judgmental about Shelly's lifestyle, and her pleading with Shelly to be more discreet about her lovers in front of Parker.

"We think of it more as a temporary truce," Shelly said, giggling and putting down her gin fizz. "A halt to the hostilities."

"See, here's the way it is, kid, ya see," Parker mugged, doing his usual poor imitation of Edward G. Robinson. "This guy over here, this Shelly guy, she don't know how to handle the boss, ya see?"

Shelly rolled her big blue eyes. "All this time, and he doesn't even know I'm not a guy." She shook her torso like

9

Charro. Her spectacular body, encased in a sweater cut low enough to alarm any father, left no room for doubt about her gender.

Their father laughed, before he noticed that Lauren barely smiled. He nudged Shelly. "Cut it, kid. Don't go embarrassing your sister at work."

"She's not embarrassing me, Dad," Lauren said quickly, even a little sharply, because she knew down deep that she was embarrassed. The Lazy Bull catered to a quiet dinner crowd, and while the bar pulled in the usual number of singles on the make, decorous behaviour was the general rule. "I've just got a few things on my mind tonight. I guess I don't feel much like laughing." The bartender handed her an order sheet. She scanned it and handed it back. "Thanks, Roger."

"My pleasure," he said, but his eyes were glued to Shelly's skin-tight sweater. "Any old time."

"I think the gentlemen at the other end of the bar want you, Roger," Lauren said softly. She let her annoyance show. Shelly had a lifetime of Rogers behind her, was, in fact, living with a Roger type at the moment. She didn't need another one.

"Wanna talk to the old man?" Parker said.

"What, Dad?"

"About what's on your mind? Is anything wrong? Did you have a fight with Anthony or something?"

For a moment, Lauren was sorely tempted to answer Parker's questions in depth. Yes, she wanted to talk to someone. No, nothing was wrong, exactly. She certainly hadn't had a fight with Anthony. But here she was, thirty-two on her next birthday, and as far away from marriage as ever. . . . "No, Dad, thanks. It's nothing. And Anthony and I had a wonderful time yesterday. We mostly just sat by his pool and talked. Everything's fine. It's always hard to get rolling again after a day off." She kissed Parker's cheek again and started for the kitchen. "See you later."

She waved to a regular customer and skirted the dining

room, eyeing the entrance and coat check room to make sure that everything was in order. The light coming through the stained glass in the massive door cast a churchlike amber glow over the thick tweed carpeting. The richly stained wood gleamed in the soft light. In the background was the tinkling of ice cubes and the hum of relaxed conversation.

It was a familiar and well-ordered atmosphere. Lauren felt the tenseness slip away, and she smiled to herself. It was frequently like this after she had spent a whole delicious day and an evening with Anthony. They were so right together that she felt a lingering sadness because the idyllic hours had to come to an end. She didn't begrudge the time either of them spent at their work. What bothered her was that at the end of the day's work they would not be together.

At times like this, when the ache of separation was most painful, Lauren saw no value in Anthony's insistence that they put off marriage until their financial situation was secure. She understood his practicality in this matter. She even applauded his good sense. Sometimes she even congratulated herself on the good fortune of having a man who was not only a sensitive artist, but methodical and level-headed.

But when her body was still tender from his passionate embraces, as it was today, she cared little for the harsh realities of money. She just wanted to be able to know that at the end of her shift she could go home to the man she loved. Right now. Tonight. Not when and if his opera gave them the security he insisted they have. Perhaps at heart she was the true romantic, not he. What about that line in the marriage vows "for better or worse, for richer, for poorer, in sickness or health, till death do us part"?

Lauren, still smiling, walked on to the kitchen to begin her usual inspection tour. Lovely as the vow was, both she and Anthony had seen good marriages crumble under economic pressures. They had waited this long; they could stand it a little longer.

It wasn't as if she didn't love working. She had a terrific

job. Only her salary check reminded her she was not a full partner in the Lazy Bull, so great was her control over the business. She liked that. She had always been ambitious, thrived best under pressure. It was a pleasure to know that this restaurant reflected her capabilities. But with the pleasure coexisted a certain degree of heartache.

Parker had once owned two restaurants, which someday would have been hers. She had worked hard in them and had done a spectacular job of making them quality operations. Under her hand, their little family chain would have grown. Right now she might be in charge of four or even more restaurants, with money problems a thing of the past. She knew she had the energy and skill to go on to bigger challenges. Part of her personal grief was that she had allowed that golden opportunity to slip away. It hadn't been her fault, of course. As her mother's illness had dragged on, the medical bills had mounted alarmingly. Parker had panicked and had sold both the restaurants. Even in her grief, Lauren had seen other alternatives. They could have sold off just one of the restaurants and gotten by. They might have negotiated a loan. Or taken in a partner. It hadn't been necessary to bail out completely, as Parker had insisted on doing.

For Lauren, it had been like running a successful race only to be abruptly shoved back to the starting line. It wasn't fair. It wasn't right. Worst of all, it hadn't been necessary.

She, the strong one, hadn't been strong enough. She hadn't stood up for what she knew she could do. Her one big chance, and she had failed to save the restaurants. She had failed to save herself. Parker had been frantic to sell, and she, unable to bear increasing his agony, had not insisted on holding on to all she had worked so hard to achieve.

The Lazy Bull's kitchen was in perfect order, producing beautifully cooked and arranged dinners with a minimum of fuss and chaos. Lauren had implemented many of the time and energy saving methods in this kitchen she had used in the family restaurants. Pleased, she headed back to the

12

entrance foyer and reminded herself that she was young, she still had her life before her. Others with the same hot ambition she felt, the same dreams of creating something more substantial than what they had, also endured losses before moving up in the world. Anything could happen. She would never give up and neither would Anthony. They would eventually triumph. One of them would make it before long. Anthony's opera would make them rich. Or that sweepstakes ticket Parker had coerced her to buy might just be the lucky one. . . .

Lowenthal, himself old and infirm, had been understanding of Alexandra's misgivings over her original will, but helpless to suggest a more palatable solution than the bizarre plan she had in mind.

Being almost as tied to the Regis empire as Alexandra herself, the old lawyer had conducted an extensive investigation of the young woman to whom his friend and employer was determined to bequeath almost all of her worldly holdings. What he learned did not greatly relieve his mind. True, this Lauren Wells had a Master of Business Administration degree from a small local college, she had done well at school, she'd been a credit to the two restaurants owned by her stepfather, lost due to the enormous expenses caused by Lauren's mother's terminal illness and not by the young woman's mismanagement. She also seemed highly esteemed by her current employer at the successful supper club of which she was general manager. But this background in no way prepared her for what Alexandra had in mind— total control of the prestigious Regis-Royale hotel chain, a network of fabulous international establishments, with branches in every major city in the free world!

Troubled, Lowenthal had trekked across the city to the Lazy Bull to observe Lauren Wells covertly. He found her lovely and charming, apparently capable and not easily ruffled by the demands of a capacity crowd of impatient diners. Even so, he had tried to reason Alexandra out of what he considered an impulsive and most likely disastrous whim.

"When Brett died, he worried about your coping with his large estate by yourself, Alexandra. And that was before the Regis-Royales were anything more than a handful of mediocre hotels. He thought that big business should be in the hands of experts. But he went ahead because he knew you had competent help available."

"So you'll help her," Alexandra had replied. Then she'd laughed at Norm's concern, because they both knew that she alone had built the Regis-Royale empire to what it was now. She had done it, every bit of it, using more cunning and business instinct than any man she knew, including her husband. She had created a legend from almost nothing.

" 'I inherited it brick and left it marble,' " she quoted, applying Emperor Augustus' comment on the city of Rome to herself and her hotels. And now she was supposed to turn over her creation to her enemies. No. She had found a solution, one that frightened her, true, but one that also filled her with hope and peace.

Alexandra Regis was a woman who always paid her debts, and she had one outstanding debit on her private ledger. It was a secret she had kept for fifty years, and now it was time to settle up.

In college Alexandra had had a disastrous affair with a young man whose name she could now barely recall. But at the time it had shattered her. She had believed herself pregnant, and when she told the young man he had fled. Alexandra was the only child of an influential, society-conscious family, and she had believed that when her condition and the fact of her lover's departure were discovered, she would be scorned, ridiculed. In her panic, she had impulsively attempted to take her own life by swallowing a handful of phenobarbital tablets one night. She had been rescued by her roommate, Barbara Madison, who not only salvaged her life but also her mind, calmly talking her out of her

*panic and pledging to help her through her ordeal, if she
was indeed pregnant.*

Her fears had been in vain—she was not pregnant and,
thanks to Barbara, no one ever knew about Alexandra's
suicide attempt or the loss of her virginity. Barbara had
appealed to Alexandra's lover and had won his pledge to
be discreet about the affair. Alexandra had vowed to repay
her friend, but when the time for repayment came some
months later, Alexandra had done nothing to help. Barbara
was forced to withdraw from college due to financial re-
verses in her family. Alexandra could easily have afforded
to pay Barbara's tuition and expenses, but she let her friend
go with only a tearful parting. Buried in those tears was
a trace of relief. With Barbara gone, no one would ever
know her secrets.

Through the years, Alexandra often thought about Barbara with love and regret. She continued to vow to repay
her roommate someday, but she was loathe to stir up the
dust that now covered her past. She met Brett Regis, fell
in love, buried herself in the role of wife and pushed Barbara
out of her mind.

In time, her idyllic relationship tarnished. Brett had an
affair and was careless enough to let news of it reach Alexandra. He became absorbed in business, and his young
wife, disheartened about love, matched him in acumen and
eventually surpassed him entirely, becoming the force behind the Regis wealth. She was still a comparatively young
woman when Brett died, and she threw all the bottled passion she might have invested in a second marriage into
making something unique out of the hotels they had owned.
She became shrewd and single-minded, with a rare talent
and love for empire building. She trusted only herself and
gambled with an open hand on her hunches. It paid off
magnificently. Everything she touched turned to gold.

As long as she remained in active control of the hotel
chain, everything went according to her plan. But cancer

was blindly democratic, cutting down the mighty as well as the weak. The board of directors of the Regis-Royale hotel corporation, of which Alexandra was chairperson, was in the process of pressing for a merger she detested. The investment corporation that sought the merger wanted to add a line of motels and to divest the hotels of their graciousness and old-world elegance in favor of slick efficiency in order to squeeze even greater profits from the operation. Alexandra, herself a thoughtful student of the J. Paul Getty method of business administration, well understood the wisdom of being cost-conscious and profit-minded. But she also knew that her hotels had something unique to offer in a world being consumed by plasticized pap. Her hotels were islands of genteel comfort and personal service, with all the trimmings and pampering that her affluent, quality-conscious patrons demanded. True, they would settle for less if that were all they could get, but Alexandra was convinced that she and her investors would continue to show the same handsome profit as ever by remaining faithful to the high Regis-Royale standards, by resisting this campaign to modernize and distort.

Even so, the slick statisticians from the investment corporation had constructed dazzling graphs, and Alexandra was no longer positive that enough of her people shared her opinions and concerns. Quality seemed less important than numbers. She knew that if money talked, big money shrieked the loudest. The Regis-Royale was a vested interest business with stock owned by its employees through an excellent profit-sharing program, and the board of directors, who owned a considerable portion of that stock, could not help but be influenced by the statisticians' graphs.

After she was gone, if her will wasn't rewritten immediately, they would stampede to merge with the investment company. Before the flesh had completely fallen from her bones, her beloved Regis-Royale chain would be turned to a mere shadow of what she had created. She would have *left no monument, no mark. The vast fortune she had ac-cumulated would buy her no immortality.*

Only by leaving her money and hotels to one individual could she hope to circumvent or delay the merger. But there was no one. The only family she had—and that by mar-riage—was Earl Regis, Brett's nephew and only living rel-ative. He was currently general manager of the Beverly Hills Regis-Royale and a member of the board of directors, but only on the strength of his blood tie and Brett's deathbed wishes. Alexandra would have gotten rid of Earl long ago if not for respect for her late husband. He was lazy and inept. His sole ambition was his expectation that Alexan-dra's death would give him more power, which he would no doubt misuse.

And, in truth, the way her present will read, Earl would benefit as would a score of other top executives, each in his own way as undeserving as Earl.

In the moments between drug induced sleep, she had sought a solution to her problem. It seemed so unfair. She had sacrificed a normal life of love and family for her business. It pained her to think she had made a poor choice when it was far too late to do anything about it. She won-dered how other old women spent their last hours. How did they count their wealth? In the accomplishments of their children, the sustaining contentment of their marriages, the smiles on the faces of their grandchildren? Traditionally, men created dynasties, women families. Men built monu-ments, and women gave those monuments meaning. Men accumulated great fortunes, and women inspired the great accumulaters.

Alexandra had been ahead of her time. She had done the accumulating, the monument building. And now the marble would be crushed back to brick.

Alexandra had begun to think more and more often of Barbara Madison. The time for paying outstanding debts was at hand. But a quick investigation revealed that Barbara *had died two years before. Alexandra thought herself eternally condemned to the gross imbalance on the credit and debit sheet in her mind. Frustration burned hotter than the pain of the cancer eating away at her organs. How could she endure this debt?*

At that point, almost a week before, Alexandra had turned her attention to Barbara's only child, Lauren Wells, now a woman.

Alexandra removed Lauren's photograph from the desk trolly and studied it again. The lovely, fine-featured face with the clear green-blue eyes, strong chin and beautiful teeth displayed in a good smile pleased her by its resemblance to Barbara, although her roommate's daughter was far more beautiful. A silvery coronet of braids, not brown and not quite blond, coiled neatly on the graceful head, lent a faintly European effect that went becomingly with Lauren's unpainted beauty. It implied a confident self-image, so rare in this day when young women all seemed to have been stamped out of the same trendy mold. There was intelligence in the lovely eyes, determination to the chin.

The idea had come at once. She tasted it as if it were a choice but unfamiliar delicacy. Why not take the ultimate gamble in a lifetime of playing hunches? She was dying, but she had yet to lose her Midas touch.

Why not leave everything to Lauren Wells?

What could she possibly lose that wasn't already lost?

Leaving everything to Barbara's daughter would tie up all the loose ends. It would strike a vengeful blow to those who were happily anticipating Alexandra's death, thinking it would give them control of the Regis-Royale stock. It would be an effective vote of no confidence to the board members who were waiting for the moment when they could sell her out and merge with the investment corporation. It would serve as a severe rebuke to Earl Regis who had long ago milked dry his family connection to the conglomerate. She would repay Barbara by making her daughter one of the wealthiest and most powerful women in America.

Why not?

There was something poetic and emotionally satisfying in the fantastic idea of making a total stranger her heiress. The photograph of this particular stranger, who so closely resembled her mother, implied character strength which did not exist in the people more logically in line for such an inheritance. Barbara had been good and wise, quick to find truth and perceive hidden motives in people. Why shouldn't these traits have been passed on to her daughter? Norm Lowenthal's investigations revealed that Lauren wasn't entirely unequipped for the job. Yes, she would be overwhelmed at first. She might bow out of the business entirely and simply enjoy her newfound wealth. But she also might take active control of Alexandra's empire. At the very least, putting this outsider in charge would keep the board of directors in limited power, unable to alter the direction of the hotel chain without the new majority stockholder's support. That alone would be worth this desperate move. It would buy time, throw a wrench in the works. Her enemies would have to rally and begin their campaign all over again.

Lauren Wells was admittedly an unknown factor, but Alexandra's other alternatives were known. And despised.

Her mind made up, Alexandra had told Norm Lowenthal her decision was final and set up today's carefully planned meeting.

"Elana," she called, aware of the wheezy, fragile sound of her own voice. It reminded her of a rusty piece of machinery, grinding to a halt. "When Mr. Lowenthal and his staff arrive, please show them right in. Wake me, if necessary."

"Yes, Mrs. Regis."

While she waited, Alexandra turned to the window and luxuriated in the golden light. The smog had burned off, leaving the sky as clean and clear as her conscience. Then her contented smile faded as her mind drifted of its own accord back to her earlier dream. Should she have a clear conscience? What was she really about to do to the lovely young woman with the sweet old-fashioned coil of braids? In effect, Alexandra had traded away her personal life, one that might have been rich in love and passion and children and fun for the harsh and often bitter struggles of big business and power. What would this Pandora's box of wealth and intrigue do to Lauren Wells, who at this moment might unsuspectingly be cradled in the protective arms of a lover?

Alexandra cast the question out of her mind. The answer was in the future, a future to which she had no claim.

Chapter One

It was one of those perfect, rare smog-free days in Los Angeles, the kind that Lauren usually celebrated with a picnic in Griffith Park, a walk along Zuma Beach or even just by coaxing the first tan of the season by floating on a raft in the pool outside Anthony's apartment.

Not this year! she thought, fighting down a gigantic wave of panic as she dragged her eyes from the broad expanse of tinted window to gaze numbly around the luxurious office suite that now belonged to her. *Maybe never again!*

For a terrible moment, Lauren felt as if she might be sick right in front of these superbly tailored, immaculately groomed men. She set her lips tightly and took a deep breath. She refused to disgrace herself and risk the veiled amusement of this select group. She desperately wanted Anthony by her side, holding her hand, steadying her with his delicious sense of humor. She might be intimidated by these men, but Anthony would be merely amused. He would say they were too perfect, too in control of themselves, like distinguished robots in a Disney exhibit. They were robot-like, smoothly gliding about their business, conferring with each other in low voices, scribbling urgent notes, going over paperwork, lighting cigars or cigarettes, refreshing themselves with sips of coffee or iced tea from expensive hotel cups or glasses, each of them wearing exactly the right kind of expression for whatever he happened to be doing.

Well, she would have to be a robot, too. At least for a little while. An actress playing a part. She could do it. She could do anything. After all, she had just been awarded the starring role in a miracle. Anything was possible after that.

She caught her reflection in a beveled glass mirror and was grateful to see that she looked cool and businesslike, that her face was also properly composed. Other than a touch of mascara to bring out her long lashes and a dab of gloss to freshen her mouth she wore no makeup, so there was nothing to smear or run. Her hair was never a problem. It was so long that hanging loose it was a silvery mane tickling the backs of her shapely calves. But after years of practice she could weave it into a braid so neat it almost seemed artificial. She wore it her usual way, spun into a coronet around her head, the front trimmed into graceful bangs to soften a face she thought too strong, too determined.

The sleek tweed suit she was wearing was exactly the right touch. Anthony had helped her select it especially for this important meeting of the board. It had been fun shopping for it with him.

He had teased her about the effect she was trying to achieve. "Wear your hair down and we'll get you a leopard-skin sarong. Throw 'em off-guard. They won't know if they should salute or ravish you."

"Who?" she'd teased back. "You, or the board of directors?"

That's when it stopped being fun, because Anthony had tightened up, the smile freezing on his handsome face. "Don't expect me to treat you any differently than I always have, Lauren. No matter how that meeting turns out to-morrow."

She'd been surprised by his reaction, then angered by it. She turned from the suits she'd been considering to gaze at him, as always a little bit amazed by the way his presence affected her. It was more than his wonderfully carved features that excited her, or his lean, beautifully muscled body. Other handsome men had wanted her, had made elaborate efforts to incite in her the wild emotions she felt just by Anthony's nearness. But there was an intensity in this man that canceled out the fire she had seen in other men. It was more than his immersion in his creative work. It was as if the sweetness and passion of his music were a part of his being. He somehow managed to master the intensity, but it leaked out of his soulful eyes. He reminded Lauren of a young Orson Welles, at times moody, at times charming, but always magnetic and unashamedly himself.

"Anthony," she'd said warningly, forcing herself to be immune to his effect on her, "where did that come from?" They knew each other too well to play games. They had been engaged for almost a year, lovers for almost two.

He shrugged. "I'm a little tense. This thing has hit me hard, too, you know. I guess I'm terrified that all this money will change us." He laughed then and pulled her to him.

She could feel the heat of his body through their clothing, and quickly she turned their attention back to the rack of expensive suits to hide the surge of fear his words generated in her. She wouldn't let anything change between them— he was too precious to her.

Remembering, Lauren wondered why she had been disturbed by the incident. Naturally her new inheritance would take some getting used to on both their parts. It was . . . breathtaking, to be abruptly lifted out of obscurity and relative poverty to find herself immensely wealthy, her face in every newspaper and magazine. They were both still stunned by the news, reeling from it as if from a blow, unsure if they should kneel and give thanks, or grab an armload of cash and hide away on some desert island until they adjusted to the shock. Of course Anthony would fear that Lauren would expect him to treat her differently. They'd hardly had a moment alone since the reading of the will five days ago.

Someone put a glass of iced tea within her reach and Lauren took it gratefully. She had to forget about Anthony for the moment and concentrate on what was happening now.

This was a tiny lull in the meeting, the natural pause between the presentation of one piece of business and the preparation of the next. It was the first time since Lauren had stepped into this office that she had not been the focal point of interest to the nine men assembled around the expansive and highly-polished conference table. She held the frosted glass of tea and smiled her thanks to the one secretary present, then took advantage of the moment to look out again beyond the tinted windows. Her windows. In her office. Would she ever get used to it?

All of Beverly Hills and Westwood were laid out at her feet, with the columns of Century City gleaming metallically in the distance. The view was spectacular from the top floor of the stately Beverly Hills Regis-Royale hotel. She'd never seen it before, although the popular Rembrandt Room, also occupying the top floor, offered the same view for the price of a dinner or a drink. Shelly had been to the Rembrandt Room several times with various lovers and husbands. Even Anthony had brought his parents there for dinner when they'd visited from New York. She'd had to work and was unable to join them until later that night—in a coffee shop. Had Anthony called his parents to tell them, or had they read of her inheritance in the papers? What would Anthony have said?

Hey, folks, remember Lauren, the girl I'm going to marry? Remember that fancy hotel I took you to for dinner? Well, Lauren owns it now. Yeah, and dozens more just like it.

She turned from the window. The view was making her giddy.

"All right now, if everyone is ready . . ." prompted a large, balding man with that orange tan Lauren always associated with the rich, although these days anyone could afford an indoor tan.

He was Alden Chambers, senior partner of a large international law firm, one of the four members of the board who was not otherwise connected with the hotel chain.

"One more moment, Al, please," objected the younger and impressively handsome François Lamogue, the Regis-Royale's vice president in charge of international affairs. He turned his attention back to whatever he was writing.

The low-key conversations started up again. Lauren envied the board members their casualness. She glanced over at Norman Lowenthal for reassurance. He was the oldest man in the room, frail and slightly stooped, and the only one not on the board. Not even the excellent cut of his gray suit concealed the ravages that time and disease had wrought on his ailing body, yet there was a strength and clearness to his dark brown eyes that encouraged Lauren and helped her put this meeting and these polished men in perspective. He had informed Lauren of her fantastic inheritance. In a way he was like the family physician who had delivered her, because he had brought her to a new life, a life so far beyond her dreams that she had yet to grasp the full significance of it. She had spent most of the past five days with Mr. Lowenthal and she felt he was almost a friend, especially at the moment.

The old man smiled back at her, one weathered eyelid drooping in a conspiratorial wink.

She and Anthony had spent three hours in Mr. Lowenthal's office the evening before, going over the agenda for this hastily called meeting of the board of directors of the Regis-Royale. If Anthony hadn't been at her side, asking the right questions, going over the answers step by step, Lauren might have bolted from the office. She understood that she had an enormous choice to make at once. She could elect simply to enjoy her newfound wealth and leave the

25

direction of the hotels to more experienced hands, or she could boldly jump headfirst into the meeting, and claim the chairperson seat that Alexandra Regis had held until her death.

"You're under no obligation to involve yourself with the business, Lauren," Mr. Lowenthal had told her. "There are no strings attached to your inheritance."

"But Mrs. Regis did say that she hoped I'd take over her seat as chairman . . . chairperson of the board?"

"Yes, she did. That was her desire. But you are not bound by her wishes. Alexandra was an amazing woman, as hardheaded in business as they come. But she was also something of a gambler with an uncanny knack for picking winners. She played hunches like any confirmed gambler, and her hunch was that you might just want to take up the reigns she was dropping. Of course, she had specific reasons for wanting this. . . ."

Lauren had listened attentively while Mr. Lowenthal explained the proposed merger to which Alexandra Regis had been vehemently opposed. "My becoming head of the board would kill the merger?" she asked uncertainly.

"Not necessarily. The final decision would be yours to make. Mrs. Regis knew that it would take time for an outsider to understand the issues at stake, which would certainly delay the merger for a good while. And she hoped that you would eventually agree with her that the merger would be a mistake."

"Is it a bad idea?"

The elderly lawyer chuckled. "That, young lady, might well be something for you to decide on your own. Alexandra believed it to be a very bad idea indeed."

Anthony stepped in then, waving his hand through the air as if clearing a chalk board. "Mr. Lowenthal, as I understand it, Lauren can have everything, all the houses, the private hotel suites, the stocks and bonds and liquid assets, the . . . everything, and not be involved in the actual running of the Regis-Royale empire, right? She doesn't have

to do a thing except spend money for the rest of her life?"
He shook his head. It was almost more than he could digest.

"Absolutely correct, Mr. DeGiacomo. Mrs. Regis had
no natural heirs. She felt a great sense of gratitude to
Lauren's mother, for reasons explained in the will. It was
an emotional debt and this is her way of settling old scores."
The attorney was obviously enjoying himself. "Would you
like a dollar figure on your inheritance, Lauren?"

"Not quite yet. I might faint away." She already had a
good idea, and the figures devastated her. In one form or
another, her personal fortune now ran into astronomical
numbers. She couldn't cope with it all. There were a million
questions she wanted to ask. On the top of the list was a
big *why me?* She had been as surprised as everyone else
present at the reading of the will to learn that her mother
had once saved Alexandra Regis's life when they were
roommates in college. Lauren had known that her mother
and the famous Mrs. Regis had roomed together for a few
months before Barbara had dropped out of school, but her
mother had never put special emphasis on the friendship
and certainly never hinted that she had played such a key
role in Mrs. Regis's life. Every once in a while her mother
would talk about how she and Alexandra—then Alexandra
DuPar—had gotten the best of a pompous professor or
outmaneuvered some overeager beaus. For this reason, Lauren always read articles on the hotel millionairess when they
appeared in *Newsweek* or *Time*, and more than once she had
secretly wished her mother had maintained her friendship
with Alexandra Regis. But her mother had never been one
to look back.

Before Lauren could say anything else, Anthony was
fiddling with his watch and suggesting that there was no
need to worry about the meeting then—let the experts handle the business, Lauren would soon become an expert
herself . . . at spending money. "I'm sure she has a great
latent talent for it," he had teased.

His response rubbed Lauren the wrong way and she had

to force the expected smile. Is that all he really thought of her, that she was the kind of woman who would be content to lead an idle, pleasure-seeking life? Sure, it would be wonderful, having whatever she wanted. But not twenty-four hours a day. It would be like existing on a diet of candy alone. Even the most delicious chocolates would eventually sicken the stomach. She had worked every day of her life, and work, doing a job well, was important to her.

But it was more than that. Once before, she had been given a chance to realize her ambitions with Parker's restaurants and she'd allowed the opportunity to slip away from her. She had vowed never again to allow such a thing to happen, no matter what. It wasn't only the money. She had talent and a vast amount of untapped energy. The control of a small chain of restaurants was exciting, but to oversee a hotel empire! To be tossed the shiniest brass ring of all and not grab for it! No, she couldn't step aside. To do so would invalidate a life of precious dreams.

"I'm sure I can spend with the best of them, but I haven't decided about this yet, Anthony." She had kept her voice cool. "I admit that I'm completely unprepared to fill Mrs. Regis's shoes, but I can't say that I'm not excited about the opportunity that's been dropped in my lap. To guide a world-wide chain of hotels . . ." It took her breath away. "I'd have to learn from the bottom up," she said, her mind racing. "I'd need help, lots of help."

Norm Lowenthal studied her quietly for a moment. "You have some interest in filling Alexandra's seat then?"

"I know it sounds preposterous," she said quietly, with dignity. "But I'm a career woman with a business degree. It's like just passing the bar and being invited to become senior partner in your law firm, Mr. Lowenthal," she said with a grin. The attorney was the senior partner in one of the most prestigious law firms in America. "You can understand why I'm not so ready to let this opportunity pass me by."

The old man looked agitated. "There's so much you

would have to learn. . . . Of course I'd be at your disposal, just as I promised Alexandra I would. But my doctor insists that I take it easy. There are others, of course, who could guide you. . . . A good secretary would be vital. Too bad Linda Rogers quit. She was Alexandra's right hand. But possibly, she'd be willing to work with you, help you train someone. You would have time to learn, I suppose. . . ." He'd lapsed into a debate with himself, fretfully taking both sides.

Anthony had been staring at her quietly, ignoring the ramblings of the attorney completely. "But why, Lauren? Why ask for problems? Big business is murder, you know that. You'd be a lamb out there among the lions. God knows, you never have to work again."

Lauren had felt a great sadness then. "You don't understand, do you? It isn't just for the money, Anthony. It's what I could do! Just think of it! To be able to shape the policies of an enterprise like the Regis-Royale!" She was vital, alive, intelligent. What a thrill it would be to become one of the lions herself.

Norm Lowenthal looked over at the couple. "It's an enormous job, young lady."

"I can learn! I'm an excellent student, you'll see," she insisted energetically.

The old man smiled. "You don't have to convince me, Lauren. This isn't a job interview, you know. You are the major stockholder in the company. You have merely to demand your right to chair the board, and no one can squeeze you out of it. If you're sure that's what you want . . ."

Ignoring the troubled look on Anthony's face, Lauren nodded. "Yes. It's what I want. If I can't learn, I'll step down and let someone else take over. But I want my chance first."

"Very well. Then here's what we do tomorrow . . ."

Remembering all Mr. Lowenthal had said the night before, and feeling grateful that the elderly lawyer was at the board meeting with her, Lauren lifted her glass of iced tea and silently toasted him in return to the exaggerated wink. She noticed immediately that the exchange had been observed by the only other woman present in the office, Christina St. Dennis, personal secretary to Earl Regis, general manager of this particular hotel, and a member of the board. Chris had been commandeered to act as minutetaker for this emergency meeting, a job normally held by Alexandra Regis's longtime secretary, Linda Rogers, who had quit immediately following her employer's death.

Lauren tried to interpret Chris St. Dennis's expression, but the lovely face revealed nothing. Except for a certain noticeable spark in her arresting, almond-shaped eyes, the secretary might have been another perfect robot, tastefully garbed in a beige Lanvin suit, her dark hair caught up in an impeccable chignon at the back of her sleek head.

At a signal from Lamogue, Chambers began to speak once again. "The main purpose of this meeting, as we all know, is to fill the seat vacated by the death of Mrs. Regis. I know that several of you are in favor of putting the name of James F. Reardon, Jr. to the stockholders at the meeting directly following this one. I believe that Jim Reardon would be an excellent choice to chair this board. He's proven his ability as Vice President in charge of finance for the Regis-Royale corporation. Strong financial leadership is the name of the game these days, and I can't think of anyone stronger than Jim. Are there any other names to be presented to the stockholders at the next meeting?" Chambers looked around the office, smoothly gliding his eyes past Lauren as if she wasn't there.

This was her signal. She cleared her throat as much to draw attention to herself as to relieve the tension mounting in her. Lauren had rehearsed the short speech half a dozen times during the night, but now that the moment had arrived she was petrified. She told herself that it didn't matter as long as she didn't let her nervousness show. *Be a robot,* she told herself sternly. *You can do it!* "I don't think it will be necessary to present names to the stockholders, Mr.

Chambers," she said evenly, pleased and relieved to find that her voice wouldn't give her away. "I intend to fill Alexandra Regis's seat."

The silence was marred by a quick intake of breath, but Lauren didn't look up to see who had made the sound. She kept her face serene during the silence which stretched on and on.

Alden Chambers was about to say something when a young woman hurried into the room and whispered in François Lamogue's ear. His face clouded over and he stood up.

"Excuse me. I'll only be a moment. Some trouble at the Tel Aviv Regis-Royale." He followed the messenger out of the office.

The other men seemed grateful for the interruption although Lauren caught several remarks about the frequency of trouble in the Middle East recently.

Mr. Lowenthal leaned over to say something, but the real estate developer—was it J. D. Hollenbeck? No, S. D. Hollenbeck—beat him to it. "What does a pretty, young thing like you want with such a stuffy job?" He had a Western twang to his voice, and his smile was fatherly, even kind. "Don't tell me some smart young fellow isn't taking up your time in better ways—if not, the boys today don't hold a candle to their fathers' generation."

It was difficult to resent this patronizing attitude as much as it deserved to be resented, because Hollenbeck managed to toss out the offensive thoughts in a winsome, even charming manner. "Women today can have a social and a business life, Mr. Hollenbeck," she countered, noticing the cold, calculating eyes that belied the paternal smile.

"Have you seen the view yet, Miss Wells?" Mr. Lowenthal waited for her to get up, then guided her lightly to a distant window, his hand on her elbow.

The office was immense. The conference table was in a separate alcove that could be closed off by louvered doors, leaving a rectangular office dominated by a massive desk behind which was the window with the best view. But once they reached it, the attorney didn't take the time to so much as glance at the huge slice of city below them.

"You're doing fine, Lauren," he said softly. "I wanted to rescue you from Hollenbeck. He was responsible for the initial approach by the investment company that wants the merger. I suspect he'll get the contract to build the motels, if the merger is effected. Hollenbeck put up some of your newer hotels. Reardon is strongly in favor of the merger. He's a good man. The value of your stock would be sure to rise with him at the helm. But he was diametrically opposed to Alexandra's position on the issue. His judgement is sound, and I believe he'd be an asset to the board, but not as chairman, at least not with the merger unresolved."

Lauren looked over at the people grouped around the conference table. There was so much to know. So many hidden motives. Mr. Lowenthal had assured her that she had only to establish her position as chairperson of the board and president of the corporation for now. Then she could take things one at a time, get down to learning her job. Anthony had been right—she was a lamb among lions. She could feel the resentment and antagonism in the room, all directed at her. She was an outsider, an unknown. She had inherited something she didn't deserve to have. Any of these men had to believe themselves more deserving and capable of filling Alexandra Regis's shoes than she. At the very least, they would want her out of their way so that they could manage the corporation in their own way. It angered her.

"Have you ever read any of Kurt Vonnegut's books, Mr. Lowenthal?"

"Reading is on my top priority list for my retirement, young lady. No, I don't believe I have."

"A lawyer in one of his books once observed that during that mystical moment when great wealth is passed down from its creator to an undeserving and therefore unconsciously guilty inheritor, there's a golden opportunity for clever intermediaries to syphon off some of the fortune for themselves." She smiled. "I feel like this is one of those moments. I may be a lamb, but these lions will have to scratch damn hard for their meat. I may not be the best person for this job, but I'm all that I've got. I'll get better."

Lowenthal laughed delightedly, years seeming to fall from his worn features with the outburst. "How could I have doubted Alexandra's talent for choosing winners? Get back over there and give them hell, Lauren. I'm behind you every inch of the way."

Lamogue reappeared just as Lauren slid into her seat. "It is resolved. A terrorist bomb threat in the hotel. Two young Arabs were apprehended by the Israeli soldiers, but it was only an empty threat." He took his seat.

Alden Chambers turned to Lauren. "I believe you were speaking, Miss Wells?" He regarded her darkly. "Do we understand that you wish to replace Mrs. Regis as chairperson of the board? I'd like to advise you that this is not an honorary position. It requires a great deal of expertise." He kept his voice pleasant, but his words were a direct insult to Norm Lowenthal, who would have been bumblingly inept if he hadn't already informed Lauren of this fact.

"Mr. Lowenthal has explained the position in depth, Mr. Chambers." She fixed a cordial smile to her pretty lips. "I realize that I'll need the guidance, experience and best wishes of all of you in the uphill struggle ahead of me. I'll need to learn the hotel business inside out. It will take time, and meanwhile I intend to make no changes. Everything will continue as it is now, the way Alexandra Regis left it. I have no objection to Mr. Reardon joining the board as suggested, but only as a member, not as its head."

Hollenbeck rose to his feet, two dark smudges of red mottling his flaccid cheeks. "This board doesn't have the authority to elect a new chairman!"

Smiling because most of the charming Western accent was now gone from his speech, Lauren nodded at the real estate magnate and took a leisurely glance at her watch.

"That technicality will be taken care of within the half-hour, Mr. Hollenbeck. At the stockholders' meeting. The stockholders will of course vote in the new chair*person* of the board of directors, and the board will then name the new president of the corporation. Since I hold seventy-two percent of the stock, the vote is—as I know we all agree—a mere formality." She paused to let her words sink in, noticing that at her emphasis on chair*person* the formerly fatherly Hollenbeck had thrown her a murderous look.

This was not exactly the speech Mr. Lowenthal had given her, the one she'd practiced over and over. That had been a modest little announcement of her rights. But she could feel the lawyer's delight in how she had handled herself. She was also aware that one other face in the room was semaphoring congratulations with the twist of a lip and the lifting of a brow. Lauren turned to Chris St. Dennis and returned the smile. At least she had one ally in this foreign camp.

Still retaining a trace of the smile, she turned to the eight members of the board. "Now that that's settled, shall we move down the hall to the stockholders' meeting? I have a great deal to do yet this morning."

She stifled an excited giggle until she was alone in the office with Mr. Lowenthal.

"Round one," he said with grave amusement, "is all yours."

She refused to think about the rest of the battle right then.

Chapter Two

Although it was barely five o'clock by the time she reached her apartment, Lauren was so exhausted that she considered going right to bed. It was cool and dim in the small one bedroom apartment in the Silverlake area. A bird was cooing a warning to Tuxedo, her fluffy gray-striped kitten, on the tiny patio beyond the dining nook.

Lauren felt a strange sadness as she looked through the patio door with its many panes of colored glass. The apartment was a find at under 400 dollars a month, and she had labored to make it really attractive and homey. Soon she would be leaving it behind. There was a big, beautiful mansion in the exclusive Holmby Hills section of Beverly Hills that was all hers, fully staffed and awaiting her arrival. There hadn't even been any need to leave the Beverly Hills Regis-Royale—she had a suite there, also, for her use at any time. She still had almost three full weeks rent on this apartment, not to mention a last month's credit, but what did that matter now? She was so rich that money meant nothing any more.

The kitten gave up its grandiose quest to bring down the bird that was almost his size and likely far better equipped for battle. He pawed daintily at the patio door to be let inside so he could greet his mistress properly.

She unlocked the door and scooped up the little animal, nuzzling him under her chin. "Hi, little hunter. Hungry, huh?" She wasn't fooled by his effusive greeting. She deposited him on the tile floor she and Anthony had installed themselves only a few months earlier. The kitten promptly set about delaying his own dinner by bumping against her legs as she tried to open a can of cat food.

Holding the can at arm's length—she detested the pungent fishy odor—she prodded the kitten out to the patio to his dish and water bowl. She fed him carefully, not wanting to stain her new suit. Not that the suit mattered, either. She could get a new one. She could get a dozen new suits, if she wished.

Lauren left the cat to his feast and sank into the red canvas butterfly chair under the old avocado tree whose branches shaded almost all of her patio. She was sorry that she had promised to visit her stepfather in the evening. Anthony would be coming for her in a few hours. She would have liked to be alone with Anthony tonight. There was so much to settle, so many plans to make. But she hadn't seen Parker since she'd been summoned to Alexandra Regis's house—her house—for the reading of the will. She had talked to him several times on the phone, but he wanted to see her. Shelly would probably be there, and the four of them would quietly celebrate this amazing thing that had happened to her. To all of them, really, because she could deny nothing to her stepsister, stepfather and the man she loved. Parker and Shelly were ecstatic. Why wasn't she?

But she was happy, wasn't she? How could you not be happy when you'd gone to bed poor one night and had awakened the next day to learn that you had been given everything you could possibly want—and more. Wednesday night she had been like everyone else she knew—worried about the future, exhausted from a hard day's work, dreaming about getting out of the rat race. She remembered driving home on the freeway in her faded little Toyota and spotting an Excalibar nosing out a vintage Rolls Royce. She wondered about the owners of those luxury vehicles, and why a special few had in abundance what others only craved.

And now she was one of those few, and not even by any effort on her part. She should be shouting from the rooftops with joy. Instead she was moping on her postage stamp sized patio. But everything had a price. She could have the mansions and hotel suites, but she'd have to give up this little apartment which she'd fixed so painstakingly, where she'd made such wonderful love with Anthony, where she'd been so happy.

Would things change between Anthony and her now? She wouldn't change. She wouldn't let that happen. But her money might change him. Money had been a problem between them before. But always the lack of it.

The worst argument they'd ever had had been about money. Anthony had turned down a commission to compose a score for a television special, not wanting to take time away from his opera. If he'd accepted the work, they could have gotten married right away. Lauren had accused him of not wanting to marry her at all.

"I want to marry you, Lauren. I want to wake up in the morning with you in my bed. Sometimes I wake up in the middle of the night aching for you. Then I want to say, the hell with everything, let's get married. But I've seen what the lack of money has done to other marriages, and I won't let it happen to us. But I won't compromise my work for money, either."

Their angry exchange had ended in an all consuming embrace. When they were together, no matter what happened, it was impossible for them to stay out of each other's arms.

But the argument and the reconciliation had left them no closer to acquiring the nest egg they had agreed upon almost a year earlier. Lauren squirreled away as much of her salary as she was able, but with Shelly and Parker so dependent on her there was always some unexpected expense. And Anthony was living on what was left of the money he'd been paid for the two scores he'd written for the prestigious Marwood Symphony and the option money from the British production company. So there was little enough for him to spare.

Sometimes they had made up stories for one another, pretending there had been a windfall that would have permitted an immediate marriage. In their fantasies it hadn't mattered if the money came from Anthony's opera or Lauren's career or a fairy godmother. But since the fairy tale had become a reality there had been no plans for a wedding. Why hadn't the subject been mentioned yet? Lauren knew that she wasn't being quite fair—they were still in shock, and there hadn't been time to talk about anything other than the inheritance. What was holding them back? They loved each other. She wanted to be with him forever. There had been no other men in her life since Anthony, and none before that had really mattered. And she knew the same was true for him.

A gentle wind fanned the fat avocado leaves. Lauren took a deep breath of the unusually sweet air and her mood lightened. In the place of her earlier exhaustion, she felt eager to be with her family—although it would be nicer to be alone out here with Anthony, perhaps making love under the stars on the daybed tucked between two mounds of night-blooming jasmine.

It had been almost two weeks since they'd been together like that. But there, too, Anthony was the reasonable one. Much as he desired her, he firmly resisted the temptation to let intimacy become a habit between them. He seemed to feel that unless he kept a tight check on his passion for her, it would overwhelm them both.

She shivered, although the breeze was warm. The thought of being erotically overwhelmed, swept out of her-

self for a little while was tremendously appealing. Her fingers longed to stroke Anthony's muscular chest, to feel the
delicious weight of his body pressing down on her. He made
love as if he were coaxing a special music out of her soul,
infinitely patient, immeasurably gentle. And then, with little
warning, he would be a fire burning out of control, claiming
her over and over again while she clung to him helplessly,
eager to merge into the storm at the center of his being.
During these rare moments Lauren felt as if she could give
up the world for this man, and she knew that he shared her
feelings. But such emotion also frightened him. His opera
required the same kind of passionate involvement, and he
had to remain faithful to his work until he had gotten from
it what he wanted. Only then would he be free to take a
bride of flesh and blood.

Tuxedo had become bored with his gluttony and began
to rub against her ankles for attention. Lauren stroked his
furry body absently, her mind far away. She couldn't help
wondering if money was really the only thing that stood in
the way of her marrying Anthony. He had his music, and
now she had taken on an unexpected career that would drain
her energy and gobble up great bites of her time. She should
have been eager to leave the management of the hotel chain
to the experts and opt for a deliriously luxurious life. Then
Anthony would have all the time in the world to work on
his opera, and she could be there to lend a constant ear,
give encouragement, be a sounding board. But she didn't
want to live in the shadow of his greatness, much as she
believed in him. She wanted something important for herself.

The day had gone surprisingly well. She had handled
herself admirably, under the circumstances. She was a little
drunk on her success. Both meetings had come off without
a hitch. She was officially the chairperson of the board of
directors of the Regis-Royale corporation, and president of
the organization as well. Her name and picture would be
in every major paper and magazine in the nation. She hadn't

expected the changing of the guard of a conglomerate to be so exciting. It had been almost sensual, the tight excitement in the conference room when the assembly of fifty stockholders, along with the board of directors, formally elected her to their highest offices. They'd had little choice, of course, but that hadn't made it less thrilling.

She had taken her first step up in the world, and it was the step of a giant. She had Alexandra Regis to thank, a woman she had never met. She hadn't told Norm Lowenthal how she felt about Mrs. Regis's avowed desire for her to take over in her place. She hadn't even shared her feelings about that with Anthony. Lauren wasn't sure she could put it in words. She didn't deserve such confidence, but she was very touched by it nevertheless. She desperately wanted to show herself to be worthy of what she had been given, and competent to sit in Alexandra's chair.

The antagonism she'd felt from the members of the board had not deterred her. In fact, it had only served to sharpen the intoxicating challenge of taking active control of the hotels. With a start, Lauren realized how glib she had been at the first meeting today, suggesting that with only a little help and time she could do the job she had insisted on taking. In reality, she didn't know where to begin. It couldn't have been more confusing if she'd agreed to take on all 172 Regis-Royales personally, doing everything from the bed-making to the cooking to the baggage carrying herself. Her degree from Landover College and her experience at the restaurants were not sufficient preparation for what was ahead.

But she had acquired an ally today in Chris St. Dennis. Between the two meetings she had made a quick call to the personnel department for her records. She was surprised to find that the lovely young woman had an MBA from Harvard and had been employed as Earl Regis's secretary steadily since her graduation.

"Jobs are hard to come by," Norm Lowenthal had commented dryly when she told him. "There are many young men and women working beneath their level." Then he'd chuckled. "Well, well, well. An excellent . . . hunch, Lauren. You and Alexandra may have more in common than she'd guessed."

Satisfied that Chris's background and experience merited it, Lauren invited the dark-haired beauty into her office and offered Chris a job as her assistant.

Chris had accepted without hesitation. "Earl Regis won't like this," she'd said with a decidedly impish grin. "But I do."

Indeed, when Lauren had informed the general manager of her piracy, she'd seen him struggle with himself to disguise his resentment. But the new chairperson-president was firmly the captain of the ship, and she had already beaten back one attempt at mutiny that day. Earl Regis was not one to try where others had failed.

With or without Chris St. Dennis, it was going to be a long, uphill struggle with enemies at each step. Starting tomorrow, she would bury herself in her opulent office and begin the toughest educational program of her life. But that was tomorrow. Right now, she didn't want to think about it. Or about moving to Holmby Hills. Or about the unspoken tension between herself and Anthony.

She would think, instead, of something to eat. She was starved! Big business was tough on the appetite, something she would have to watch. Although she looked like one of those lucky women who remained enviably thin no matter what she ate, it wasn't so. Her body had a tendency to soak up calories, and she exerted a great deal of self-discipline to keep her svelte shape even though clothing made her appear light and lithe. She could have made a success of modeling, if her interests had gone in that direction, because whatever she wore took on a touch of elegance just by being draped over her delicately boned body. But stripped naked there was a surprising fullness to her high-nippled breasts, a womanly roundness to her limbs and belly, hips and buttocks. There was a firm cushion of flesh between her finely developed skeletal structure and her velvety textured skin. Her figure was a constant source of delight to Anthony who had initially expected angles and sharp ridges and instead had discovered an animallike suppleness. Lauren was grateful that she possessed such a sensuous, lush body, and she guarded it carefully from deterioration. She exercised every day she could, not only because she wanted to look her best but also because she had always been a busy person and was terrified of being slowed down by illness or excess weight. She also made a conscious effort to feed on health foods, and had almost reached the point of convincing herself that she preferred such food to junk fare. Almost. Not quite. At the moment she could have eagerly devoured a hamburger with all the fixings, a mountain of greasy fries and a couple of gooey chocolate bars.

Resisting such urges, she carried Tuxedo back in the house, deposited the kitten on his little wicker bed in the corner of the living room, washed and made herself a snack. She knew Parker would be sure to have a feast ready on their arrival—he was a marvelous chef and loved to feed people. But this was an emergency, so she settled for a small banana cut into a half cup of plain yogurt to tide her over.

It was a delight to sip her herbal tea and spoon her yogurt, with the obligatory sprinkle of wheat germ, in the tiny breakfast nook where she took most of her meals. A few rays from the dying sun penetrated the avocado boughs and the little patio looked enchantingly sweet through the stained glass door. She managed to fend off her earlier melancholy, but it wasn't easy. She was sorry that Anthony wasn't coming for another hour. Much as she had looked forward to being by herself after the tension packed day, she was now inexplicably lonely.

She was rinsing her dish and spoon and mulling over the fact that she never had to wash another dish as long as she lived, unsure if she loved or hated the thought, when she heard the tapping on her door. "One minute!" She turned off the water and hastily wiped her hands on a towel. It was too early for Anthony, but she welcomed any distraction.

She opened the door to a large bunch of bright red roses fringed with lacy ferns, all wreathed in stiff florist's paper. "Oh, Anthony!" She took the bouquet and threw her arms around his thick warm neck. The powerful scent of the flowers tickled her nostrils, and she was aware of an onslaught of conflicting emotions. Her first response was a familiar agitation—they had agreed to be very practical about money, and expensive roses came under the heading of unnecessary indulgences. Then, almost but not quite instantly, she had to shove aside such considerations. All that was in the past. There would be no more scrimping and saving. She was free to react, as any woman might, to a surprise bouquet of roses. "Oh, Anthony," she repeated, pressing herself to him, having to stretch to fit her head into the cradle of his neck.

"Hi, princess. Posies for the new president and chairman of the board." He kissed her soundly, then stepped back to pull several newspapers from under his arm.

Lauren tried to take the papers, but her hands were too full. She hurried to the sink instead, giggling because she didn't own a single vase big or elegant enough to do justice to the roses. She never thought she would have use for one. Hastily, she filled a glass pitcher with water, peeled off the green paper and unceremoniously dumped the flowers into it, hurrying back to Anthony, who was seating himself at the little table where she'd just been daydreaming over her yogurt.

He'd already folded back the papers to expose her picture and the brief article under it. It was a good picture of herself in the suit she was still wearing. She looked amazingly fresh and businesslike, though it must have been snapped after the draining meetings. Her eyes skimmed the story about her ascent to the head of the Regis-Royale company and board. "Wow!"

"You haven't seen anything yet, chairman Wells. The

Examiner must have assigned their society editor to the story."

"Chairperson," she corrected, grinning. "No, make that chair*person*." She quickly gave him a briefing on her run-in with S. D. Hollenbeck.

He clicked his heels together under the brightly enameled yellow table. "Chair*person*," he amended with an exaggerated toothy German accent.

"Make that *chayer*person, partner," she advised, tugging at an imaginary cowboy hat. Then she scrambled for the other paper. "Let me see!"

She read this one more slowly, torn between excitement and embarrassment at the emphasis on her beauty. The reporter had seen something more than a newsworthy business event in Lauren's story. He turned it into a Cinderella fantasy come true, stressing Lauren's unexpected elevation from the masses to her present position of power and plenty. He enchanted his readers by holding up Lauren as proof that at any moment and through nothing more solid than a sentimental whim, any wish can come true. In the close-up shot that accompanied the story Lauren looked charmingly quaint, like a fairy-tale maiden. The perfect, oval face under the ash-brown coil of braids, the bright eyes and aristocratic features belonged to a long-lost princess who suddenly has been touched by a magic wand and restored to her rightful place in the palace.

"You're going to be very famous, Lauren," Anthony said softly, reading along with her. "Are you ready for it?"

"I don't know," she answered gravely. "Are *we* ready for it?" Her laugh was shaky. "Oh, hell, this is just one romanticist having a little fun." She waved a slender hand, dismissing the reporter.

"Don't be too sure, baby. This is the kind of stuff people love. The world will make you its sweetheart for a while. They like to believe someone's pulled one over on the big guys. And you make one fine example." He lingered over the picture that had captured Lauren's unique beauty so well. "It's *Rocky* all over again, with the people rooting for you from the sidelines and the guys at the top trying to grind you into the canvas."

"Stop. You're scaring me," she protested, attempting to sound carefree and hearing her voice come out strained and thin. She had wanted to give Anthony a minute-by-minute account of her big day, but now she wanted to put the whole thing out of her mind. "Why are you so early?" She pulled the papers from him and dumped them on the window box.

"Sorry to see me?" He outlined her firm chin with an ink stained fingertip.

She got up and moved to him, pulling his curly-haired head to the curve of her belly and tightening her arms around his neck. "I never wanted to see anyone more in my life."

He pressed his lips to her hip and even through the layers of clothing she could feel the warmth of his breath. An electric shock of desire ignited her blood.

His big hands encircled her, moving with a soothing firmness over her back, her waist, the round crescents of her firm bottom. "Easy, Lulu. It's okay," he promised, evoking a smile with the use of the cartoon strip pet name she detested. "Little Lulu, I love you-ou, yes I do-oo."

She ran her fingers through the dark curls and traced a line to the warm flesh of his cheek that no amount of shaving could make absolutely smooth. "Let's stay here tonight, Anthony. Let's call my dad and tell him we'll make it another night. I want to be with you, darling." She knew that some of her intense desire for him was due to the tremulous uncertainty she felt, but it didn't matter. She needed him close to her—his lips, her body, his tense masculinity. She wanted him to consume her, blotting out the rest of the world and its confusing demands.

Very gently, he pushed her away, the bruising strength of his fingers confessing an equal need to which he refused to succumb. "We can't, honey. Shelly called me this afternoon. She's desperate to see you. I think she and that bum she's living with have been at it again, although all she could talk about was you. And Parker's been cooking all day." He looked up to meet her eyes, his own glazed with unmistakable passion. "We'll get away early, I promise. We need to be together tonight."

She stopped to press her lips to his, anguished by everything that was keeping them apart.

"You're right. Damn you, Tony, you're always right." Having gotten back at him for the "Lulu" by using the diminutive of his name, she was able to smile and put her desire on hold for a few hours.

"Tony? Tony?" he postured, lifting his hands in despair, "what kind of a name is that for a composer of operas?"

Lauren suddenly remembered that she'd not asked him a single question about the progress of his work that day. It was usually the first thing out of her mouth. "How's it coming?" she asked, glancing at his watch to avoid his eyes. "Damn, it's later than I thought. I'd better shower and change. I feel grubby. You have no idea how soiled you can get in a spotless board room. I might as well have put in a day in a coal mine. Emotionally, I mean." She bit her bottom lip in shame. She'd finally asked about his work, then rambled on about herself without giving him a moment to answer. "Talk to me while I get ready."

If the rest of her apartment were small, her bedroom was little more than an airy closet, just large enough for a double bed and a dresser. But it opened onto the patio, and the adjoining bathroom was comparatively enormous.

She hurried to her room, only partially closing the door behind her. It was something she always had to think about, leaving doors open or closing them when she undressed with Anthony in the apartment. She felt self-conscious about her nudity unless they were going to bed together. Their feelings for each other were so volatile that Lauren sensed she would be taking unfair advantage of his hard-won control to do so. He tried to keep himself in tight emotional check, holding back until he had a legitimate claim on her. And for all his sophistication, she suspected that some part of his sensitive being wanted her pure and virginal for their wedding night. When she had once mumbled a love-struck yearning for her lost virginity so that she might have presented it to him, he had softly laughed. "That's the ultimate beauty of a good woman, Lauren. She has the power to spiritually renew her virginity as often as necessary for a man she sincerely loves."

It was the most sexist remark he'd ever made, and she'd loved him for it.

As always, she compromised by leaving the door casually ajar and undressing beyond his line of vision. She might indeed have to wait until they were legally mated to find out just how much passion was in that crazy, beautiful Italian heart, but she was willing to bet that it would be worth the wait. "So did you fix up that rough spot at the end of the second act?"

As he talked Lauren hung up the suit that now exuded the heady aroma of the Premier Enfant perfume she'd sneaked off to buy on her way to Beverly Hills early that morning. She slipped out of the raw silk blouse and underthings that were almost as new as the deliciously expensive perfume. "Miss Gotrocks," she whispered to the naked vision in the mirror, her fingers flying through her hair, pulling pins and carefully loosening the braid. "Sounds good," she encouraged as Anthony talked. He loved to talk to her about his work. It helped him define problems, find solutions.

Every ritual with her hair was complex enough to drive another woman to take up scissors, but Lauren had worn her hair at its fantastic length for so many years that she could do every chore in her sleep, if need be. Even though her hair was so long, it was delicate and not overly thick for a single braid, but let down after a day of being woven together it unfolded like a cloak of oceanic waves. If she so desired, she could mask her entire body in its strands, every movement an intoxicating preview of the tantalizing body underneath. Perhaps later, she thought, she would surprise Anthony by appearing like this right after they returned from Parker's apartment. She'd tease him a little until he could stand it no more. He loved her with her hair down, but she'd rarely worn it loose and never during love-making. Hair might be a woman's crowning glory, but hers could strangle two passion-swept lovers. . . . She could hardly wait to put it to the test.

"Don't be so impatient, Anthony," she called to him before going into the bathroom for her shower. "The classical operas weren't so awfully strong on story line, you must admit. Even the Italian operas." Lately he had had the same thing to say about his work. He had musical ideas in abundance, but the libretto limped along. He'd even talked of scrapping his story line and starting from scratch, reworking the music to fit the new characters and events he would devise. "Wait," she called before he could fire back a volley in defense of Verdi and equivocate about Puccini. "I'll be out in ten minutes."

She rarely washed her hair before going out for the evening, but perhaps, for once, Anthony would spend the entire night with her. She knew she wouldn't want to get out of bed tonight for anything less than a blazing fire. She quickly washed it, poured on a rinse and used her wide-toothed comb to gently loosen the tangles under the shower's needle-like spray. Finished, she soaped her body, unable to keep from thinking of the way Anthony's hands would feel on her. She let the water hiss over her back, amused by the power of her mind. It shied from thinking about the ramifications of her newfound fortune and stubbornly clung to fantasies about lovemaking. But it was easier for her to cope with passion than unlimited power. She thought of the disbelief on the faces of the board members that morning and made a face at the cracked bathroom tile wall. She would learn to cope. Tomorrow. Tonight was for her and Anthony.

Chapter Three

Flashbulbs popped and people shouted excitedly. The packed apartment smelled like the kitchen of an overachieving gourmet before the Silver Spoon award dinner. But all Lauren saw when she and Anthony arrived at Parker's was the living comedy and tragedy masks on the faces of her stepfather, who was grinning broadly, and Shelly, who was dissolved in tears.

"Oh, Lauren!" The curvy body in the skintight, low-cut red dress pressed into her. "I'm so happy for you," her stepsister whispered in her ear.

Lauren hugged the shorter woman and planted an affectionate, worried kiss on Shelly's heavily rouged cheek. "What's all this?" she asked Parker, whose wide smile revealed most of his suspiciously perfect teeth.

Before he could say anything, the others in the room rushed forward.

"Good show, Lauren!"

"Atta girl! Congratulations!"

"Surprise! Oh, Lauren, I still can't believe it's true!"

"That makes two of us," she squealed, exchanging cheek kisses with Dolly Berger, a waitress from the Lazy Bull.

"Did we surprise you?" Parker demanded in his usual hardy bray. He put a strong arm around her waist.

Lauren kissed him, disturbed by the weight he'd lost in the scant two weeks since she'd last seen him. "What's the matter? Haven't you been eating your own cooking?" she whispered.

"Not to worry," he answered fondly, releasing her to pat Anthony on the shoulder and give his guests a chance at her.

"You rat!" Lauren shouted to Anthony as he walked away with Parker. "Not even a hint!" She looked down at her simple outfit of a tan and brown long sleeved jersey and jeans. "Not even a lousy hint!"

He laughed and her friends joined in, tickled that their surprise hadn't been ruined.

"You look great," Charlie Anderman, one of the Bull's owners, insisted. He gave her a hug. "I've been interviewing replacements for you all day, and I'm so angry about losing you, I almost didn't come tonight."

"Oh, Charlie," she sighed, aware that he was only partly joking. She stifled a little pang of jealousy of whomever he would eventually hire. She had liked her job and those with whom she had worked. The contrast between them and the men on the Regis-Royale staff was enormous.

Larry Fay, Charlie's partner, elbowed him aside and scooped Lauren into the bearish embrace befitting his massive frame. "Don't listen to him. He's just worried that he'll have to leave the track for work now and then, since you won't be there to do everything." He looked at her in awe. "We plastered your newspaper clippings all over the Bull. Gives the place a little class."

Trish Fay gave Lauren a kiss. "And that doesn't go for you, Larry, I suppose?" she teased her husband. "A little work will do the both of you some good, to say nothing of our bank account." She smiled warmly at Lauren. "I'm so happy for you, honey."

"Thanks." She looked at the supercharged faces of her

family and friends and felt slightly disoriented, as if she were at the tail end of a dream and couldn't decide if she wanted to awaken to reality or not.

She was propelled to a long table laden with a truly astonishing assortment of foods, from hot delicacies in chafing dishes to creamy bowls of dips in a rainbow of colors. A separate table groaned under its burden of cakes and other desserts. Once again she had to stop herself from thinking about the expense of such a feast. She hadn't realized that money had been such a large part of her life before. Only with its new abundance could she begin to understand how the lack of it had regulated everything else.

Lauren grinned at the irony. How often had she said that she'd love to be so rich that she'd no longer have to think about money? Not true, she was discovering. If anything, money would have to take on a far more important role than ever before. Wealth did indeed carry responsibility, and great wealth even greater responsibility. As head of the Regis-Royale corporation she was responsible for the salaries of each and every person connected in any way with her hotel empire. Worldwide that could run into tens of thousands of people.

Feeling weak, she sipped at a glass of champagne and let Parker personally fill a paper plate for her from his mouthwatering buffet. "Oh, no! I'll need a new wardrobe after this," she wailed, accepting the heaped plate.

Parker waved his hand with cavalier abandon. "So? You'll buy a new one tomorrow. Ten new ones."

Before Lauren could respond, he was called away to give a list of the ingredients of one of his masterpieces to a guest. For the moment, she was alone with her food while everyone else swarmed the buffet or the small open bar on the other side of the large room. Spying a Morris chair her mother had loved, she snaked her way through the mob, gratefully sinking into its faded red cushions. The chair was next to one of the stereo speakers, and the clear sound of Charlie Parker's horn pushed the party noises into the background.

Her stepfather was a jazz buff and had a large collection of rare old records. Music and cooking were his greatest passions since her mother's death. Listening to the plaintive cry of the saxophone caused Lauren to wonder how much time Parker had been spending locked up in the large but rather bleak apartment with such melancholy company. This party would do him good, however much she wished he'd have saved it for a time when she was more prepared for merrymaking.

"Eating already, huh? It figures. Good. I bet you didn't have time for more than a handful of trail mix or alfalfa sprouts today," Anthony accused, coming to her side for a moment on his way to the buffet table.

She bit into a little ball of pastry oozing with a flavorful cheese filling and shook her head fondly at his familiar shot at her health foods. Anthony was typically Italian in his attitude about eating. He was happiest when she was stuffing herself, as if there were no connection between the body he adored and her usual spartan fare. But her self-discipline was no match for Parker's kitchen wizardry, and she tore through her plate like a starving lumberjack.

At last, she set her plate aside and looked up again. Everyone was still eating except for Parker, who was urging still more food on everyone in sight. Anthony was holding his barely touched plate and bending a sympathetic ear toward Shelly, whose heavily made-up face showed sadness and pain.

She was surprised to see Shelly talking to Anthony in the intense, desperate way that she usually reserved for Lauren. It pleased her, though, that her sister had developed such a high degree of trust in Anthony. But Shelly was her sister and her responsibility, and after she'd digested her dinner a bit she'd find out what was going on. Lauren already suspected that Shelly had had another fight with Dick, her current lover, with whom she'd been living for several months. He was another of the long list of Shelly's unsuitable men who brought her nothing but unhappiness.

Sometimes Lauren thought she was wrong to be footing the bill to keep Brian, Shelly's twelve-year-old son, in a private school near San Diego. Being responsible for Brian might be just what Shelly needed. It might make her think twice about the men she chose. On the other hand, she hated the thought of her nephew living in such an unstable home. When Brian had been too young for school Shelly had gone from the boy's heartless father to a second and equally destructive husband. Having the child to care for hadn't stopped her then, and Lauren had no real grounds for suspecting it would now. As always Shelly sidestepped her way through a life that was bewildering and filled with things that went bump in the night. And Lauren would continue to try to smooth her way. Even though Shelly was the older of the two, Lauren had always been the rock, and the blond sister a delicate reed, perpetually ravished by the changing wind.

Lauren smiled over at Brad and Linda Everly, musicians who were good friends of hers and Anthony's, wishing they'd come over and talk to her. Linda, an ardent feminist, would love hearing the details of her tangle with Alden Chambers and S. D. Hollenbeck. Brad would probably think she was crazy not to take the cash and run since he was anything but a workaholic himself, but his teasing would be good-natured.

It suddenly seemed odd to be sitting there alone while surrounded by friends. Everyone had come to see her, and yet, she was sitting alone with her empty plate. She thought back to other parties held in her honor, birthdays and casual get-togethers. She didn't remember ever being alone, not even when she'd had a bad day and hadn't wanted to be sociable.

Her friends were treating her differently! As if she had somehow changed overnight! She was no longer Lauren Wells, friend and fellow working peon. She was now Lauren Wells, millionairess, president of a corporation, chairperson of an empire! It was absurd. A part of her was angry, another part hurt. She had an impulse to jump up on the treasured old Morris chair and shout a declaration of her unchanged identity. She might have done it if Shelly hadn't picked that moment to edge away from Anthony and sidle up to Roger Shilling, the bartender from the Lazy Bull. Lauren liked Roger well enough, but he was a perfect example of the kind of man she hated to see anywhere near Shelly. Handsome, trading on a vulgar but undeniable sex appeal and totally unable to keep his act together. He was dodging alimony from the two families he'd already betrayed, and he'd shown an interest in Shelly on several occasions. Until tonight, Shelly had heeded Lauren's advice to give him a wide berth, but her walk and eyes betrayed the amount of alcohol she'd consumed already. If she was on the outs with Dick, she'd be easy prey for Roger.

Lauren caught her attention and flagged her over. Roger shrugged and threw his former co-worker a grin of temporary defeat. He was well aware of her disapproval of the way he ran his private life but wasn't sensitive enough to let it bother him, or let it stand in the way of what he wanted.

"Pull over a chair and talk to me," she said, motioning toward a folding chair within reach. "What's wrong?" she asked without preamble. "You and Dick fight?"

"It's over between us," Shelly admitted in the little girl voice she'd never quite outgrown.

"I think I've heard that before." Lauren kept her voice light.

"This time it's for good," she said with a wobble to her chin. She opened her mouth to explain further, then closed her eyes and shook her head.

Lauren took a closer look at the face transfixed with agony, seeing for the first time that night that the right side of Shelly's jaw was faintly discolored. Dick had hurt her. "Okay." She made her voice firmly optimistic and took Shelly's hand. "What comes next?"

"I don't know! I can't stay with Dick another minute,

but I don't have any money to move on." She opened panic-filled eyes.

For the first time since coming into her inheritance, Lauren was wholeheartedly grateful for her massive pot of gold. "Oh, yes you do! Are you kidding? I wish all of our problems were this simple. Listen, Shelly, I didn't want to criticize Dick before, but I'm really glad you're getting away from him. I'm happy to help and just tickled that I can. A few weeks ago, it would have been a whole different thing. I'll slip you a check before I leave tonight. Don't worry, it'll be enough so you won't ever have to go back there." In her fear that Shelly might be in jeopardy if she returned to Dick's house at all, Lauren impulsively offered a second solution. "Look, I've got a great idea. When you leave here go to the Beverly Hills Regis-Royale, hear? I'll call and set it up. You can stay in my suite there until you can get a place of your own. Have whatever you need sent up to the suite. Don't even get your clothes. Buy what you need for now, and pay to have someone go to Dick's for your stuff later. The check will cover everything. Okay?"

In spite of the dumbstruck expression on Shelly's face, there was also a hint of complacency, like an indulged child who feels certain she's going to be pulled out of any mess she gets herself into. "Oh, Lauren, darling . . . you're so good to me." The hint of smugness dissolved as tears filled the round blue eyes. "I don't deserve you. I was so afraid that everything would change now that you're . . . you know . . ." she lifted her shoulders helplessly, reluctant to use the word that had come to mind.

"Rich," Lauren laughed unabashedly. "Filthy, wonderfully rich! And that means that the money is an outright gift and don't you dare argue with me." In the past the checks Lauren wrote to bail Shelly out or for Brian's school fees were called loans and as such became embarrassing to both women. Now, perhaps, they could dispense with such pretensions.

"Well . . ." Shelly took a deep breath, swelling her already straining bodice. "If you're sure."

"Wait here. I'll be right back." She got up, then noticed the drink in Shelly's hand. "No, better still, go get some dinner." She didn't like the idea of Shelly driving to Beverly Hills drunk. Or, for that matter, of having her weave her way through the elegant lobby in that condition. Maybe it wasn't such a good idea to send Shelly to the hotel. But Lauren didn't want to disappoint her now. "Please. Besides, Dad will be crushed if his own daughter doesn't sample his goodies."

Lauren waited to make sure that Shelly got something to eat. Then she grabbed her purse and slipped into the bathroom where she could write a check. Mr. Lowenthal had arranged for a large amount of cash to be immediately available to her some days before, and she wasn't bounded by practical considerations as to the size of the check. Even so, it required some thought. There had to be enough for a first, last and perhaps extra month's rent on an apartment. A cleaning or security deposit. Money to move her things. Money to get by on for a while. And money for a few articles of clothing until she could get someone to pick up her things from Dick.

In the end she wrote a check for three thousand dollars. With that kind of money Shelly would probably get a very expensive apartment, but Lauren, trying to think ahead, wasn't sure that wasn't a good idea. If Shelly got a place she really liked, she might not be so quick to give it up for some man. Lauren wouldn't mind accepting the upkeep of such an apartment if it kept Shelly safe and secure. She felt a little guilty, anyway. She could have suggested that her sister move right into that big Holmby Hills mansion with her. Or she could at least have invited her to spend the night in Silverlake. But she had other plans for the remainder of the night.

She scribbled a note on a scrap of paper and folded it over the check. That way Shelly could read Lauren's offer to permanently pay for an apartment and there would be no need for further discussion about the subject.

Parker's bedroom was a minor disaster area, depressing Lauren further about him because she knew him to be a basically tidy man. She would have to do something about him. He had a part-time job cooking for a small restaurant in Hollywood, which left him too much time for brooding and not enough money.

Shelly was just finishing dinner when she returned to the party and Lauren was pleased to see that Roger Shilling was oiling up to someone else. Anthony was at the edge of a group listening to a funny story Parker was telling. "I just called the hotel, and it's all set. Just give your name at the lobby." She slipped the folded note and check into Shelly's hand, smiling at the greedy way her sister tucked it far into her strapless bra. "Sure it's safe there?"

"For the moment."

Relieved to see Shelly smiling again, she turned her attention to Parker, who was just finishing his story, almost destroying it by prematurely laughing at the punch line. "I'm worried about him. Do you think he'd like a vacation? He could go check out some of my new digs in Europe or something. Just to get away for a while. I think he's brooding too much. What do you think?"

"Pops?" Shelly looked at him thoughtfully as she lit a cigarette. "I don't know. Maybe." After a moment she shook her head, exhaling a trail of smoke. The food had done her a world of good. "Nope. You want to know what he needs? A good, full-time job. Work. He needs to keep busy."

Lauren could hardly keep from smiling. Unlike her own close relationship with Parker, Shelly's dealings with him were fraught with tension. They obviously loved each other deeply, but they were frequently snappish toward each other. Parker was troubled by Shelly's discordant life, and Lauren suspected he felt responsible for Shelly's weaknesses. His first wife had left him and Shelly for another man. Parker had tried to be a good father, but he'd had to work to support himself and his child, and Shelly's care had fallen on relatives until she was five. Then he had married the widowed Barbara Wells when Lauren was almost three years old.

Lauren's mother had loved Shelly without reservation, but the distrustful five-year-old clung to her father, fearful of being turned out yet again. But a trust relationship had developed between Barbara and Shelly. And Shelly and Lauren had come to an early truce after Shelly gave up trying to punish Lauren for assuming any claim to Parker. Lauren could hardly remember a time when she wasn't watching out for Shelly, fighting her battles, taking her along on her activities.

Yet for all the closeness in their family, Shelly and her father never overcame their feelings of unease toward each other. Even so, there were times when they surprised Lauren with their perceptiveness, like the time Parker had explained their occasional wars with a curt "We're too much alike." And now, Shelly had taken one look at her father, pinpointed the problem and offered a solution. Shelly and Parker might not have the same easy relationship Lauren had with each, but they knew each other in some instinctive way.

"I don't think I can grab a job for him out of my hat. Not at the moment, anyway," Lauren mumbled.

For the next two hours she and Anthony mingled and talked. She was able to share bits of her news with different people present, and by the end of the evening, she was able to laugh over the write-ups she'd gotten in the press, which all had seen and most had carried to the party. She was relaxed and generally happy by the end of the evening, pleased that she'd been able to help Shelly. She'd stuck a check for one thousand dollars on Parker's dresser with a note wishing him a happy father's day. "It's not father's day," she had written, giving into the impulse to gift him, "but you're not an ordinary father, either. Make me happy by squandering the money on a new stereo or some fallen woman who can appreciate those lousy jokes of yours." She signed it with her love, tremendously gratified that she was now in a position to make grand gestures.

He'd found it before she and Anthony were able to make their escape. "It'll take more than that to get anyone to laugh at my jokes," he said huskily, trying to get her to take back the check.

"Please, Dad. I want you to have it. Today's a special day for me. Please let me make it as good as possible."

They were in the tiny hall by the door, whispering softly so as not to be overheard by lingering guests. "When you were a little girl," he murmured, a fond smile on his craggy features, "you used to say you wanted to grow up to be a genie. You said it often. Your mother and I thought you meant that you wanted to grow up to be like Jeannie Kirby, a very attractive friend of your mother's whom you admired. Then we realized that you meant you wanted to grow up to be a genie like in the story books we read you. Someone who could grant wishes for people." He kissed her cheek. "You still have braids, and you're still the same sweet girl, honey. Only please be careful. Giving people what they want isn't always the right thing to do."

He cleared his throat and put her check in his pocket. "Okay, my genie, I'll check out those fallen women. Somewhere there's one with a real sense of humor."

They drove home in the leased Mercedes Mr. Lowenthal had arranged for right after the reading of the will. He had spotted her old Toyota and discreetly asked if she would allow him to see to another vehicle for her, since she would be driving to the hotel frequently in the next few days. Anthony was at the wheel and drove with the skill of a man long used to fine cars. She wanted to make some remark about how handsome he looked in the beautiful chocolate brown sedan but stopped herself. Anthony was often quiet, but tonight there seemed to be something bothering him.

Finally, he muttered a few words, laughed and turned to her, a rueful smile on his face.

"What?"

"Oh, just something that creep Roger said before we left." He shrugged, as if it were nothing more than the temporary annoyance of a pesky insect.

"Yes?" Getting him to talk was like pulling teeth, but she wanted everything to be perfect when they got back to her apartment.

"That I'd sure fallen into a soft pile. That's just what he said. 'Lucky bastard, you sure fell into a soft pile. Why don't these things happen to me?' Something like that."

Lauren's stomach tightened. "Roger's a jerk. You know that, Anthony. He's just mad because I gave him a dirty look for trying to close in on Shelly again. She's got enough troubles without Roger."

"Roger's definitely a jerk. No question about that. But there are a lot of jerks out there."

She tried to read his face as the red light changed to green. He looked younger than thirty-two in the red glow, older with a greenish tint. "We can't worry about them," she said firmly.

Anthony said nothing but continued to drive in silence. He pulled the Mercedes to a stop behind his six-year-old Ford with its crushed rear fender. Lauren reached for her purse but not the door latch because Anthony made no move to leave the car yet. Instead his eyes were trained on his crushed fender. A nearby streetlight on the opposite corner illuminated his face. It seemed stormy, brooding, his intense dark eyes focused inward. "Anthony?"

"I'm sorry, Lauren. It's all getting to me. This is going to take more adjusting to than I'd realized. Your inheritance. It's wonderful and all, but it's thrown me. I'm not sure why. Last week I'd have been crazy happy at the thought of either of us striking it rich. Then it happened. To you."

She stiffened. "I see," she said tightly. "If it had come to you, it would have been fine, huh? Happily ever after.

But it happened to me, the woman, so that makes it . . ."

"You know that isn't my ax, Lauren." He tried to take her hand. "I'm not talking about that."

"Aren't you?" She pulled back from him, peeved at having to back into a corner of her own car.

He slumped over the wheel. "I don't know." When he turned to her again, his face was full of confusion. "Look, sweetheart, I've got to be alone. I've got some homework to do. Let me sort this out, okay?"

The last thing she wanted tonight was to be alone.

"You're exhausted. I'm pretty wiped out myself," he said before she had a chance to answer. "Let's sleep on it. What's your schedule tomorrow?"

"I'll be in the office all day," she mumbled. "I'd planned on spending the night in Holmby Hills." It was impossible to say "at my house" just yet. "To get the feel of the place. You know. See if I need to do anything, get to know the household staff." She felt empty.

"Okay, I'll call you."

She wanted to ask him to come with her to the mansion. It would have been so much easier that way, on both of them, coming to it together. But she couldn't talk any longer, not with him just dropping her at the door like this. She merely nodded and got out of the car with him.

He handed her the keys. "It drives nice."

"Yes, I know."

He started to say something else, thought better of it, waited for her to unlock and enter her apartment and then went to his car.

Lauren undressed numbly, putting her clothing away out of habit rather than conscious effort. She felt very lonely. Even Tuxedo, after his greeting meow, had gone back to sleep.

She washed quickly and unwound her coronet. Usually she left her hair in one long braid for sleeping. Otherwise it tangled hopelessly around her neck and body. But she couldn't forget how she had planned to start this night, so she opened the braid and brushed the trailing mane loose. With her fingers she urged the cascading locks to cover most of her body. In the bright bathroom light she looked like a desperate siren, preparing for her nightly call to distant ships. She touched Premier Enfant to the warm velvet curve under each breast, the insides of her thighs, the hollow of her sculptured throat.

Her bedroom was dark but for the night light on the dresser. She moved toward it to see herself in the large mirror attached to the dresser.

She gasped at the sight of herself half-hidden in the wavy silvery strands that covered her shoulders, most of her high breasts, her shapely torso, the smudge of her genitals. Only her thighs, thrusting forward as she moved, escaped the lush tendrils. She was like some sensual creature of the night, surprised by her reflection in a pond. She stopped, wondering how Anthony would have reacted, seeing her like this.

Very slowly she lifted an arm toward the center of her throat. She extended one finger and cut through the hair, parting it deftly between her breasts and ribs, on past her slender waist and stopping below her navel. Then, with both hands, she threw back the divided sheets of her glorious mane with a sudden gesture, revealing her completely naked, rosy, trembling body.

She looked at herself for another long moment, feeling rather than seeing the ripeness, the eager stiffness of her flesh.

"Anthony, why aren't you here? I need you so much," she cried aloud.

In the wake of her voice the room was very quiet.

Biting back tears, Lauren quickly braided her hair and went to her lonely bed.

Chapter Four

"Stop! Enough! I quit!" Lauren pushed back from the desk and moaned with exhaustion. "Feed me or I'll die!"

Chris St. Dennis moved aside the closest mountain of folders and rested her cashmere-covered elbows on the corner of her boss's desk. "More grass and bark? With some nice berries and bushes for dessert?"

"Sounds about right. Maybe a few wilted lettuce leaves on the side." She gave her effortlessly trim secretary a measured frown. "Have you any idea just how very much women like me hate women like you? I've gained two pounds this week just by eating in the same room with your lunches."

"Hate? Just because I eat real food?" Chris looked hurt.

"Real food!" Lauren threw her forearm across her brow in mock horror. "It's real, all right. Real fattening. And real delicious, damn it. If I ate like you I'd be enormous in no time." After a week Lauren still wasn't over her amazement at the amount of food Chris could put away at one sitting. At night, she had begun to dream about Chris's lunches.

"I've always had a big appetite. Any day now I expect to wake up and find myself hanging over the edges of my bed." She puffed out her cheeks and patted her nonexistent belly under its Welsh tartan plaid skirt. "There. Now are you happy?"

"If only I could believe it!" Lauren got up, stretched, then walked over to the beveled glass mirror to the left of her desk to see if she needed any repair work before breaking for lunch.

"As if you had anything to worry about, yourself." Chris stared appreciatively at her employer as Lauren readjusted a hairpin. She was struck by the woman's rare beauty again, the clean lines of the classically molded head, the long, graceful body looking superb in soft, pleated beige trousers. A rich brown velour sweater revealed surprisingly full breasts and emphasized the smooth golden tones of Lauren's flesh. "I'd be a wealthy woman if I used as few cosmetics as you."

Lauren looked up at Chris in the mirror. The dark-haired secretary was so stunning she could have been a model. "If they did for me what they do for you, I'd pour them on." With an artist's touch, Chris applied pencil and powder and cream to accentuate what was already there—a beautiful, intelligent face. Her outfit today—the tartan skirt and vest, the Italian woven-straw accessories—like everything she wore, was smart, expensive and straight out of *Vogue*.

"Hey, let's get this mutual admiration show on the road. I'm starving." Chris barely glanced at herself in the mirror, blandly confident that her flawlessly arranged hair, face and outfit would pass muster anywhere.

"It figures." Lauren pulled on a tweed blazer and grinned at Chris in the mirror, deeply pleased with the warmth that was developing between them. Chris was proving herself a marvelous asset already. Although she looked even younger than twenty-seven, she had the cool competency of a seasoned executive. She knew the Beverly Hills Regis-Royale inside out, but also had a broad understanding of the conglomerate as a whole. And she knew where to go to get the information she didn't have. Her scheduling of meetings was so artful that an executive seen at three in the afternoon would provide the vital data for an intelligent grasp of the four o'clock meeting. She courted reluctant sources to get straight answers and made sure Lauren was assimilating all she was being exposed to.

At first, Chris hadn't wanted their intimacy to be obvious, either. "You're going to have a hard enough time commanding the serious respect of the Hollenbecks and the Chambers," she warned. In front of others she and Lauren were polite but formal with one another. But alone in the huge office, they lightened their heavy work load with frequent joking and kidding. As the week passed they felt more confident about appearing in public together.

"Where shall we eat?" Lauren held up a hand. "Anywhere but in the immediate vicinity, please. For a change." For the better part of the week they'd taken their meals in the office. There was so much to do, to learn, that both had decided to work through the weekend. "And let's take a nice, long lunch break."

"You're the boss." Chris snapped her fingers. "Hey, I know just the place! A view of the ocean. All the privacy you could ask for. Excellent service. And the specialty of the house just happens to be this wild Mexican salad that's loaded with berries and bushes."

"Sounds like my kind of a place," Lauren grinned, dipping a fingertip into a small tin of lip balm.

"Well, actually, it's my kind of place. To tell you the truth, it *is* my place!"

Chris drove them toward the beach in a mint-condition white Thunderbird with two worn but immaculate leather seats. The car was a surprise to Lauren, although it fitted the designer clothing and Chris's Ivy League education.

The house where Chris stopped was also a surprise—an undistinguished frame house, narrow and high, old and dilapidated. In spite of extensive and sincere efforts to ren-

ovate this part of Venice beach, the neighborhood seemed
unable to shake off its aura of depression. Many of the other
buildings wore shiny new fronts. Newly planted trees and
plants added a festive touch. But Lauren saw a tattered old
man nursing a bottle in a doorway, and the children playing
in the street had wary, old-looking faces.

She followed Chris up a flight of exterior stairs, stepping
lightly on squeaking boards and clinging tightly to the railing. They finally arrived at the top floor and paused to look
at the gorgeous view from a brightly painted balcony which
was the same teal blue as the sea beyond. Foamy whitecaps
dotted the water and the scalloped yellow beaches sparkled
under the sun.

"Pretty, huh? Worth the climb and the grime below, I
think." Chris turned and unlocked the door, which had been
sanded and stained a glossy, rich mahogany brown.

Still winded, Lauren stared down at the watermelon
wedge of Pacific Ocean below. "Lovely. Did you do all this
yourself?" She gestured at the baskets of cascading flowers,
potted trees and intricate strings of vines growing in and out
of a variety of hand-thrown clay pots.

"The balcony? Oh, yes." She opened the door and tucked
her keys back in her purse. "With my own little hands. I
had some help with the view, though. I've got a green thumb
and I'm pretty handy with a hammer. You should have seen
this when I moved into the place. One wrong step and you'd
be on the ground floor in record time."

"I can imagine," Lauren said, thinking of the rest of the
deteriorating building.

"My next project is that lousy staircase."

Lauren followed Chris into her apartment reluctantly,
hating to leave the charming balcony and the cool, invigorating salt air. She gasped as soon as her eyes adjusted to
the dimness inside. "Oh, this is beautiful!"

Chris had worked wonders with the roomy attic apartment. The walls had been painted a subdued cinnamon color

66

wherever possible, and covered with a delicately patterned fabric where the decay was beyond redemption. Lampblack moldings tied the two wall treatments together and emphasized the oriental flavor of the room. Magnificent antiques—including several highly lacquered black enamel Chinese tables—sat on sumptuous Persian carpets. It was a perfect setting for Chris. Despite her French surname, the exotic cast of her dark eyes and flat cheekbones suggested an oriental ancestor.

"Incredible!" Lauren shook her head in wonder and turned to Chris, a tawny eyebrow rising.

Chris laughed. "My parents had a lovely home not too far from your house in Holmby Hills," she explained lightly. "The T-bird was my sixteenth birthday present. After my father left my mother for a girl not much older than I was, things went downhill for all of us. I ended up with what was left of the furniture and barely enough money for my education. When I got out of Harvard, I was like everyone else—over-educated and under-experienced. A friend of my father's sent me over to see Earl Regis. He liked what he saw and hired me on the spot. Lucky for him, I also knew what I was doing." She shrugged. "I wanted to get into the Regis-Royale organization because I thought there would be a chance of advancement for a woman, since Alexandra Regis was at the top of the heap."

"But you did such a good job for Earl that he hid your light under his lampshade," Lauren finished.

"To say nothing of his undying hope of eventually luring me into the sack."

She walked into a roomy kitchen that could have graced the pages of *Architectural Digest*. Chris had worked with wood and clay for a country flavor, enhanced by an attractive display of copperware and a profusion of leafy ferns and palms. A center island built of clay bricks was topped with butcher block and flanked by rattan bar stools, serving as a work area and a kitchen table. The floor was tiled with handsome clay squares. A variety of appliances made it the culinary workshop that gourmets dreamed about.

"My stepfather would have to be dynamited out of a kitchen like this." Parker's birthday wasn't too far off. Maybe she'd surprise him with a whole new kitchen. Or, better still, buy him a little house. He loved to putter. Or even better than that, find him a job.

Chris, busy at the copper double-doored refrigerator, noticed Lauren's cloudy expression. "Something wrong?"

While Chris worked, Lauren perched on one of the bar stools and told her about the change in Parker since the death of her mother. She held back the fact of his drinking out of loyalty, but omitted nothing else. "Chris, do you think we could find a good job for him at the hotel? He's had a lot of experience as a professional chef, but I'm not sure his health is good enough for him to stand all day long."

Chris deftly folded diced green chiles into the large salad and then tossed in brightly gleaming kidney beans and canned garbanzos. "There is one opening that comes to my mind, but it might be too much for him," she suggested tentatively. "The head of kitchen operations is on extended leave, but it's a complex job. Somewhere between army general and psychiatrist. There's a lot to organize and good chefs are so touchy." Tiny cooked beets went into the huge glass bowl along with slivered avocado and squares of white and yellow cheeses.

Nose prickling with the fragrance of sliced green onions and crisp tortilla chips, Lauren nodded eagerly. "I'm sure he could do it. He owned two restaurants." She watched Chris sprinkle the salad with hamburger meat that had been warmed in the microwave, then toss the whole thing with creamy French dressing. "I don't know what that is, but if it holds still long enough, I'm going to attack it."

Chris removed two thick stoneware plates from a cupboard, took out two wine glasses, some silver and napkins, then hipped open a door to a second balcony off the kitchen.

She quickly put together two place settings on a wrought-iron umbrellaed table, doggedly refusing to allow Lauren to do a thing. "I'm having the boss to lunch. This is my chance to polish the apple." After serving generous portions she poured a good cabernet sauvignon and sat down. "There. My world famous Taco salad." She flapped open her linen napkin and smoothed it over her skirt.

"This is actually as delicious as it looks," Lauren said with some surprise, taking a long sip of her wine. As she ate and sipped her wine, Lauren's eyes lighted on a most extraordinary structure. "What's that?" She pointed to an odd building with a dome and forked up some hamburger, a garbanzo bean and a fat red cherry tomato.

"Isn't it wild? You should see it inside. It used to be the home of a wrestler called the Baron Michele Leone. A beach character. My, uh, friend David Bryan lives there now. He's a lawyer and nothing like the Baron, but he gets a kick out of the place. If you think this view is nice, you should see it from David's dome." Her voice had a warm, special tone.

"Is David your lover?" Lauren held up the glass of wine. "Curse of the grape. I'm not usually so nosy. He sounds nice."

Chris smiled. "No, not yet, anyway. I don't know why not, either. He's a wonderful person, I really like him, and he's terribly attractive—sincere in a way that's only a game with most men." Her deep brown eyes clouded over. "He's too nice. It would have to be a very serious thing. I sense that already."

"Is that bad?" Lauren thought of Anthony. They hadn't seen each other since the night of the party. They had talked on the phone several times, but each had allowed the pressures of work to keep them apart. Tonight he was picking her up and taking her to her new home. She couldn't put off moving any longer. "Don't you want to get married?"

Chris picked up a chip and nibbled at it. "Sure. Yes. Of course." She appeared to think about it. "Someday."

"Career first?" Lauren smiled knowingly. "I think it was easier when marriage was a woman's career. Fewer options means fewer confusions."

"You'll laugh if I tell you why I'm afraid of encouraging David too much."

"So make me laugh. I need a good laugh. It's been some kind of a week." She grinned at the other woman, feeling very close to her and very grateful to take her mind off the hotels, her inheritance and Anthony.

"I'm looking for the perfect man."

"Perfect? Translate." Lauren touched the napkin to her lips and glanced over Chris's shoulder to the dome. A man had just stepped onto a balcony. He was too far away to see clearly. She had the impression of a solid body not overly tall and hair dark enough to pass for black. He was wearing a business suit.

Chris forked aside some spinach greens and exposed a cube of cheese. She stabbed it but didn't lift it to her lips. "Perfect. I mean it. If I get seriously involved with a man, he's got to be the living incarnation of this image I've carried around for years. Gentle but firm. Handsome. But not too handsome, not so handsome that it gets in the way. Devoted. That's a big one. Loyal. The kind of a man who knows what he wants and won't risk losing it on some whim once he finds it. A man who will be an excellent father and husband." She laughed self-consciously. "And rich. Mustn't forget that."

Lauren smiled. "Sorry. I've already got him. Anthony. Except for the rich part, and I suppose that doesn't matter any more. Besides, he'll have money enough when his opera is completed." She looked over at the dome again. David had removed his jacket and was hosing down some good-sized trees.

Chris turned and grinned. "The gardener's at it again. Actually, that's how we met, because of our gardens. We'd noticed each other working on our plants and bumped into each other at a local nursery. I didn't recognize David right

70

away, but he looked vaguely familiar. I admired a stunning basket of ivy but couldn't afford it. When I returned home the basket was on my balcony with a note saying it was from the other member of the Venice Rooftop Beautification Association. I've been seeing David fairly steadily since then. I keep wanting to let him down easily before we get too involved, but, actually, I like him too much."

"And he's not perfect?"

Her laugh was faintly embarrassed. "Well, he certainly isn't rich." Chris turned her attention to her food. "Are you moving into the house tonight?"

"Yes. Anthony's meeting me after work. I've put it off as long as I could." She pushed her plate away and picked up her wineglass, breathing in the mingled aromas of wine and salt air. "It's insane. I should be overjoyed at moving out of my cramped little apartment into that mansion. But it's all going too fast. If you hadn't made the arrangements, I'd have put it off even longer."

Chris nodded. "The movers called this morning to say they were finished. I talked to Mrs. Hastings and she said that everything would be put away by the time you arrive."

Lauren felt faintly embarrassed at the thought of the housekeeper going through her personal items. Her visit to the Holmby Hills house earlier that week had proved that she would need to bring little more than her clothing with her. Still, she hadn't been able to part with certain treasures—furniture and prints she especially liked, gifts from Anthony and mementos that had belonged to her mother. And her cat. She had personally transported Tuxedo to his new home the night before, staying only long enough to get him settled. "Isn't it funny. I've stalled moving as if it were a fate worse than death. When I do go to the mansion, I feel as if I'm imposing on Mrs. Hastings and her staff." Her voice had a hesitant quality.

"Not funny, and not strange, either. Anyone would be thrown for a loop in your position. Everyone dreams of walking into a street paved with gold, but no one bothers to think about what they'd do once they were there." Chris smiled and helped herself to another spoonful of taco salad, judiciously selecting only the most fattening items. "Just remember, it's no longer Mrs. Regis's house. It's yours. If you're not comfortable with Mrs. Hastings fire her and find someone you like. Otherwise you're going to have to be very sure of yourself in her presence. Believe me, she wants to keep her job. But she'll bully you and try telling you how things are run—if you let her." She smiled to take the sting out of her words. "In a month's time you'll feel as if you've lived in that mansion all your life. By the time we leave for Europe, you'll hardly remember what your life was like without servants."

Lauren wasn't sure she wanted to forget her old life. "Maybe I should have turned this whole thing over to Shelly. She looks as if she's more prepared for a life of luxury than I am."

Both women laughed, thinking of Shelly's visit to Lauren's office the day before. She had been splendidly attired in a neat and closely fitted Guy Laroche suit and she had bought a standard poodle to complete her new look. Her makeup had the mark of a professional, someone who had encouraged Shelly to enhance rather than flaunt her natural beauty. Her hair was a softer blonde and handsomely cut. She looked smashing and she seemed calmer, more self-assured. As soon as she was alone with Lauren, she'd sweetly but unabashedly asked for money.

"I got carried away." She dimpled, glancing down at her costly wardrobe complemented by Gucci shoes and a purse of soft leather. "I wanted to get rid of the old Shelly. Turn over a new leaf, you know?"

Lauren knew that she should say something about Shelly squandering the money she'd given her less than a week earlier, but she was so delighted with Shelly's changed appearance and attitude that she stifled her misgivings and dashed off another check.

"I think I'm a little jealous of Shelly. She knows how

to enjoy a good thing." Lauren finished her wine and smiled. "But maybe I'll be doing well by the time we leave on our trip." She hadn't had time to allow herself to get really excited about the trip she and Chris would be taking in June. But thinking about it now sent shivers up her spine. She would visit most of her major hotels abroad, traveling in the Regis private jet. Tonight she would ask Anthony to come with her. If only they could make the trip a honeymoon. But she would be so busy, and it wouldn't be right to expect Anthony to wait patiently for the rare moments she would be able to spend with him. But she desperately wanted him with her on this trip. She wanted to share everything with him. But once again, she was haunted by the selfishness of her desire. He had a deadline to meet. And he deserved to have his wife completely to himself, especially on their honeymoon.

Lauren glanced at her watch. "Time to get back to work." She sighed.

"Right." Chris began to clear the table. "You have a meeting with Mr. Reardon at three. We'll barely make it." She grinned impishly. "But that's one of the nice things about being boss—they have to wait."

Without asking, Lauren began to help put things away. "The apple's been polished. And stuffed." She brought the remains of the salad to the butcher-block table.

After rinsing the dishes, they prepared to leave. Lauren noticed Chris glance over at the ornate dome where David Bryan lived. He was not in sight. She caught the wistful look on the dark-haired woman's lovely face. The expression mirrored her own confusion about her relationship with Anthony. It was a touching, questioning look. But there was one big difference between Chris's dilemma and her own—Chris didn't want to love her David, and Lauren did love Anthony. But she couldn't forget his startling over-reaction to Roger Shilling's stupid remark. It had bothered her all week. And honesty forced her to admit, if only to herself, that she had felt impatient with Anthony since that moment in Norm Lowenthal's office when he had assumed that Lauren would be content to spend an idle life. Did that mean she secretly wished Anthony would settle for such a life himself? Living in her shadow, content to exist merely to give her love and assistance?

"Hello . . . are you in there?" Chris was smiling at her from the front door.

Lauren shook her head, as if to dislodge the disturbing thought that she had ever wanted her strong, committed Anthony to accept the role of her prince consort. "Okay, tell me about this James Reardon."

Chapter Five

By the time they returned to the Beverly Hills Regis-Royale, Lauren understood Jim Reardon's job and his value to the organization. Chris confirmed Mr. Lowenthal's opinion that he was an excellent financial director. But this had not prepared her for his considerable charm.

Nor was he prepared to find his new boss so stunningly attractive. His surprise was obvious and appealingly boyish. "Your photographs in the newspapers show a beautiful woman. They don't begin to do you justice," he said softly, almost reluctantly, as if his admiration had overcome his normal decorum. "Being overwhelmed is no way to start a business relationship."

Lauren was a little embarrassed by this greeting, but also pleased by his honesty. "I'm afraid I don't know how to answer so flattering a hello," she said, smiling as she ushered him to a seat across from her desk.

He laughed. "Well, we could just sit here and stare at each other for a while. I'm very pleased to meet you, Miss Wells."

ROYAL SUITE

She gave him her hand, conscious that he held it a trifle
longer than necessary. She was also conscious of being a
woman rather than just the president of the hotel corporation.

Lauren hadn't looked forward to this particular meeting.
Reardon had to be aware that she had kept him from being
voted in as the new chairman of the board after Alexandra's
death. She had expected the same measured and barely
concealed disapproval of her that had been shown by Chambers, Hollenbeck and some of the others, but the financial
director was direct, helpful and encouraging instead. He
also had a sharp wit that disarmed and delighted her.

He was in his early forties, tall and well-built, a busy
man who took the time to keep himself in shape. His meticulous dress and grooming spelled success but not excessive vanity. His brown hair was well cut and not as dark
as his brows and deep-set thickly-lashed eyes. He had a
nice smile and a good laugh. He was also magnetically
masculine, but did not play on it. Most of all, his eyes
interested Lauren. They exuded self-confidence but not
egoism; they were clearly the eyes of a man who believed
himself both practical and idealistic.

"If there's any way I can help you, Miss Wells, I hope
you won't hesitate to call on me. You must be overwhelmed
by all of this," he said, gesturing to the paper-laden desk.
"I'm impressed by what you're attempting to do. I know
there's been a great deal of pressure on you." A smile tugged
at his lips. "But from what I've heard, I believe you just
might be able to hold your own."

"That's nice of you to say, Mr. Reardon." She looked
deeply into his dark eyes. "Especially since it appears I've
taken away your seat on the board. I was a little apprehensive
about this meeting. No hard feelings?"

"Of course there are," he answered after a moment, his
jaw creasing with a completely unaffected rueful grin. "At
the risk of alienating a woman who is not only in a position
to fire me on the spot, but who also happens to be the most

76

beautiful boss I've certainly ever had—and just to set the record straight—I think I should be sitting in that chair. I'd make one hell of a chairman of the board. By not grabbing me up for the job, Miss Wells, you've already made one big administrative error. But I think the chain will be able to absorb the mistake." He laughed again, easily and fully. "I'm generally far more tactful. I do suffer from one administrative weakness myself—I prefer even unfriendly truths over the most endearing of lies. Forgive me, will you?"

"I'll do my best." She was delighted.

Lauren's active imagination conjured a Superman outfit under the expensive gray business suit. She sensed that Jim Reardon was a rarity in her new world, an honest man. She also knew that he was in favor of the merger her benefactress had so strongly opposed. For that reason alone, she tried to be wary and critical of this man, but by the end of the meeting she was convinced that he sincerely believed the merger would benefit the conglomerate financially.

He didn't try to push her to a decision. "Look over the reports I've brought, Miss Wells. There's no great rush in making up your mind. It'll keep until your return later this summer." His expression revealed a surprising depth of compassion. The moist velvet eyes stroked her in a way that was above reproach and oddly comforting. "I know you're very busy, but perhaps you would join me for lunch sometime this next week?" Two deep creases showed in his jaw as he smiled. "No lobbying through the meal, I promise. Well, maybe just a little. Just enough so I can make it a legitimate business expense."

Lauren returned the smile and found herself very tempted to say yes. It wasn't a date he was proposing. Strictly business. She would be taking many meals with business associates from now on. There was no reason to decline. "My schedule is impossible all next week, Mr. Reardon. . . ."

"Jim." The dark eyes were hypnotic.

"Jim," she granted, smiling to mask her attraction to him. Not since she had met Anthony had any man affected her so strongly. She felt as if she had known him a long time, as if he were someone who was destined to have great impact on her life. She was keenly aware of hot sparks between them, that he seemed as reluctant to leave as she suddenly was to let him go. It was an effort to speak. "Perhaps the following week?"

"I'll call. . . . Lauren?" He got up.

"Yes," she said, simultaneously granting him permission to use her first name and call for a lunch date. "And I'll get to these reports at the first opportunity."

Lost in disturbing thoughts, she watched him walk out of the office.

Jim Reardon was still on her mind when Chris, ready to leave for the day, announced that Anthony had arrived. "Oh! Already? Ask him in, please, Chris." She had an image of Anthony sitting in the outer office, swallowed up by the plush furniture and carpeting, the plethora of plants in brass buckets, the heavily framed paintings, each worth more than everything Anthony owned lumped together. "No, I'll get him myself." She hurried to the door, damning herself for feeling apologetic about what she now had.

At the sight of him, all her confusion evaporated and her face radiated her delight in seeing him again. She hugged him quickly, drinking in his warmth, the familiar precious feel of his body against hers, the spicy smell of his shampoo. Their embrace negated the need for her to say any of the things that had wanted saying. It was an unspoken declaration that whatever had kept them apart for almost a week was of little real importance. All that mattered was that they were together now.

Lauren released him and turned to Chris, making hurried introductions. There was an amused expression on Anthony's face, but he acknowledged the greeting charmingly, aware that Chris was a great help to Lauren.

"I thought only men picked secretaries as pretty as Chris," he teased as soon as she was gone. "There goes another cliché. Nothing's sacred any more."

"A female boss doesn't hold beauty against an employee, joker. Only we insist on a little more, too." She took his hand and led him into her oversized office.

"Holy cow." He shook his head. "Is this supposed to be an office or a stadium?" He studied an exquisite mosaic of the hotel on one wall. "You ready?"

"Yes." He looked so uncomfortable that she decided against fixing him a drink from the concealed bar and lingering in the office for a while.

He followed her in his car through the crowded rush hour traffic of Beverly Hills, she in the Mercedes, he in the Ford with the crushed fender. She realized that she felt a little bit ashamed of his car, viewing it as Mrs. Hastings, her intimidating housekeeper, might. Annoying as that thought was, the one that followed on its heels really pricked her conscience—a conviction that Jim Reardon would drive an impeccably suitable car, not too flashy, but comfortable and tasteful. And Jim would not have been so eager to escape her office. He was used to such surroundings, could make himself comfortable in any environment.

Lauren banished the disloyal thoughts from her mind as she turned into Holmby Hills. What was wrong with her? It was natural for Anthony to feel uneasy. It had taken her days to be able to relax in her office, and she still fought blushes as she walked through the hotel, longing to reach her office without being the object of everyone's curiosity. She was barely over feeling self-conscious in her beautiful car, and hadn't she put off moving into her new home until she had Anthony to help her make the transition? She and Anthony came from a different world. It was not only unfair to compare the two men, it was pointless. Jim Reardon was merely the first handsome, appealing man she'd met in her new life. Besides, she thought with a silly grin of satisfaction, Anthony might not wear a suit as well, but she very much doubted that Jim could write an opera even badly.

She drove up to the three-car garage but not into it, leaving ample room for Anthony to park next to her. In the time it took for her to collect her purse and assemble the paperwork she'd brought home with her, Anthony parked and came to open her door.

"I feel like we're that couple in *The Rocky Horror Show*, about to enter the spooky mansion." He took the sheaf of papers from her. "Homework?"

"Financial statements." She slid over the fine leather upholstery and got out, melting into his free arm for a quick kiss. "I've missed you."

"Not half as much as I've missed you, Lauren." His eyes bored into hers searchingly. "Is everything all right?"

"Yes. Now it is." She shut the door firmly and started for the house. "Are you starving? Chris told Mrs. Hastings to have something made that could be served whenever we were ready."

He whistled. "Live-in servants and a chef on tap. This might not be so bad." He waited while she pulled out a hefty ring of keys and hesitantly selected the one for the ornate front door.

"Only Mrs. Hastings and the cook live in. The others are daily workers. Mrs. Regis had a live-in maid who retired." She fitted the key to the lock, but the door swung open before she could turn it. "Oh, thank you, Mrs. Hastings."

The middle-aged woman smiled tightly, backing up to let them in.

Lauren made the introductions, then looked eagerly into the hallway. "Where's Tuxedo?"

"In the pantry, Miss Wells. I thought it best to keep him out of the main rooms." She glanced significantly at the priceless antiques in the living room.

Lauren allowed her irritation to show. "He's to have the run of the house, Mrs. Hastings. I want his bed put in my room, with one of the scratching posts. Please see to it that cat doors are installed in at least two of the main floor doors in the morning. He knows how to use them." She smiled coldly, then turned to Anthony. "Why don't you fix us a drink, darling? I won't be a moment. I'm just going to feed Tux."

Mrs. Hastings looked horrified. "He's already been fed, Miss Wells. We feed him at ten in the morning and again at five. The cook has also given him meat scraps."

Lauren and Anthony exchanged amused glances. The message was clear—someone of Lauren's stature does not open cans of cat food. At least not with Mrs. Hastings running the house. If Lauren had a penchant for scruffy little alley cats, the dedicated and meticulous housekeeper would stifle her distaste and care for the beast as if it were a fully pedigreed Persian. "Fine. Please let him come in here, then. We'll have a drink before dinner."

"Yes, Miss Wells. Would you like Valerie to serve your apéritif in your study? Mrs. Regis always enjoyed *tapas* and a good *olorosso* sherry in her study before dinner."

To Anthony's amazement, Lauren languidly turned back to the woman and smiled a sweet, dangerous smile. Her voice had the quality of sugared poison. "That sounds lovely, though I much prefer a good *fino* sherry. Manzanilla, if we have it. If not, see that we get some. Make sure it comes from Sanlúcar de Barrameda. The vineyards at the mouth of the Guadalquiver River produce the best manzanilla. Oh, and I don't care for overly spicy *tapas*. The study sounds fine." She dismissed the nettled housekeeper with a nod, waiting until she was out of the room before allowing her face to relax into a more natural expression.

"What was all *that* about?" Anthony followed her over a thick carpet, dividing his attention between her answer and several magnificent oil paintings on the gleaming-paneled hallway walls.

They entered the large study, which had the most lived-in appearance of any room in the huge mansion. Comfortable leather club chairs and well-stocked bookcases, a tufted couch and long, low tables made the study perfect for quiet conversation or solitary contemplation. The full-sized desk near the fireplace and the companion desk at its side, equipped with the most up-to-date electronic typewriter, set the tone of the room, however. The former owner of the house had not been in the habit of leaving her work at the office after hours.

Lauren took the folders from Anthony and quickly glanced through them. "That?" she answered belatedly. "With Mrs. Hastings?" she asked absently. "Just two cats doing a territorial dance. I think she disapproves of a mere commoner taking over, but she's too well-trained to say anything directly. So she's got two choices—either she gets to intimidate me, or she gets me to prove myself worthy of her and this house." She scanned a paper and then looked up at him, her smile deepening as she dumped her armload on a corner of the larger desk. "I just won round one on the home front. She made the tactical error of challenging me about what I eat and drink. I didn't work in quality dinner houses and live under the same roof with Parker Fields to flunk that kind of a test."

She let her eyes move around the room carefully, wondrously. "Oh, Anthony, isn't it beautiful?" she asked in an awed whisper. "Pinch me. I must be dreaming. No, don't pinch me. If I'm dreaming, I don't want to wake up yet." She went to him quickly, her hand moving over the rough material of his old wool jacket. "I've already pinched myself so many times I should be black and blue all over."

He looked at her, his dark Latin eyes somber. "I'm glad you're happy, Lauren. I really am."

The sadness in his voice made her study his face. "Aren't you happy? Isn't this everything we could possibly have wanted and more? A dream come true?"

"I suppose." He made a heroic effort to disguise the gloom in his tone. "I'm an idiot, that's all. I found myself driving by your apartment in Silverlake before heading for Beverly Hills. The "for rent" sign is up already. I suppose you gave them permission? Technically, the apartment is yours yet." He smiled. What did a few months rent on the modest apartment mean in the midst of so much splendor?

"Of course I did." She looked at him questioningly, waiting for him to say what was really bothering him.

"Oh, damn it, I don't know. I'm still scared, that's all. I've been trying to laugh it off all week long." He reached out suddenly and took her in his strong arms. "I'm scared stiff you'll change, Lauren. That all this will get to you, corrupt you, make you see things in a different way." He pushed her back enough to study her face. His eyes were intense, pained. "Not other things. Me, damn it. I'm afraid that now that you have the world at your feet you won't want me."

She couldn't help it—she started to laugh. "I'm sorry, Anthony. I can't help it." She collapsed against him, laughing.

He had no choice but to hold her. His only alternative was to allow her to fall to the floor at his feet. But his arms were stiff around her. "What the hell's so goddamned funny?"

Knowing she had struck at his fierce Italian pride, she controlled her laughter. "Oh, darling, I'm sorry, really. It's just that . . . Anthony, I got scared, too, and for the same reason. I was afraid that you'd change because of my inheritance. I knew I wouldn't, but I couldn't be sure about you. And you aren't sure about me." Her pretty smile faded. "Why am I laughing?" she asked uncertainly. "Our lack of faith in each other isn't at all funny. Here we're planning to get married, and we don't even have the trust . . ."

"That's the first time you've mentioned our getting married since this whole thing happened." He said it quietly, his eyes locked to hers. "I've waited."

She tried to turn it into a joke. "To be asked? I thought the man asked the woman. Come to think of it, you never actually did ask, you know. On bended knee, promising to give me everything and telling me that you can't live without me."

"Lauren, you know what I'm talking about." His serious expression didn't falter. "I've been expecting . . ."

"Oh, there you are!" She saw the tip of a black nose and a fringe of whiskers and dropped to her knees, smiling.

The little cat stepped daintily into the room, paws sinking carefully in the thick rug. His exceptionally bushy tail, a white and gray feather, was like an exclamation mark over his haunches. "Meow?" he cried as if demanding an explanation for all the peculiar things that had happened to him since he'd last seen her.

"Oh, look at you!" She picked him up and straightened to show the small animal to Anthony. "He's so fluffy and he smells wonderful."

Tuxedo looked at her as if she were sharing his dismay over the indignities committed on his body in order to bring him to such a fine state of being. He butted his head against her throat.

Lauren found the spot behind his left ear that guaranteed instant purring and began to rub it. "I don't think he likes being rich yet, but it looks good on him. Within a month he'll be demanding fancy collars and scraps of prime beef."

"Like Shelly," Anthony said, shaking his head. "She showed up at your dad's house looking like she'd bought out all of Rodeo Drive."

"You were with Parker last night?" Lauren was surprised. Anthony had never spent much time alone with her stepfather.

"Yeah. I've gone over to his place a couple of nights this week." He shrugged. "He didn't look so good at your party, and I think he's drinking more than usual. I figured he could use some company, especially now that you're so busy making more money. And Shelly's busy spending what you already have."

Lauren flushed and kept her eyes on the kitten. She and Anthony had had their share of arguments about Shelly in the past.

"Honey, you know I care about Shelly, and I worry about

her. But indulging her isn't likely to strengthen her character much. You'd do her a big favor if you'd get her a job instead. She needs to be able to stand on her two feet for a change. She's been standing on yours all her life." He sat down in one of the big club chairs just as a uniformed maid came to the door.

Still holding Tuxedo, Lauren smiled at the stocky blond servant. "Just put the tray on the desk, Valerie," she suggested. "Thank you."

After the woman had left, Lauren poured the pale sherry from a crystal decanter into two exquisite tulip-shaped glasses. She brought a glass to Anthony and tasted her own by allowing a few drops of the sherry to warm her tongue. She recognized the distinctive dry hazelnut flavor, smiled at the unmistakably bitter but not unpleasant aftertaste of manzanilla.

"Very good. One point for Mrs. Hastings." She brought the heavy silver tray of *tapas* to the table next to Anthony, scanning the bite-sized morsels of food with approval. "They don't fool around here," she said, eyeing the *angulas* and the squid in its own ink. Instead, she helped herself to a bit of fresh tuna marinated in a piquant sauce.

Anthony toothpicked two of the tiny eels. "What's that?" he asked suspiciously, looking at the squid while he washed down the spicy *angulas* with his sherry.

She told him, watched him try the chewy squid with eagerness, smiled. Food could distract Anthony from the most serious problem, just as Tuxedo had distracted her. But she knew they would eventually get back to the earlier subject.

Lauren fed a sliver of the tangy tuna to Tuxedo, who nibbled disinterestedly at the delicacy, proving that Mrs. Hastings had taken her unwelcome obligation seriously.

Lauren took a seat on the leather ottoman at Anthony's feet. "Anthony, I do want us to get married."

He looked over at her at once, face alert, a smile forming. She instantly regretted her brief moment of hesitation.

"But not right away," she added quickly. "I've thought about it all week. Please listen to me without saying anything until I've finished."

He gave her a mock salute with his glass of sherry. But the expression in his eyes was more hurt than derisive.

Lauren did nothing to conceal her own feelings. "I love you so much, Anthony. You're the only man I've ever wanted to spend my entire life with. We've waited a long time to get married. Putting it off was your idea, and for some very good reasons. If you remember, I didn't agree with them at first. Your work, money . . . they were things I felt we could live with. But you didn't want us to do without, and we would have had to live mostly on my salary if we married before your opera was produced." She paused, aware that again neither of them had said a word about the progress of his work. She bit into her bottom lip and hurried on, unwilling to lose her train of thought. "That was reasonable. Lack of money is no longer an issue. But you still have your work, and now I have mine."

"We each had our own work before," he stated flatly.

"You're deliberately being dense, Anthony." She shrugged off her irritation. "My work was the kind that ceased to exist as soon as I left the restaurant. Now that's changed. I expect to be working twenty-four hours a day for several months. I'll be eating, drinking and sleeping with work on my mind." She made a helpless gesture. "You have no idea all I have to learn! It's staggering! The more I learn the more I find out how much I don't know." She struggled to find a way to explain so that he would understand. "Imagine wanting to be a composer and knowing nothing about music. And starting out with a tin ear." She smiled at the feeble joke.

"I would suggest a different line of work, in that case," he said stiffly, placing his glass carefully on the table and fumbling in his pockets for his lighter and cigarettes.

He rarely smoked when he wasn't working. It was a sign of his agitation. "That was a cheap shot, Anthony. I believe

I can do this job—if I give it the time and attention it requires." She sat up straight and moved her leg to give the sleeping kitten more room. "The point is, I've finally come to appreciate why you didn't want us to get married until you at least had a handle on your opera. You didn't think it was fair to ask me to share you with another passion. I really didn't understand until now. I thought if you loved me as much as you claimed, I'd always come first. I've only just realized that coming first or second has nothing to do with it. You have a job to do, and to do it properly requires great chunks of your undivided attention." She wet her lips with the sherry and smiled, pleased she had been able to express herself with clarity. "I have the same obligation to myself now. I've set out to accomplish something important, and I must give it my best. I refuse to give you the leftovers. By the time you finish your opera I should have a handle on what I'm doing."

She reached over and ran a hand over his dark curls. "Do you understand? Anthony?"

He took the hand, studied it sadly, then kissed her long fingers. "Would I be too honest if I said that I do understand and still don't like it?" He sighed and pulled her over until she was in his arms.

Her lips warmed to the caress of his hungry mouth. It caught them both unexpectedly, the shocking force of their desire for each other. Too much time had gone by. His arms held her tightly and she felt herself dissolve into parts. Her breasts swelled against the confinement of her clothing, a deeply throbbing lust pumping hot blood through her veins.

Anthony gasped and the sound of his anguished breathing was delicious music against her ear. She wanted to hear him say he would spend the night with her. The memory of that other night was still painfully fresh. But as he continued to hold her with trembling urgency, Lauren knew there was no need for reassurances tonight. He wouldn't leave her. Not tonight.

A soft ring startled them. Lauren got up unsteadily and walked to the phone on the desk. "Hello?"

Mrs. Hastings' voice was crisp. "A Mr. Parker Fields to talk to you, Miss Wells. Shall I put him on?"

"Oh, my stepfather! Yes, certainly." She sat on the edge of the chair behind the desk, her body still tingling, missing the steadying strength of Anthony tight against her.

"Your stepfather? Yes, Miss Wells, I'll make a note of it," she said with that hint of disapproval Lauren found so irritating. Oh, well, she reasoned, once Mrs. Hastings was firmly on her side, the woman would be a marvelous help, withering unwelcome visitors and callers with a word. She wondered what had happened to Mr. Hastings, imagining him departing for places unknown with his head bent and hat in hand, eternally cowed.

"Dad?" Lauren smiled at his booming hello. "Are you okay?"

"Not to worry. Your secretary told me you were moving in tonight, so I thought I'd be your first obscene phone call."

Grinning, she told Anthony what her stepfather had said.

"He could never be obscene," Anthony said loudly enough to be heard on the other end of the phone. "But tell him he has a lousy sense of timing."

"In that fancy house?" Parker's voice was comically awed. "I wouldn't touch Bo Derek in such a fancy house."

"I should hope not, you old lech." Her blood was cooling in her body, and Lauren told herself it was for the best. Her house or not, she was more than a little reluctant to put dinner on hold and race her lover to bed on the first night. Mrs. Hastings would have a heart attack. "When are you coming to inspect the new barracks, Dad?"

"I thought you'd never ask. Your Miss St. Dennis said you wanted to tell me something."

"Definitely. How about dinner tomorrow night? I'll be home by seven at the latest. Are you free?"

"I think I can work it into my busy schedule." For a

moment, the lightness went out of the thundering voice. "Tell you what. Why don't I come early and make my world-famous *Scampi alla Napolitana?* In honor of lover boy." His tone warmed as he spoke of Anthony.

Lauren smiled at Anthony, again appreciating his sensitivity to Parker's needs. "That sounds lovely. However, you're forgetting about being my guest, for a change. This time you get to relax. You get to check out the palace and the guards, especially the top sergeant. The one who answered the phone. Besides," she added, lowering her voice, "I want you should do a shake-down on this cook they got over here. How else am I gonna know if it's safe to eat in this joint?" It was an old game between them, she managing a fairly passable Brooklynese, and Parker doing a Bogart that would fool the late actor's mother. "Catch my drift, Sam?"

"I dunno. Play it again, will ya?"

The booming laugh made her hold the receiver away from her ear. "See you around seven, then? Take care, Dad. Eat something tonight. Not drink. Eat."

She was still smiling when she hung up.

Anthony held out his arms. "Come here, Sam."

"He's Sam. I'm Dangerous Dan." She looked at his arms. "Dinner?" she suggested weakly. "First?"

He grinned. "Worried about Mrs. Hatchetface out there?"

"Mrs. Hastings? You bet. You don't imagine Alexandra Regis was slipping men into her bedroom, do you?"

He got up and playfully advanced toward her. "Alexandra Regis was seventy-two years old."

She backed up until she was against the desk. "Not always."

"Well, then?" He lazily traced a fingertip over her features, dipped it down over her throat and slowly outlined one sculptured breast, ending up by teasing its sensitive nipple through the velour sweater.

Lauren caught the hand. "It's true, what you once said about women having the ability to constantly renew their lost virginity, Anthony." She breathed in the mingled perfumes of his aftershave, her Premier Enfant, the sweetish polish from the gleaming furniture, the fishy, tangy *tapas*, the sherry's bouquet, the acrid smoke of his dying cigarette. "This wild, breathless, shy excitement . . . yes, shy, somehow, like it's going to be the first time for us. Not because it's been so long. Just because it's us and I love you so much." She pressed his hand hard against her breast. "Let's have dinner and go for a walk in the garden. Let's talk about us. Not our work. And then take me to bed, Anthony. Don't let us spoil tonight. I want it to stay as perfect as this moment."

He stroked her swelling flesh through the fabric with gentle passion. "Perfection terrifies me. It's impossible to maintain. Trust me to love you through the less than perfect moments."

She didn't want to hear his reasonable words. Moving into the protective ring of his arms, she fondled the cherubic curls. "This moment is perfect. We're surrounded by treasure. Fine works of art, gorgeous furniture, this magnificent house. We're drinking the best wine from the costliest crystal. Soon we'll sit down to an excellent dinner prepared and served by a staff eager to please us. We can have whatever we want, our every whim indulged. We have each other, and we're going to sleep in an elegant bed in a room that would win the approval of a queen. Oh, yes, darling, everything's perfect."

He held her tightly and pressed his warm lips to the nape of her neck, just below the coiled braid of silver-brown. "Is it so much better than being together in Silverlake? Close your eyes, sweetheart. Don't I feel the same? Isn't the excitement the same?"

She swayed in his arms, so close to him that she was conscious of the buttons on his shirt, the cold metal of his pants zipper, the slight pull of cloth at her waistband and thighs, none of it taking precedence over her awareness of his hard, muscular body. "Yes, you feel the same. The excitement is the same. My love for you is the same." It was difficult to think but she wanted to share her feelings with him. "There *is* a price on love, I think. You can't pay to improve the quality of love, that's not what I mean. But the quality of an experience can be bought." She pulled away to wave an arm around the room. "Look at this, Anthony! Look how beautiful it all is. No more of the nagging pressures that kept me from enjoying every day. I can dress in designer clothing every day of the week. I can justifiably feel that I'm deeply involved in something important. I'm proud of me in a way I never was before. I can finally take care of the people I love, without secret resentment because taking care of them meant losing something for us. And doesn't our wonderful love deserve such elegant trappings? Why put a diamond in a tin ring when you can have gold? I like this, Anthony," she said with unexpected ferocity. "I want this."

"Don't be afraid, babe. Nobody's going to take it from you," he said quietly. "I don't begrudge you any of this. I just don't want it to be too important to you." He saw she didn't understand. "I'm not that polished diamond you're talking about, Lauren. I have rough edges. I don't know the right ways to charm a woman. If I knew them, I wouldn't use them anyway. You're going to meet all kinds of men now. I don't mean just because you're rich, but because you're in the spotlight now. Not social climbers or fortune hunters—I trust you to see through those—but successful, powerful men who will want you because you're in their world, and because you're beautiful, inspiring. They'll know what to do and say. They'll know how to romance you, make you feel you're living in a fantasy world. So please don't make all this exterior glamour become too important, because none of them will love you the way I love you. The way I've always loved you."

Lauren watched his handsome face darken with emotion, the planes and angles of his features as delicately carved as a master work by a master sculptor. The tumbling black curls, the straight line of the nose, the intensity of the hot, probing eyes. She parted her lips to issue a quick affirmation of her love, a denial of vulnerability to a suitor such as he had described. Then she thought of Jim Reardon, and how she had compared him to Anthony.

Then she smiled. "Anthony, my love. I have what I want. You. The rest . . ." she waved at the walls, ". . . just so much background music. Nice background music. No static." But his words still pricked her uneasy conscience.

They ate in a large, formal dining room, speaking in low voices as if afraid what they said would echo off the brocaded walls. Valerie served a delicious trout poached in white wine, with braised Belgian endive and broiled tomatoes. The *beurre blanc* sauce was flawless, the best she'd ever had, although she'd never admit it to Parker, who was convinced that no one else in Los Angeles could make a perfect *beurre blanc*. A light and lovely Danish rum pudding completed the meal. Since a good Swiss Neuchatel wine had accompanied the fish, Lauren decided against an after dinner drink.

Anthony poured himself a tiny portion of Framboise and held the small glass up to the light. "It takes something like twenty gallons of tiny wild raspberries to make a single bottle of this stuff." He tasted the expensive *eau-de-vie* with pleasure. "You're right. This is definitely no tin ring."

"And, contrary to what you think, you're no hunk of glass." She took his free hand. "Want the grand tour?"

He looked into her sea-green eyes. "Will it still be here in the morning?"

Heart hammering, she nodded. "Mrs. Hastings was to have my stereo put in my room. Do you think you can find it? A little music would be nice. I'll join you soon." She touched his lips with her own.

He poured a little more of the Framboise and started out of the room. He stopped and turned at the door. "Where can I find a road map?"

She didn't smile. "Let's see what kind of a great white hunter you are. See if you can find it by charting the stars."

"Will you be at the end of the trail?" He smiled as she nodded. "I'll find it."

Lauren hugged herself quickly and sent a silent prayer for the gentle repose of Alexandra Regis toward the ceiling. Then she went into the enormous kitchen, complimented the cook and wished Mrs. Hastings a good night. She was glad the two women's quarters were in a wing off the kitchen. Upstairs in her suite she would be further away from them than she had been from her neighbors in Silverlake.

Her private bath had a hallway entrance as well as being connected to her bedroom. She entered from the hall, with its old-fashioned sconce lighting, and peered into the outer room of her suite. The charming sitting area was rich with tapestry wall hangings and comfortable, brocade lounges and chairs in blues and greens, heavily threaded with gold stitching. Her stereo looked a little out of place with its black plastic facings and dust cover, plain walnut veneer and drab rectangular speakers. It hadn't been necessary to bring it. Further down the hall was an entertainment room which contained an elaborate music system with speakers in every room of the house. There was also a wide-screen television, a video tape recorder with a library of motion pictures, a complete Atari game and a small screening area for watching reel movies that weren't available on cassette. Mr. Lowenthal had mentioned that Mrs. Regis had little patience or time for such diversions, but kept the room up-to-date for the comfort of guests.

Lauren had decided against taking Mrs. Regis's bedroom suite for her own use. She tried to believe that her choice of the second largest suite was due to her preference for the really spectacular bathroom that went with it, in which she now stood. But she suspected that she was secretly uncomfortable with the idea of sleeping in the room where Alexandra had died. Norm Lowenthal had suggested having it repainted and newly furnished, but she had declined. The suite she had chosen was almost too opulent to bear. She knew it would be a while before she felt completely comfortable living with such luxury, impossible to think of a time when she would be able to take any of it for granted.

Anthony, sitting in one of the brocade chairs, sipping his Framboise and listening to Pavarotti, didn't notice her in the connecting room. She quietly closed the door, amused by how much at home he looked. While he was listening to his beloved music, head cocked to catch every note, he was impervious to his surroundings. He could easily have been alone in his run-down apartment. For the moment, even she was forgotten. Her smile was partly for the knowledge that when she came out of the bathroom and made her presence known, even the music would be forgotten.

She looked with longing at the spectacular round sunken tub of pink marble that was the main attraction of her bath, but chose the shower instead, first assuring herself that her shampoo and rinse and personal toiletries were on hand. Then she undressed, removed the pins from her hair and freed the long braid. She looked very young with her hair loose, no more than in her early twenties. She felt very young, flooded with enthusiasm for her new work, coltishly nervous with sexual expectation for the night before her.

Rosy from the water, she dried herself hastily and worked quickly to blow dry her silky hair. The hot air and brushwork made it a cloak again, a Lady Godiva cape of shimmering strands. When it was completely dry Lauren dusted her body with fragrant powder, anointed her wrists, the backs of her knees, the hollow of her throat and the nape of her neck with Premier Enfant, took a final look at herself in the mirror and then let herself into the sitting room.

Anthony looked up at her entrance. His eyes didn't change; they already had been transformed by the music. He looked at her as if she were the walking embodiment of the music, his pupils fixed on her pale face and the long, ripe body that tantalized him through the glinting tresses. He slowly rose out of his chair. "Lauren." His voice was thick, distorted by passion.

She crossed the room to him. The flat of her hand caressed his face. Then she turned and began to move backward toward the bedroom itself, toward the bed, her lips curved into a smile of promise, her eyes holding his captive.

Anthony left the music and followed her into the darkness beyond, his smile matching hers. He unbuttoned his shirt as he advanced, shrugging out of it, letting it drop to the carpet. He had already removed his shoes and socks, and his trousers slid easily to the floor, as ignored as the shirt.

She stopped when she felt the bed pressing into her calves. From the outer room the clear, plaintive voice of Pavarotti, singing of a lost but perfect love, serenaded them.

Anthony, naked at last, hidden only by the curling dark forest of hair on his chest and groin, came to her. He slid his warm palms along either side of her lovely face, pausing at the cheekbones, then sliding higher, his fingers lacing through her hair, lifting the long tresses so that they began to ripple back, freeing her body for him.

Lauren felt the covering veil spilling back over her shoulders, was intensely aware of the heat of his body, the texture of his skin, the readiness of his thrusting flesh.

"My love," he groaned, his lips bending to hers. "My own perfect love."

Her mouth yielded to his searching kiss, melting under the honey probe of his tongue. She tasted the fruity Framboise, but the brandy was far less intoxicating than the ardent insistence of his flesh moving over hers. Dizzily, she thought to challenge him about his use of the word "perfect" when he had scorned her evoking it earlier, but she wanted no victory, however small. She wanted only the exhilarating moment, the final safe haven of being consumed by his unquenchable hunger.

She felt his heavily muscled arms go around her narrow back and under her thighs. Then she was being lifted, cradled against him like a child.

He carried her effortlessly to the huge bed, setting her on top of the satin comforter with infinite gentleness. In the other room, the album came to its end, clicked a futile demand for a new record, then began to replay the Pavarotti.

Lauren reached up for him and thrilled to his greater weight bearing down on her. Her brain screamed for tenderness, whispered words, endless kisses. But her body, too long denied, beat up against his, demanding immediate satisfaction. She couldn't remain still, was powerless to keep from urging him to take her, fill her, quell the burning need that tormented her hot, trembling flesh.

He groaned as her supple limbs enfolded him, drawing him impossibly closer. His lips were bruisingly possessive, his arms tight around her, his hands spasmodically clutching at the silky strands of her magnificent hair.

She cried out with happiness as he rose and fell above her, matching his thrusts, her cheeks scalded with burning tears even as he kissed the salty wetness away. "I love you . . . I love you," she sobbed, distantly aware that the tears were a silent tribute to him because he was right, after all—perfection was a fleeting miracle. Already she was toppling from its pinnacle and try as she might, she could not sustain this absolute perfection and not die of happiness.

Much later—she knew it was almost morning because the deep blue outside the windows had lost its velvet thickness and had become more luminous—she awakened, tangled in his arms and the strangling net of her disheveled hair. Very carefully, she disengaged herself from Anthony's warm body, easing out of bed only when she again heard the rhythmic breathing and knew he was sleeping soundly.

She closed the bathroom door quietly, then put on the light. Her image in the mirror made her smile. The crushed ripeness of her passion-stained lips, the warm flush of her body, the waving hair a nimbus of gold and silver giving her a primitive, feral look.

When she returned to the bedroom, her hair in one long, combed and plaited tail, she was surprised to find Anthony awake. "I'm sorry, darling. I tried to be quiet."

"You didn't wake me." He kissed her cheek as she slid between the satin sheets and smoothed the comforter over both of them. "I had a strange dream. You were running through the woods naked, I was chasing you and Pavarotti, singing away, was chasing me."

It was light enough to see his toothy grin. "Oh, the music!" They had fallen alseep with it on. Now there was only silence. While she was in the bathroom he must have gotten up and turned off the stereo.

"It's almost five. Since I'm up anyway, I think I'll go."

"Oh, no!" Although she'd secretly feared Mrs. Hastings's unspoken disapproval of Anthony spending the night, she very much wanted him to stay. "I don't want you to go."

He ran a gentle hand over her body, cupping a sweet breast. "I don't want to go, either. But I think I'd better. I scrapped the libretto yesterday. I have to begin again, and I want to get an early start."

"Completely?" She was instantly alert to Anthony's carefully unemotional tone. Guilt pricked her conscience again. Not only had she forgotten to inquire about his progress once more, but she'd not even been sensitive enough to realize that he'd come to so important a decision. "Oh, Anthony. . . ."

The libretto had been about a young and misguided widow who tried to recreate her happy marriage with her new lover, nearly losing him by doing so. But the story had never allowed Anthony the full expression of his musical ideas. He would rather scrap everything and start again than compromise in any area.

Lauren had great faith in his work; she was positive that this opera would establish him as a great creative force. But she felt he was being overly critical where the libretto was concerned. Time and time again, she cited examples of famous operas with story lines as simple and one-dimensional as shoddy confessions stories. Over and over she told him it was his music, his powerful ability to move an audience with melody and harmony, that would carry the opera. It was an old battle between them. But Anthony insisted on greatness in every respect—no matter what the cost.

She respected him for his idealism and tried to understand his goals, but her selfishness had made her impatient. She had longed for the day when his opera would be complete and staged. Then he would have time for her and money enough for marriage. But her inheritance had turned the tables on them.

"Yes," he answered finally. "Completely. I have to find a new story. I can't continue trying to force this one to do what I want it to do." He gave her a sad smile. "Don't look so disturbed. The timing couldn't have been better. You've got your own thing to do for a while—whatever it is you're running after through the forest. It's not as if we're being kept back from getting married by this delay in my work. You keep running until you find what you want and I'll slow down and let my muse catch me. We'll steal away for moments together when we can."

Lauren knew she should be comforted by the logic of what he was saying. It offered her the space she needed and put no pressure on her in any way. They would go on almost as before, both of them pulling separately for the same goals. But she hesitated, full of uncertainty. So much was happening to her, and she wanted to share it with Anthony. She wanted him by her side as much as possible. And she knew what starting a work over would mean. He'd work night and day. She'd be lucky to talk to him on the phone more than a couple of times a week, or see him briefly on weekends. "I'll never see you." It came out an accusation, for all of her good intentions.

"Just till I get an idea, Lauren. You know how I work.

Something will come to me." He got out of bed and began to dress, retracing his steps to find his garments.

Morning was rapidly advancing. She could see him clearly, his broad, strong back, the tapered hips, the sturdy, masculine legs. He was a study in colors, the sheen of his black curls, the deep olive of his skin, the fine dark hairs on his limbs. Naked, he might have been an athlete, supple, powerful, quick in his movements. She had once told him he had the face of a poet on the body of a boxer. For the moment she didn't care that he had a tremendous talent to share with the world. She only wanted him back in her bed, ever present in her life. All hers, existing to embellish this wonderful new life she had been given.

As he dressed, she told him about the trip she and Chris were planning. "I want you to come, Anthony. Remember how many times we've talked about traveling together? In our wildest dreams we never expected to do it this way. A private jet, the best places to stay. Oh, Anthony, you've got to come," she burst out, unable to tread lightly. "You'll have your new story underway by then, won't you? Surely you can take a little vacation. You've been working so hard."

He turned a calm but cautious-eyed face to her. "Lauren, you know I can't stop until it's completed. I've got a deadline." His voice was gently reproving. "There'll be times for trips later."

The thought of sharing her first trip to Europe with anyone other than Anthony made her frantic. "Why? Damn it, the world won't stop if you don't get the opera done for another month!" She knew she was skating on thin ice, but she couldn't seem to help herself. "It's been so long anyway, what difference will a month or so make?" Didn't he realize that any man would be more than happy to accompany her on such a venture? An image of Jim Reardon came to her mind. "You've got to come!"

His features tightened but his voice remained calm. "The only thing I've got to do is finish my work, Lauren. Everything else can wait. Everything else has to wait." His eyes spoke an urgent appeal for understanding.

She met his steady gaze, but her own eyes were flinty. "There must be dozens of men who would be delighted to take this trip with me." She spat out the words, as horrified by them as he. She was hurt, angry, unbearably disappointed. Anything could happen on such a trip. She needed him with her, to love her, protect her, bolster her confidence. She had never made demands on him before. Why couldn't he understand that she was insecure and needed him? Did she have to spell it out?

Lauren knew that resentment was distorting her perspective. This was going all wrong. She'd anticipated them luxuriously greeting the new morning with more lovemaking. Anthony should have nuzzled his face against her neck, his senses inflamed by the scent of Premier Enfant she'd dabbed on before getting back into bed. And then, impassioned, pressed his bed-warmed body to hers, his grasp growing tighter as his need for her took him the rest of the way out of sleep. She wanted to go to the office still glowing, serene in every fiber of her being.

Instead he had awakened to impatiently throw himself back into his opera, forgetting her flesh as easily as he had forgotten the Pavarotti album the night before.

"Oh, Anthony," she said, sitting up in the big bed, drawing the comforter up around her breasts, "aren't my needs as important to you as your work?"

He sat at the edge of the bed, looking at her. Instead of giving the quick answer she wanted, he considered the question for a long moment. "It's not a matter of evaluating priorities. You're asking me to compare apples and oranges."

"No I'm not. I need you now. Everything's happening at once. I've taken on a lot. I know that, but I can do it, Anthony. I can. I want you to be a part of it. Don't you understand?"

His arms lifted, as if he wanted to hold her. He let them fall to his side, knowing that touching her was not the sort of comfort for which she was asking. "I made my feelings clear about the job before you made your decision. Now that you've made it, I have every intention of backing you up every inch of the way. I believe you can do anything you want to do, Lauren." He got up and went quickly into the outer room, returning with his shoes and socks. He sat down and began to put them on.

"Well, then, if you're behind me. . . ."

He shook his head, finished lacing his shoes, then turned back to her. "Being behind you doesn't mean giving up my own work. Not for a trip, however glorious, however much fun it would be for us. In an emergency, of course I'd be there and the opera would have to wait. Look, I know everything's changed for you. Nothing has really changed for *us*, though. Do you understand that? Last week I asked you not to expect me to treat you any differently now. I didn't fall in love with you for your money and power. This windfall is going to test us, Lauren."

She shook her head. "How can you say that, Anthony? We have everything we ever wanted."

"Do we? Do *we?*" He rubbed his jaw as if to remove the morning growth of stubble. "Look, babe, consider this: If either of us had inherited some reasonable sum of money, it would have been great. You could have quit your job at the Bull, we'd have gotten married, focused in on my career. Later, after we had the home front secure, my opera on the road, you'd have gone back to work, maybe a small business of your own. Instead, you get a fortune dumped on you and, with it, a position of incomparable power and a challenge. And you took it. Now you want me to put my career on hold while you work on yours. It's not a sexist issue. I think you know that. If I didn't have this option, if I'd simply had a job like you had at the Bull, you couldn't keep me from going on this trip. But I have something important going. Don't ask me to put it down to hold your hand and encourage you from the sidelines. And don't make my not putting it down a proof of a lack of love or faith.

"I'll miss you like hell. I wish I could put down my work and live vicariously for a change. Damn it, Lauren, everyone fantasizes about a free ride. But I can't do it. My opera isn't in competition with you. But it is a major part of my life. Just as you are. You must understand that I'll still be here when you return, that I'll love you as surely, steadily and devotedly as I do now . . . that I'll continue to love you that way as long as I live."

He stood up and came to her side of the bed. His hands reached down, brushed aside the comforter and cupped her breasts with possessive firmness. "If that isn't good enough for you, we're in big trouble, Lauren." He released her quickly, as if her voluptuous flesh had burned his sensitive fingers. "Because you're right: There's a world out there full of men who would give up everything for you. I can't do a damn thing about keeping you safe from them. I have to trust our feelings for each other. And I have to believe I'm the kind of a man you really want. If I'm not," he added, his voice taking on a rough edge, "then it's best we find out now."

Her breasts ached at the loss of his touch. "Of course you are," she cried, her emotions jumbled. He was answering questions she'd not asked, hadn't even allowed her mind to broach. "There will never be anyone but you, Anthony."

How could she ever feel this way for any other man? Why, then, did she feel so alone, so frightened of a future she had chosen? "Anthony. Come here. Please."

He bent over her, his face almost ethereal in the pearl-blue light of morning. "I have to go, babe."

"I know."

But as their lips clung, Lauren admitted to herself that for all the splendor of the days yet ahead, she would have frozen this one moment in time if she could.

Chapter Six

Some fun loving previous tenant—perhaps the wrestler—had given the already outlandish apartment a novel new personality. The inside walls of the dome were painted an iridescent shade somewhere between peacock and lilac. Being inside the dome was like being inside a giant soap bubble. The light flooding in from the many arched windows and glass doors hit the walls and caused the paint to shimmer like a rainbow. The effect was dazzling if a bit frightening—there was the suggestion that one windy night the bubble would pop.

Chris loved it, just as she reluctantly loved both of the dome's present tenants. It was a guarded love she felt for David and his four-year-old daughter: She feared creating any bubbles that she might ultimately have to burst. "What do you say, Nipper, shall we pick up these toys and make dinner now?" She smiled at the pretty little girl with the two ribboned pony tails.

The pixie face regarded her somberly. "Do we have to

pick up all of them?" Round brown eyes looked in dismay at the scattered pile of notched plexiglass tiles. "All?"

"It does seem like a lot all at once, doesn't it?" Chris knelt on the frayed rug, wishing she'd had the time to change before rushing to pick Nipper up at nursery school. "Tell you what, you hand me all the red and green ones first, okay?"

The little girl happily complied, pleased with her ability to discriminate between the colors. "Here's one, hiding under the chair. Bad boy," she scolded, digging it out and handing it over to Chris, who was replacing the tiles into their slots in the styrofoam box.

"Very good. Now how about the blues and the yellows?" She watched as David's daughter completed what she had thought would be a difficult chore. It astounded Chris how much Nipper resembled her father, those same clear, dark eyes, the generous mouth, the clearly defined straight nose. Her little body had David's sturdy structure, less a blessing in a female than in a man, perhaps, but adorable at four. She was a little teddy bear of a child, cuddly and dimpled. Chris couldn't imagine a mother who would abandon such a little girl, even to as loving a father as she knew David to be. He had neither talked about his ex-wife nor discussed how he had come to have total custody of Nipper. Chris didn't feel it was her place to probe, but she couldn't help feeling curious. If Nipper were her daughter, no force on earth could take her away.

"Now there's none left! And I did it all myself!" Delighted, Nipper scrambled off the floor and came to tug at Chris's hand. "Can I help you make dinner now?"

Chris nodded. "When your daddy called and asked me to pick you up after nursery school, he said he'd make dinner when he got home from the office. So we're going to surprise him by having dinner all ready. As a matter of fact, since it's your dinner, you can be the cook and I'll be the helper." After a hasty check of the kitchen while Nipper played, Chris had decided on a macaroni and cheese casserole, with sauteed mushrooms and chunks of leftover chicken. One of the many things she liked about David was his unspoken determination to be both father and mother to his little girl. He admitted to being a poor excuse for a cook, but he labored over recipes and delved into cookbooks in an effort to produce tasty meals and establish a sense of family life. He shunned TV dinners and take-out meals, often spending a Sunday afternoon concocting and freezing dinners for the rest of the week while Nipper cut shapes out of bread dough at the kitchen table.

The dome was one huge room in which David had erected partitions—a low wall to designate the kitchen, a curtained off nook to create a semi-private and very feminine room for Nipper. His own bedroom was concealed behind a floor to ceiling bookcase, solidly filled. Other living areas bled into each other—a study for David next to a play area for Nipper, the living room with its TV and stereo on the other side to offer as little distraction from work as possible, a dining room facing the largest window, with its spectacular view of the ocean framed by David's jungle of plants and trees.

Chris improvised aprons for each of them out of kitchen towels and brought all the ingredients for the casserole to the old blue table in the dining room. While she boiled water, Nipper tried her hand at grating cheese and stripping chicken from the bones. She bravely took a turn at grating onion, but like any good head chef, soon learned how and when to delegate authority.

Nipper chattered while they worked, telling Chris all about the busy life of a four-year-old who had a great many friends in school, a sprinkling of enemies, a favorite teacher. Chris sensed a desire in the child for the special camaraderie between a mother and daughter, something that not even David could fulfill.

She listened carefully, asked questions and made encouraging responses, but she tried to steel her heart against the tug of maternal compassion she felt. Even as she had agreed to pick Nipper up after school, Chris had told herself she was making a mistake. She dared not involve herself in the family picture, and here she was, making dinner with David's daughter, in David's home. He was ordinarily careful about not imposing on anyone in regard to Nipper, but today had been an emergency. He and two friends had opened a storefront legal clinic, and he had been alone when two distraught parents had rushed in just as he was leaving. Their son had been innocently involved in a gang shooting, and David had been unable to leave. Because she knew that his calling her meant that he had exhausted all other possibilities, she had been helpless to refuse. Not that she wanted to. It disturbed her to realize that she was immensely enjoying playing momma to the sweet little girl.

When the macaroni was nearly soft, she "helped" Nipper assemble the casserole, watched her decorate it with toasted bread crumbs and put it in the oven. She cleaned up while Nipper set the table for two at her direction.

The stereo was softly playing a Neil Diamond album and the dome was fragrant with the smell of melting cheese and onion when David walked in. Nipper ran up to him with open arms.

"Daddy! I made dinner! But Chris helped really a lot." Her voice changed to a squeal as her father lifted her high, then tickled her chubby neck with an onslaught of kisses. Still holding her and his worn black briefcase, he crossed the bubble dome to where Chris was hastily removing the towel apron from in front of her plaid skirt.

"You mean I've been doing all the cooking when I had a real chef right in this house all along?" He smiled over the black pony tails at Chris, his dark eyes warm, obviously pleased with the domestic scene which had greeted him. "Thank you, Chris. I hated to impose, but I was really stuck. You didn't have to go to all this trouble." He put Nipper down and gave her his briefcase to put on his desk.

"No trouble at all. I got to be the cook's helper." She smiled and refrained from telling him how much she'd enjoyed the past few hours. "How did it go?" She had just fixed herself a cup of coffee and got up to pour one for him. Black. With a half teaspoon of sugar. How had she come to know his habits already? In the past two months they had seen more of each other than she'd intended.

"Fine, thanks. The boy wasn't involved at all. He was released to his parents without too much trouble. Thank God. The hardest part of this business is having parents come to you swearing that their kids are innocent, and you have to be the one to tell them that the kid is guilty as hell, with a rep as black as a hardened criminal." He took the coffee gratefully. "Thank you! It's been a long day. Too damn long." He sat across from her at the table and gingerly sipped the steaming coffee.

The record ended and Nipper raced from the desk to his side. "Can I watch TV, Daddy? Until dinner?"

He tugged affectionately at a pony tail. "Want to rot your mind, huh? Well, Jennifer Lynn, every working woman needs a little mind rotting." He got up, turned off the stereo, replaced the record carefully in its jacket, and put on the TV. Without being told, he tuned in the Muppets, Nipper's favorite show.

Chris tried to finish her coffee hastily, but it was still too hot to gulp down. She wanted to get away from this apartment with its warm family atmosphere, its cozy affection, even the scent of simple but hearty food. She reminded herself that all this had nothing to do with her. She was simply a friend, helping out in an emergency. Nice as this was, it had nothing to do with the kind of life she wanted. David was good, kind, caring, but she could not be content as the wife of a struggling lawyer, raising some other woman's child. She had not lied to Lauren earlier: She was looking for perfection, some earthshakingly romantic suitor who would give her a glamorous life and carry no old ghosts into their lives.

Just then Nipper laughed at the antics of Miss Piggy. Chris glanced over at the child in confusion, knowing that it would be very easy to love the little girl as if she were her own. Who could ask for a more perfect daughter? She lifted her coffee cup determinedly, no longer caring if she scalded herself. She had to get away.

"Aren't you joining us for dinner?" David looked down at the two place settings.

"Oh, I can't, David." She finished the coffee and put the cup down.

"I wish you would. We wish you would, don't we, Nipper?"

The little girl looked away from the TV screen. "What did you say, Daddy?" But before he could answer, Nipper noticed Chris getting up and reaching for her purse. "Oh, you're not going, Chris, are you? You have to stay and have dinner! You helped cook!" She ran to the table. "Please?"

David grinned. "Two out of three constitutes a majority vote, lady. You big business types know all about that." He reached up and loosened his dark blue tie, then undid the top button on his white shirt. His eyes met hers in a special appeal. "Will you stay?"

Chris was touched by the gentle quality of his asking. She had rebuffed his one attempt at deepening their relationship beyond a friendly kiss or hug without explanation. Most men would have pushed for one, but David was sensitive and patient enough to know that if she were to come to him, it would be in her own time.

Chris fumbled in her purse for the keys to the T-bird and shook her head, smiling at Nipper although the appeal in her eyes was only slightly easier to refuse than David. "I'd love to, but I just can't."

"Oh, please," the child begged, butting her head against Chris's thigh as if to physically keep her from going.

Chris felt as if she were choking. She knelt and held Nipper for a moment. "I just can't tonight. Some other time. I had fun, sweetie. Maybe we can do it again, okay?"

Jennifer Lynn had none of her father's tolerance. "No, tonight, please. Don't go yet, okay? I'll teach you how to make cookies if you stay."

Grinning but managing a firm tone, David lifted his daughter to his lap. "Maybe Chris has something she has to do, Nip." He looked at her questioningly. "She knows she's welcome to stay. Since when do you know how to make cookies?"

"I do have to go, Nipper. I . . . I have a date. But the next time we can bake, okay? We'll learn how to make cookies together." She moved quickly through the crazy bubble room to the door.

The night air was moist and chilly, heavy with salt and the lingering odor of sand baked all day by the sun. Chris hurried down the endless staircase that, like her own, was in sad need of repair. She unlocked her car on the driver's side, checked the interior before getting in, then sank gratefully into the leather seat. It was a short drive to her own apartment, but her mind was churning with emotions, and it seemed to take longer than usual.

She parked in her rented garage, locked the door and hurried up her stairs, flashlight in hand. More than once she had found people lurking in the shadows along the way, lovers looking for privacy, a sprawled drunk, once a potential prowler frightened off by the strong beam of light. She had learned to lose her fear of the neighborhood long ago, telling herself she would be no safer in Beverly Hills than she was here, where there were slim pickings for burglars. She never let any locals into her apartment, not even the landlord or delivery men, so no one knew how profitable it would be to break into her private world.

Chris liked to surprise people with the contrast between the inside and outside of her home. She remembered with pleasure how stunned David had been the first time she had invited him to her apartment. But then he'd asked where she learned her carpentry skills. Her pleasure had evaporated

109

and she avoided the question. Her father had been her teacher and she didn't like to think about him, much less talk about him. He had spent many hours with her in his home workshop, teaching her to turn odds and ends of scrap wood into something beautiful and useful. All that came to an end, of course, once he met Adair. After that, his young girlfriend became his hobby. It was ironic: Until then he had given Chris lessons in how to create something worthwhile from trash. Once he took up with Adair, he had just as effectively shown his only daughter how easy it was to take something worthwhile and turn it into trash.

She let herself into the apartment and switched on the lights. The stereo FM radio came on automatically, right in the middle of an old and much loved Beatles song. It struck her for the first time that she had installed the automatic starter to make her homecoming less lonely. She never considered herself lonely before. Certainly, she was no lonelier than she wanted to be. She could have had a frantic social life, if that had been her wish. She regularly turned down dates, parties, all sorts of invitations, going out only occasionally when something particularly appealing was offered.

She went to her bedroom and undressed, hanging up her plaid outfit and slipping into a comfortable pair of jeans and an old black sweater.

As she ran a brush through her dark brown hair after releasing it from its chignon, Chris gave some thought to her looks. She had always been considered extremely pretty, even beautiful. But her appearance meant next to nothing to her now. When she had been a girl, before her parents broke up, she had placed a great deal of value on the accident of breeding that had given her so acceptable a visage. Boys had called her constantly for dates, other girls wanted to be her friends. She had loving parents at home, the best clothing, her brand-new Thunderbird to go with her brand-new driver's license. Then it had been important that she was pretty, that her developing body was lean in the right places, swelling at hips and breasts. The popular boys at school—the football players, the fair-haired jocks—were the idols of her peer group, and she had her pick of them.

Her life was everything she thought it should be—until her father became openly involved with Adair. Then her life became a shambles. It was a long time before Chris had become sufficiently detached from that pain to resume her normal life. By that time, she found that she had matured. She was no longer swept up in girlish play. She wanted a good education, a career, a solid life of her own. She dated now and then in college and in graduate school, slept with a few men when the urge became strong enough, but kept her heart intact and her goals firmly in mind. Men were drawn to her, and she met one or two who would have given her a decent enough life. But always there was a flaw, more a general dissatisfaction, the knowledge that something was lacking, than any particular deficiency. If she were going to commit herself to a man, he had to be very special.

Part of her motivation for going east to college was a desire to get away from her parents: The bewildered expression in her mother's eyes as she tried to adjust to her new life as a greatly impoverished divorcee. The absurd clothing her father had begun to wear to be less conspicuous in Adair's world. The way each parent had started to look to Chris for advice and help. When she left California and her parents behind to throw herself into her studies, she was far from equipped to handle their confusion. She had been the child up until then, indulged, adored, comforted. By the time she returned, crossing the country for the second time in her little car, Chris was a woman, well able to deal with the emotional demands she'd fended off before.

Her mother had taken a job in an office and was living in a furnished room in a small guest house in Santa Monica. She wanted no reminders of her life with Chris's father and was paying to keep her beautiful things in storage. In the years that Chris had been away, her mother had changed. Outwardly content and self-contained, there was a bitterness in her eyes. The loss of her marriage and secure home had etched itself permanently on her face, destroying the beauty that had once been there.

Her father was still married to his young wife, but he made only token attempts to keep up with Adair. In some ways, he was even less happy than his ex-wife. He had lost control of his business and was in poor health. A friend of his had gotten Chris her interview with Earl Regis, and her dire need for a job had forced her to accept the position that was far beneath her capabilities. It was only when her father had died of a massive heart attack two months later that Chris realized just how much she had resented his foolish love affair, his destruction of their comfortable home. He had left her a small inheritance, enough to renovate the Venice apartment and pay to have the furniture moved in. What was left she insisted on sharing with her mother.

At first, she had expected to find a more suitable job, but the marketplace was flooded with new graduates clutching impressive degrees. She settled for doing more and more of the work that should have been done by Earl Regis. She knew the hotel manager imagined himself in love with her. She had no respect for him, was in no way tempted by his offers of fine apartments, furs, jewels if she would take him as a lover. He was bland-faced and dull, playing on his blood tie to the Regis's for his success. He had no objection to Chris doing his work, only to her taking the credit. He compensated by paying her well.

Through the years of working at the Regis-Royale she had defined her image of the perfect man, the only man she would marry. No one she dated or met came close to challenging this image until she met David Bryan. She couldn't understand her vulnerability to him. He was physically attractive but not exceptionally so. She couldn't deny his goodness, his solidity. But he was far from her dream lover. He had been married before. That meant he had experiences he couldn't share with her. He had already been a father. He couldn't devote himself entirely to her, even if she had wanted him to he had a child and a career in his legal clinic. She had no intention of filling someone else's shoes, however appealing his child might be.

Why then, she wondered as she made herself some dinner, did she react as she had earlier? Why had she lied about a date and all but fled from his apartment? She knew he offered more than simple friendship, but he would never force himself on her. He was too decent, and he respected himself too thoroughly to push in where he wasn't wanted. And he would never subject his beloved Nipper to a woman who would resent that the child was his daughter by another woman. Why hadn't she stayed on in that funny fantasy of a dome bubble and spent a warm, comfortable evening with them?

Now, more than before, she was safe from involvement. Lauren Wells had come into her life, and at last she would have a chance at a real career. Working for Earl had been demeaning, faintly degrading, but Lauren's need for her was real and uplifting. Together they could become a dynamic force in a mighty organization. David was no threat. She had merely lost her perspective.

It was too chilly and windy to eat on the balcony, so she took her solitary meal at the butcher-block table in the kitchen. She ate quickly, with little of her customary pleasure. She cleaned up, turned the stereo louder, took a long bath and slipped into a fleecy gown and robe. She fixed herself a brandy and soda and sank down onto the couch, her legs tucked under her.

She was sleepy and relaxed from the hot, fragrant bath. The raspy voice of Kim Carnes was singing "Bette Davis Eyes." The brandy had a smooth taste and a warming bite. She had enjoyed her day thoroughly, and she was looking forward to tomorrow. Working with Lauren was exciting, rewarding. The future was unbelievably rosy. Soon they would be taking a glamorous trip, practically all the way around the world. Perhaps there would even be a man in romantic Europe, the man of her dreams. . . .

Why, then, did her eyes keep drifting over to the dimly lit dome across the way? The branches of the small trees on its balconies swayed in the wind, giving the illusion of a great soap bubble in the sky, ready to pop.

Chapter Seven

It took another two full weeks before Lauren was completely comfortable moving through the hotel at will, but once she had overcome her reluctance, she found herself enjoying her daily inspection tour immensely.

Her routine started with a cup of coffee in the Cafe L'Orange on the main floor. From there, she would make her way floor by floor to her office at the top of the Beverly Hills Regis-Royale, a roundabout journey that took better than two hours but taught her more than ten hours at her desk. She'd had no idea how many separate parts it took to build a smoothly functioning hotel. Food and beverage service alone required an army of people and a complex organization to supervise their work. Entertainment required a separate department, as did maintenance, security, laundry, the arcade of specialty shops on the main floor, baggage handling, reservations, registration, recreation, transportation and all other services essential to catering to a select public. In familiarizing herself with the hotel, Lauren had to meet the people who did the work. Any concern she felt about their attitude toward her was quickly relieved. Like the general public, the employees seemed delighted with the idea of having one of "them" in charge. It had been impossible to identify with the wealthy and powerful Alexandra Regis. But Lauren had worked for a living herself; she knew what it was to worry about a job, to scrimp and wonder about raises and inflation. On a more personal level, they seemed to like Lauren and went out of their way to be helpful. Many thought her foolish to work when she could have the kind of good life they could only dream about, but they also admired her for it.

Lauren experienced a tremendous rush of pleasure at the efficient movement of every cog in the enormous machine that was but one cell in the body of the hotel conglomerate. That she herself was the ultimate force behind these giants was a concept almost beyond her grasp. Just being a part of it all was a thrill.

Like a connoisseur of fine jewels or great art, she recognized the excellence of the Regis-Royale chain. Her occasional visits to other hotels, particularly newer ones, made her passionately pleased that the fates had decreed her to intersect with the Regis-Royale. Being in the hotel was a little like taking a journey into another time. The service was more sincere and personal, the rooms larger and more opulent, even the lighting softer and more romantic. Lauren felt it was this same quality that she, as a woman, found so appealing that Alexandra Regis had been fighting to maintain. But could this unique atmosphere be maintained and still earn the kind of profits Regis-Royale stockholders were accustomed to making? She couldn't imagine a line of motels being faithful to the Regis-Royale image, nor could she see the need for structural improvements in the Beverly Hills hotel. She was aware that she couldn't afford to base her judgement on this one Regis-Royale. This was the corporate head of the chain and it would always receive the most attention from management and staff. That was why her impending trip was so necessary. She had read many reports on the other scores of hotels, but she wanted to visit many of them herself. There was so much to learn and she was working hard, yet sometimes she felt she knew little more than she had the first time she had set foot in her office.

But she had changed in some ways. For one thing, she found herself becoming used to being in the public eye—something she thought would never happen.

At first the almost constant attention had rattled her composure so badly that she had even considered altering her appearance on one or two occasions when reporters were persistent or photographers stuck their cameras only inches from her nose. But her sense of self allowed her to ride out the initial storm of acute embarrassment. In the beginning, she tried hard to appear calm and unruffled at the open curiosity, but one day she realized the stares no longer affected her. These people were not aware of her as a person, only as a personality. They were appraising her facade, not her soul. She might have been a new and deluxe automobile, a fabulous jewel, a sumptuous fur.

Chris had stressed the value of publicity. "The hotels are a product. You've become that product. Every time someone mentions you or the Regis-Royales, it's money in our pockets, so to speak. Look at the Hilton family. Talk about the positive rewards of publicity and celebrity status. People like to talk about the individuals behind huge businesses. It gives them a sense of identification with product."

Then she had lunched with Jim Reardon—taking Chris along at the last uneasy moment. He, also, had encouraged her to capitalize on the publicity. "It's free advertising at the very least. But there's another aspect that I think will be advantageous to us. The Regis-Royales have been the choice of old wealth—people used to having money—for a long time. We need to establish a younger clientele as well. Your appearance and age alone can be a drawing card. I suggest you use it to the hilt."

Because Lauren saw the value in both points of view, she'd allowed herself to be photographed outside her old

Silverlake apartment and inside her house in Holmby Hills for a national magazine. And she had appeared on two local television talk shows. Although she'd been nervous about both appearances, she had handled herself creditably and was grateful for the experience.

But she knew she was not prepared for *Highlights*, a national television show that focused on the everyday lives of prominent personalities. Lauren had seen the show dozens of times, with mixed feelings. It had been interesting to see how the celebrities lived, but now that she was to be the object of Steve Easley's probing camera and no-holds-barred questions she felt apprehensive. Was it worth letting millions of viewers into her life for the sake of renting a few more hotel rooms?

"We'd like to play up the fact that you're becoming known as 'the princess,'" Easley's producer had told her over the phone. "Our own princess at the Regis-Royale. The viewers will eat it up."

To her great embarrassment and to Anthony's equally great amusement, the sobriquet was beginning to catch on. It had been started by media people clever enough to capitalize on the recent royal wedding in England, knowing that Americans secretly longed for such storybook glamor.

As the day of the taping approached, the thought of allowing Steve Easley and his camera crews into her home and her office challenged more and more deeply her natural instinct for privacy. She tried to talk to Anthony about it, but he was oddly complacent.

"It's part of the package," he told her. "What did you expect? Don't let it get to you, Lauren. Some new comet will soar through the heavens and the press will latch onto it and give you a break soon."

His reaction disappointed her—she didn't want to be a falling star, either. In truth, she didn't know what she wanted. But she did know that Anthony was not offering the kind of support she needed right now.

Norm Lowenthal had been much more encouraging, telling her he was certain she would make an excellent showing. But she was still nervous about the show and hated to impose more on the old attorney. He had already spent many hours with Lauren and Chris, very much against his doctor's orders. His health was worsening steadily. He'd been noticeably thinner when he'd come to dinner at her house two weeks earlier, merely tasting his food yet putting energy he couldn't spare into laughing at Parker's jokes.

Other than a few moments in bed before drifting off to a well-earned sleep, her most relaxing times were the six mornings a week when she took coffee at the Cafe L'Orange. Sundays so far had not been very relaxing. Everyone seemed to want a piece of her, or perhaps she was only noticing the demands on her time because she now had so little of it to spare. Friends seemed to need frequent affirmation of her continuing interest in them, Parker and Shelly missed not having her at their beck and call, there was much to do in the house for it to become completely hers, and she was suddenly besieged with invitations and solicitations that required her personal attention. On Chris's advice, she had hired a social secretary to handle these matters, a competent middle-aged society matron who had a remarkable ability to decode the mumbo-jumbo in the mail. At Vera Blanchard's suggestion, she committed herself to very little now, but she suspected that she would eventually be attending many charity functions and social gatherings that required an appearance by the head of the Regis-Royale. Every aspect of her life was changing, despite her best intentions. It had to change, would continue to change. At times, it frightened her, and secretly she wished to be back in her Silverlake apartment, curled up with Tuxedo, worrying about money and Anthony finishing his opera.

At other times—sipping coffee in the Cafe L'Orange and watching the activity on the cavernous main floor of the hotel, exquisitely dressed and bathed in a delicate cloud of Premier Enfant—she felt absolutely happy, at peace with herself and the world.

On this particular Saturday morning, she felt happy in a keyed-up, tense way. She would finally see Anthony that night. In the past two weeks, she had seen him for only a few hours, and even during that limited time his absorption in his own thoughts had been like a wall between them. She understood that the budding flower of his creativity necessitated self-involvement. But understanding did not lessen her resentment. He had warned her that he wouldn't treat her any differently than before, and she had accepted it. But there was so much she wanted to discuss with him, so many feelings that she longed to share.

Her excitement over the celebrities who stayed at the Regis-Royale was met with polite indifference. He was interested in her interviews only from the standpoint of how they affected her, not in their effect on the audience. He was not star struck, had never been impressed with superficial glamour. Lauren understood that Anthony preferred genuine quality to glitter, but she would have liked, just this once, to have him loosen up and gape along with her at the movie stars that came through her doors.

His reaction to her stroll through the hotel with Robert Redford was a distracted "Oh?" She longed for the day when Luciano Pavarotti would take a room at the Beverly Hills Regis-Royale, but she supposed Anthony would be above excitement even then. *I'd go out of my way to see Pavarotti perform any time, but I wouldn't walk across the street to watch him drink a cup of expresso.* She would bet her inheritance on his saying something like that.

She drank her coffee and thought of Anthony, her lips curved in a slight smile. How was it possible to love and hate a man for the same characteristics? It was that solid, realistic, sensible core, that sense of knowing the difference between what was important and what merely seemed important that generated her respect for him as a man. What did she want him to do, spend every morning with her in the Cafe L'Orange stargazing?

"Considering inflation, would you take a dollar fifty for your thoughts?"

She turned to see the smiling face of Jim Reardon at the next table, his head resting with feigned weariness on his splay-fingered hand as he elbowed an empty chair to look at her.

"How long have you been sitting there watching me stare off into space?" She was embarrassed but pleased to see him, surprisingly pleased.

"Not nearly as long as I should have. I was distracted by the competition." He inclined his rather handsome head toward a table nestled in an alcove of dwarf orange trees.

Lauren looked over and recognized Suzanne Sommers breakfasting with three other women. The cafe was fashioned like a small French eatery, open to the main lobby but with an illusion of privacy caused by the profusion of the little trees with their bright dots of fruit. The charming orange motif was carried through in vivid tablecloths and awnings, and some of the wrought-iron tables had orange umbrellas. The lean young waiters wore orange vests and white slacks, and Lauren thought distractedly that the actress, with her almost white hair, and the waiter bending over to pour coffee, with his shock of bright orange hair, were a perfect complement to the decor.

"I'm flattered." She smiled at Jim. Then, because it was silly, their taking up two tables on a busy Saturday morning, she invited him to join her. "I can't stay long," she warned him, a little too strongly. "I've an especially busy schedule today."

"Bosses don't work on weekends. Bosses don't have to work at all." He sat opposite her, his back to the actress he'd professed to have been admiring.

"Was that a commercial message?" She said it teasingly,

but she was still sensitive to inferences that she belonged on a perpetual holiday rather than in a board room.

"Oof! Touchy, aren't we?" His grin exposed straight white teeth. "I retract and apologize. But haven't you noticed? It's almost eighty outside. The beach is calling. This is a nice place to visit, but I wouldn't want to live here." He looked up at the high blue ceiling. "The color's close, but that's not the sky up there. While we sit here jangling our nerves, countless others are lazing in the sun. Wanna go swimming?"

She didn't know if he was kidding or not. A vision of them at the beach, sprawled shoulder to shoulder on a blanket, their nearly naked flesh glossy with sweetish suntan oil, made her flush. "You're the devil, tempting an overachiever. Work calls and I must obey." But she couldn't quite shake her image of him in a snug pair of trunks. There was something aggressively masculine about Jim Reardon, but she knew most of the ache came from wishing the invitation for a day at the beach had come from Anthony. If only she had taken the money and not thrown herself into this job, she and Anthony could be sunning themselves in the South of France.

"Now I've scared you off." Jim said it very nicely, little-boy hurt but forgiving of his tormenter.

"Thoughts of suntans are scaring me off." She got up and reached for her purse. "Tempting. Very tempting." She wondered if she were talking about the beach or Jim. He made her uncomfortably aware of herself and reawakened the desires that Anthony had been too distracted to satisfy.

He stood up with her and sighed. "Won't you change your mind, Lauren? Despite your good example, I'm still heading for the beach."

"Enjoy," she said with exaggerated disinterest. "When I know my work as well as you know yours, I, too, will dedicate my weekends to hedonism." She waved and crossed the patio, heading purposefully toward the kitchen.

The main lobby was packed. Outside the massive glass

doors, long black limousines were lined up, discharging incoming guests and receiving departing ones. It was such a glorious day that everyone seemed especially good-tempered and wore a healthy glow. Her guests had the pampered radiance of those accustomed to the best of everything. They walked with the measured gait of people who knew who they were and where they were going. The people who served them were crisply uniformed, immaculately groomed, properly trained. The air reeked of costly after-shave, wickedly expensive perfume, the distinctive odor of fine leather goods, the best tobacco.

The rich even smell different, Lauren thought, nodding to employees and quite a number of guests who recognized her as she worked her way through the luxurious labyrinth. The lobby had an international flavor—its gothic interior a slice of Buckingham Palace, oriental carpets, a United Nations of guests. An almost black Indian gentleman wearing an exquisitely tailored western business suit urgently speaking with a silent woman dressed in a two-pieced sari; a party of traditionally robed Japanese women hurried by. A very blond couple in smashing tennis togs parted company to create a path for Lauren; behind them four young men and a girl wore identical designer jeans, tee-shirts and suede tennis shoes. A very tall woman threaded her way through the youths, looking as if she'd just stepped out of the Christian Dior boutique in Paris and didn't quite know how she got to Los Angeles.

By the time she reached the kitchen, Lauren's good spirits were restored. She smiled at the cook's helpers closest to the door and skirted the edges of the huge room, heading for her stepfather's office. As she neared the back of the kitchen, she was aware of tension in the air. Looking around at the bustling hive of activity, though, she could discern no cause. "Good morning, Dad." She kissed Parker lightly on the cheek.

"Morning, honey." He had been talking to Chef Raymond and two of his chief assistants, but he turned his back to them without a word and steered her over to his office. "Come sit and talk awhile."

"Oh, I can't. I just stopped in to say hello. And I know you're busy." She looked at him carefully, not liking his pallor or the tight set of his jaw. "Anything wrong?"

His mouth relaxed into a big smile, but his eyes remained hard. "Nothing I can't handle. Not to worry, little girl. Everything's wonderful now that you've made me a millionaire."

She smiled, remembering his awe at the salary that came with his new job. She was almost sure she detected a whiff of gin on his breath. Glancing at the clock, she silently chided herself. Parker never drank in the mornings. "So tell me," she said, affecting the familiar Brooklynese, "the food any good in this joint?"

"Not bad. Could be better. I'm working on it." For him, it was an uninspired Bogart performance.

"So go to work. I'll call you tomorrow morning. Maybe you'll come over, okay? Shelly's stopping over in the afternoon."

"Yeah, sure, baby. Call me. If I'm not too busy spending money, I'll be home."

As Lauren left the kitchen, she glanced over at chef Raymond, but he avoided her eyes. She shrugged and attributed his behavior to temperament. Raymond was a well-known prima donna. She only hoped that Parker hadn't been tactless with the high-priced and internationally renowned chef. Her stepfather had a way of throwing his considerable skill around, as if when all was said and done, only Parker Fields knew the first thing about constructing a decent meal.

It was close to noon by the time Lauren reached her office.

Chris looked up and grinned. She'd been working for hours and was obviously glad for a break. "You're here! I gave up on you. I decided that Anthony had kidnapped you in the wee hours. I had you pegged for being halfway to the South Pacific by now."

Lauren walked through to her office, holding the door open for Chris who had her arms full of paperwork. "Not quite. Although I did almost get shanghaied to the beach a little while ago."

"Anthony actually stopped working long enough to think about getting a suntan?" Chris dumped her papers on a corner of Lauren's desk and sat down. She leaned over to remove a bit of lint from her olive green Courrèges sweater suit.

"Heaven forbid. The invitation came from Jim Reardon."

"Worse things could happen, you know." Chris grinned at Lauren. "What a catch you would be for him. The woman who captured his chair on the board, gobs of Regis-Royale green, and a beauty queen to boot. Oops, pardon me, a beauty *princess*."

Lauren made a threatening gesture with her hand, then sat behind the desk, her fingers aimlessly straying over the papers Chris had brought in. "If he's such a prize, he's all yours. I can't vouch for his perfection, though."

"He doesn't want me. He had his sights set for bigger game the minute he saw you."

"Then he's going to be damn disappointed."

Chris looked up in surprise at the harshness of Lauren's tone. "Hey, what did he do to you? He's really a very nice, attractive man, even if he isn't perfect."

Lauren was equally surprised at her own reaction. "Wow. I don't know. He sets off something in me. I'm attracted to him, and I don't want to be," she said with painstaking honesty. "I blame it on Anthony, I think, because he is putting his music above me."

"Hasn't he always done that? Oh, I don't mean put the music above you. But doesn't he always have periods of involvement with his work, and haven't you always understood and accepted it?"

Lauren cocked her head and studied the other woman. Then she grinned. "Not bad. For one price I get a terrific assistant and a shrink." She patted her braid, then anchored a pin more securely. "Work now, therapy later, okay?"

"Consider my couch out of order." Chris suppressed a giggle. "Unless you and Jim want to borrow it."

"Me and Anthony, maybe. Not Jim. And I don't give a damn how he looks in a bathing suit."

"I don't see why not. Put Anthony in a Brooks Brothers suit and you've got a matched pair."

But Lauren wasn't listening. She was instead staring pointedly at the paperwork piled on her desk. "Doesn't this stuff ever stop?" she wailed. "My brain is stretched to the limit."

"Good. Fold it back on itself and use the blank side. Today we start on familiarizing ourselves with the European hotels."

Lauren moaned. "Just a few preciously short weeks ago we didn't even know each other. Now you've become my conscience. Even worse, you've turned into a slave driver!"

Chris nodded, matter-of-factly accepting her role. "You bet. And if the whip won't motivate you, how about the carrot? Think about that trip ahead of us. You don't want to make us look like a couple of dummies, do you? When they start throwing around facts and figures, we've got to know the roses from the manure. And after we return, you've got to begin making a decision about that merger. The board is already breathing down your neck. From the work you've done so far, I know you're inclined to go along with Mrs. Regis's opposition to it. But the merger would also provide the funds to modernize the foreign hotels. You've got to know how much work is needed and what it will cost. Can the corporation raise the money without the merger? The managers over there are going to try to show you only what they want you to see. You've got to be prepared for every eventuality. Being bored with the tedium will get you nowhere. Unless, of course, you want to let someone else do the real work for you. Jim Reardon would be only too happy to advise you every inch of the way. He'd probably let you keep your titles, as long as he made the real decisions. Everyone would know, of course. . . ."

"That's some carrot." Lauren studied the cool-faced brunette, a grudging smile tugging at her lips. "I'll work, honest."

Chris grinned, her face a pale cameo against the royal blue of her stylish jumpsuit. "The real carrot is stomping those European Hollenbecks and Chambers types into shape, then taking the continent by storm after hours. Personally, I expect to be sensational in Europe. After turning a few cool millions at a meeting or two, we'll wriggle into something slinky and allow ourselves to turn into a couple of good-time girls. I intend to be wined and dined and . . . whatever. Doesn't that sound good? No paperwork and burning the midnight oil on facts and figures, because we'll already have done our homework. If we goof off now, we'll disgrace ourselves over there and instead of partying, we'll slink off to our rooms in utter humiliation. Any slinking off to hotel rooms is going to be for other reasons."

Lauren raised an eyebrow. "Do you have someone special tucked away in Europe?"

Chris looked surprised. "Of course. Prince Charming. Where else would I find him? In Baltimore? New Jersey? Maybe in West Covina?"

"I'm sure there are scores of perfect men in each of those places. It's simply a matter of defining your terms, you know." She smiled gently. "I think there's a pretty perfect one right in Venice, California."

"As you said," Chris answered after a pause, "it's a matter of defining your terms. Look, I shut down my couch. Let's get off yours, okay? Take a close look at page two on this first report. . . ." She bent to the top file.

Knowing she had struck a sensitive nerve, Lauren shrugged and got down to business.

Chapter Eight

They pored over fact and figure sheets until late into the afternoon, Chris devouring toasted cheese sandwiches and Lauren picking at a salad. By the time they were prepared to call it a day, both women were exhausted.

"I know what will fix us up." Chris tapped the last pages into a neat pile. "It's about time you started enjoying some of the nifty features of this place."

"All I want to do is go home and sleep for about ten hours," Lauren moaned. Comfortable as her chair was, she ached from the small of her back to the nape of her neck. She felt like a human computer with a short in its wiring. "Anthony's coming over and I'm going to be dozing on his shoulder. If you're suggesting a nice stiff drink, be warned that I'll probably have to be carried out of the bar."

"A drink! Such a limited imagination. When we're a mere two floors away from nirvana? Think of the *Arabian Nights*. Contemplate a few hours of the ultimate in pampering."

Alexandra Regis had installed spas in each of her largest

hotels even before health clubs were sweeping the country. The Regis-Royale spas were magnificent retreats occupying a full wing of each building, and no expense had been spared to make them the pinnacles of luxury.

For the male guests, there was the atmosphere of a deluxe training camp. Curly-haired athletes with rock-hard bodies gave guidance and encouragement to businessmen who were usually tied to their desks. Gleaming machines did most of the work, rotating limbs, stretching muscles, flexing fatty waists. Everything was intensely modern, almost futuristic. Gideon Frank, the architect-designer hired by Alexandra, believed that men were most comfortable looking ahead, visualizing an uncluttered tomorrow. For them he created clean lines, used an excessive amount of stainless steel. The men's spa encouraged a good-health-is-good-business state of being. Regardless of how little a male guest actually worked out, he was guaranteed to leave feeling like a new man.

Gideon Frank's concept for women was quite different. For them he created an atmosphere reminiscent of the ancient mideastern bath houses, a perfumed harem hot-house replete with pools of water adorned with floating lily pads. The spa's few mechanical devices were consigned to a side chamber. Instead Swedish masseuses were very much in evidence, ruddy priestesses robed in white, contrasting agreeably with the nunlike sylphs in black tights and leotards who gave instruction in aerobic dancing in little private rooms. A large fountain was in the center of the vast main room, its focal point a white sculpture of three naked maidens pouring water from buckets held aloft. Soft music played without ceasing.

At this time of the day the women's spa was at its peak of activity, with masseuses pummeling the oiled bodies of females preparing for the rigors of a demanding Saturday night ahead. There was an air of eager masochism, of glad submission to all manner of indignity, torment and inconvenience, in a hopeful attempt to pay now so that they might indulge later. Women moaned and sighed as their flesh turned rosy under kneading hands. Other towel-draped figures waited their turn in the sauna or Jacuzzi. Still others refreshed themselves in the pools, hot after an aerobic dancing class or working out on the machines.

In the cloistered salubrity of the spa, Lauren found it easy to let her mind drift, bounding at random from one subject to the unrelated next. Chris sat next to her in the cedarwood sauna, apparently caught up in her own thoughts.

Lauren wondered why her friend held onto her hopes of finding some impossibly perfect lover when she was so obviously attracted to that very nice lawyer in Venice. Chris was quite a contrast to Shelly, who loved too easily and too unconditionally. And where did that put her, Lauren? In the middle, the so-called healthy middle? She had not set up any impossible requirements, but she'd never been easy. She gave herself without strings once she was in love. And once in love, she was inclined to be scrupulously faithful. Why, then, hadn't she jumped at the opportunity to marry Anthony? Wasn't his love enough for her? Was she caught up in the myth that every woman had to have a meaningful life beyond home and family? She hadn't exactly enjoyed her day. Most of her work was nothing more than inhaling dry figures and facts.

On the other hand, she felt a keen satisfaction in knowing that she was beginning to make sense of what she was reading. She was starting to grasp what her major responsibilities encompassed, what her powers were and why, and even where she might be most effective after this intensive period of training was over. She was still too terrified of failing miserably to preen herself, but it was thrilling to begin to see a light at the end of the tunnel.

Loosened up from the sauna, they stretched out face down on two empty massage tables to await their turn for service. Lauren was enjoying herself. She'd been too busy lately to pay much attention to her body. At the Lazy Bull she'd been physically active and now most of her time was spent behind a desk. Fortunately, she'd managed to fend off the temptation of Chris's lumberjack meals, but she made a resolution to come to the spa often. After all, she wanted to look her best in Europe, didn't she?

Europe. For the first time, she allowed herself to really think about the trip. A wave of happy excitement ran through her. Business would take up most of their time, but there would still be blissful hours for sight-seeing. A world full of treasures was waiting for her. Everything would be first class now. She was Cinderella and the clock would never strike midnight.

But it was only after Cinderella lost everything that she ended up with the Prince. Well, princes were Chris's business, not hers. She would be content with Anthony. And a family.

From there her mind slid back to her brief moments with Parker. He hadn't looked well. "Maybe I should have given my stepfather some money and insisted he take a vacation instead of giving him a job," she speculated, turning her head toward Chris.

"Well, there's that old saying, 'Give a man a fish and you feed him for a day; give him a net and you feed him forever.'" Chris winked and lifted her chin to indicate a particularly muscular masseuse heading purposefully toward Lauren.

"I hope we pay these women enough. What a chance for vengeance." Lauren closed her eyes and waited for the first cool dribble of scented oil on her warm back.

The kneading hands worked like magic drawing the supple flesh away from her bones, rolling, patting, pressing until Lauren was numb to everything except the pounding of her blood and the pulsing of her heart. The masseuse was returning her to infancy, taking over the control of her limbs, moving her body from one position to another with the confident ease of a mother manipulating her baby for its own comfort. She wanted to tell this magician that she was a credit to her profession, but the power of speech also seemed to be gone. The best she could do was encourage the coaxing fingers with soft moans and sighs.

Her thoughts were like butter under the sun, melting and dripping down into open pockets of pleasure-sensitive pores. Erotic images swept over her with the same soothing rhythm of the masseuse's hand: voluptuous memories of moments of unbridled lust, each so intense that she had to bite down on her bottom lip to restrain a telltale whimper of longing.

Anthony, over her, his face distorted with passion . . . hips racing . . . fingers steel traps on the backs of her thighs while he made the earth move to the frenzied throb of their rapid heartbeats. . . .

She, playful, dignity forgotten, giggling as she towered above his supine torso, riding him with excessive vigor as she had once ridden a wooden rocking horse. . . .

Asleep, then waking to find their bodies touching at the crucial juncture. And then merging together, strangely delighted that the inky veil of night blinded them, forcing them to concentrate on the sense of touch alone. Speechless, sightless, concentrating all the love and lust into their joined flesh . . .

And one more night, the moon so full they made love with their naked bodies bathed in silver light. Anthony's vivid face, the tight set of his jaw as he ceased his tantalizingly slow invasion of her body. One last breathtaking thrust, then refusing to move at all, heavily rigid on and in her. Those hypnotic eyes watching the anguished parting of her lips . . . until, at last, she came alive under him, crying out like a wounded creature impaling itself on the knife that brought life rather than death.

On her way home, Lauren felt reborn. All traces of exhaustion had evaporated in the spa. She was primed emotionally as well as physically for the night ahead. Not only had her sexuality been aroused by the memories of those special nights with Anthony, but she had regained her sense of proportion. True, he was preoccupied with his opera. She had done her part to allow the special closeness between them to fade. She could talk of nothing but her fascinating new world. And she hardly listened to what he had to say. She brought every conversation back to herself and the hotels, as if all roads led to her private universe.

She slowed for a light and watched a handsome couple cross Sunset Boulevard arm in arm. The woman was looking up at her escort, laughing at whatever he was saying. There was a lightness about her step, a languidness that suggested that the evening on which she was embarking promised fun and romance. Her date was grinning, enjoying the walk, the balmy evening, the woman by his side. As the light changed, they disappeared into a shop.

Lauren drove on, envying the couple and remembering the times when she and Anthony had taken walks with the same casual enjoyment. Her good fortune had complicated their lives. When had she last really talked to him about his work? It had always been so important to them both. It wasn't that she'd lost interest. Far from it. His music enthralled her, his genius excited her. She doubted that she could love him with the same fervor if he lacked that great compulsion and passion for his music. He *was* his music.

It was music that had brought them together. Lauren had met Anthony at a Silverlake music store, both of them pawing through a sale bin of opera scores. When they found themselves on line at the Shubert Theater the next night, waiting to buy tickets to *Evita,* they had been struck with the similarity of their musical tastes.

On reflection, Lauren supposed that their love had begun in the usual manner: a strong physical attraction, common interests. They were old enough to move cautiously, and young enough to take a chance. Lauren's two major emotional involvements prior to Anthony had prepared her to be disappointed in love. She had discovered that men would either resent her for being brighter, more capable than they, or they would feed on her superiority, in which case she would resent them.

Anthony had been an entirely unique experience. He managed to strike that most delicate balance of all: He was capable of appreciating her as a woman and not be threatened by her as a person. Until her inheritance, he had been supportive and impressed with her ability to handle herself in challenging situations. She had never hesitated to talk about her work at the Lazy Bull. There had been a comfortable exchange between them. Certainly, they had spent more time dealing with his music—it was something that would live forever.

And that, she realized as she entered the Holmby Hills section of Beverly Hills, might be the problem now. He was no longer the only one doing something of major importance. Perhaps Anthony was only able to indulge her in her career when both of them knew it was nothing more than a job.

She caught herself and broke off that line of thinking. It was so much easier to put it all on Anthony, make him shoulder the blame for what had happened between them. Fresh from her invigorating workout at the spa, feeling rejuvenated, her mind clear, she could face a few basic truths. She'd become distracted by all she'd experienced in the last month or so. She had become a star, and as a star she had already grown to expect special attention. A part of her resented Anthony for treating her as if she were still the unimportant manager of a local restaurant. She had expected him to give her the same star treatment, but how could he when his work required so much devoted attention?

As she guided the Mercedes past the park on Beverly Drive, turning left at Maple Drive, Lauren realized that something very important had happened to Anthony since she'd seen him last. Now that she thought about it, there had been a definite change in his voice during their phone conversation last night. He hadn't said anything specific, but it had been in his tone. A special edge of excitement, a controlled rapture.

She drove faster, more eager than ever to be home. Why hadn't she understood earlier? Anthony had his story! Nothing else could have caused this undertow of exhilaration. How distracted she must have been to have taken this long to notice! Lauren sped into Charing Cross Road. Anthony had his story!

Her excitement dimmed at the realization that he hadn't offered this precious information to her directly. It should have been the first thing out of his mouth. Had he forgotten that she felt his anguish over his work? Why hadn't he shared this with her at once?

Lauren let her foot lighten on the accelerator. She frowned at herself in the rearview mirror. She knew why Anthony hadn't told her about finding his story at last. It pained her to face it, but face it she did—she hadn't given him a chance to tell her. She had been too busy nursing injured feelings because he hadn't acted excited enough about her brief meeting with a screen idol the day before.

Okay.

The road was empty, so she took another peek at herself in the mirror, smiling self-consciously as she promised that tonight would be Anthony's. She wouldn't say a word about the hotels or herself. It would be like before that first phone call from Norm Lowenthal. They would drink wine, dim the lights, sit very close and just talk. He would tell her his new story, and she would congratulate him with kisses. The kisses would become a celebration of his opera and then of their love. It would be a very long time before they would finally fall asleep in each other's arms. . . .

Her house—she was now able to think of it with such familiarity—was just up ahead. She was always amused by the formal approach to the property. The neat gardens, the perfectly manicured shrubbery, the grandiose pathways leading to the immense house sprawling beyond the lawns, all so pretentious and overdone. And yet it was a strikingly handsome home, albeit in the Hollywood mold of ostentatious excess. Anthony liked to tease her about it, dubbing the house "Kingdom Come." All it lacked were pearly gates and a bearded gateman wearing white robes.

Yet for all her self-consciousness about living in such a monument to wealth, she had grown to love the house. It had everything she could possibly want. Acres of beautiful things to look at, use, enjoy. All the privacy a public person could reasonably expect. It was the ultimate in luxury, with every tool at hand to make each aspect of life more pleasurable and productive. Sometimes Lauren had the eerie thought that Alexandra had built the house with her in mind. Why else had a woman who was reputedly terrified of water put in an Olympic-sized swimming pool, cleverly domed to permit year-round use? Swimming had always been Lauren's favorite exercise and relaxation. She was very good at it, propelling her sleek body through the choppiest of oceans with speed and grace.

The house, she decided, was a perfect example of how utterly her life had changed. The best of everything was hers, served up on a silver platter. And not a dish to wash. She drove into the huge garage that opened soundlessly at her approach, recalling the evening when she had rinsed her yogurt bowl in her Silverlake apartment. She had been maudlin over the prospect of never again doing such simple chores for herself, in reality horrified by the immense changes the freedom from washing dishes represented.

Although there was an entrance into the house from the garage, Lauren had rarely used it. She relished the short walk from the garage to the front door along a pathway outlined with brilliant clusters of tiny orange and yellow flowers. Not yet dark, the day was on the outer fringe of that magic time when all colors were most vivid under the fading light of a melting sun. She fumbled for her key but knew she wouldn't get the chance to use it. Whatever time she arrived, the alert Mrs. Hastings was always there to greet her, relieve her of whatever paperwork she'd brought home, or just spare her the inconvenience of unlocking the massive door.

Even Mrs. Hastings was coming around. The frost was disappearing from her eyes and her diligent approach to the house and her new employer's needs had lately become less professional, more personal.

The change had begun when Lauren, noticing that the housekeeper was limping slightly, insisted she see the doctor immediately. The housekeeper's problem turned out to be nothing more serious than a touch of arthralgia, but Lauren had wanted the woman to take a few days off.

"Thank you, Miss Wells. But I'll be fine in the morning. Really. But thank you."

The peculiar expression in Mrs. Hastings's usually impassive face spoke volumes. Lauren understood then that however scrupulously polite and considerate Alexandra Regis might have been to this valued servant of long standing, she'd never shown the slightest hint of real concern about her welfare.

There had been an agreeable melting of Mrs. Hastings's reserve since that day. Lauren was pleased, mostly because it helped further convert Alexandra Regis's home to her own home.

As expected, the housekeeper let her in before she could sort through her keys. "Thank you, Mrs. Hastings. How are you? Were there any calls?"

"Fine, Miss Wells, thank you. Only one call. Mr. Anthony will be slightly delayed."

"Good. I want to change. Will there be any problem about keeping dinner until he arrives?" The daily menu had been a bone of contention between herself, the housekeeper and the cook during the first week of her residence in the house. Lauren had been firm in her insistence that meals be kept simple and calorie conscious. The cook, righteously protesting the denial of her considerable talents, had been appeased with permission to construct dazzling menus for company dinners. Consequently, even casual guests like Anthony would be treated to state dinners.

"I don't believe so, Miss Wells. If there's a problem, I expect we'll all hear it soon enough." Mrs. Hastings gave a rare grin.

"I'm sure we will. Is there any mail?"

She glanced through a half-dozen envelopes while standing in the hallway under the large stained-glass window. The waning sunlight pushed through the colored glass, tinting her hand dark rose, the envelopes blood red. There was nothing important, but the return address on one caught her eye. She opened it and scanned the sloppily written note inside, her face darkening. "Did he say why he would be late?" she asked, impatient to show Anthony this particular letter. It was a veiled demand from Dick, Shelly's last live-in boyfriend, whining that Shelly had removed a few possessions that rightfully belonged to him. Would Shelly's problems never stop being dumped into her lap, Lauren wondered with exasperation. Of course, she would have her lawyer take care of Dick, but she still wanted Anthony to know about it.

"I don't believe Mr. Anthony gave a reason," Mrs. Hastings answered rather primly, as if it were unthinkable that she'd delete anything in relating a message.

Lauren started for the staircase, a smile tugging at her lips over the housekeeper's refusal to use Anthony's family name. They had settled on the "Mr. Anthony" on the grounds that Mrs. Hastings couldn't pronounce DeGiacomo. Lauren suspected that the woman found it too ethnic, too discordant with the gilded anglo image supplied by the mansion and the genteel wealth behind it. To her, the name DeGiacomo probably conjured up images of crude laborers struggling with crates of fruit on the docks of the New York waterfront. Yet Mrs. Hastings was visibly impressed with Anthony himself, in obvious awe both of his being a gifted and already recognized composer, and his marked resemblance to one of her personal idols, Orson Welles in his prime.

Tuxedo appeared out of nowhere, meowing at the hem of Lauren's skirt. He was rapidly losing his kitten look, turning quickly into a tom of promising size and beauty. His tail was fuller than ever, a great white and gray plume.

"Hello, monster cat. Read any good mice lately?" She put the mail on the table and bent to scratch between his ears.

Mrs. Hastings disappeared discreetly. Lauren's interest in this animal of undistinguished ancestry made her uncomfortable.

"Hey, don't do that," she scolded, grabbing Tuxedo's paw before he was able to make a successful leap into her arms. "Wait until I change. You shed, kid, and this suit cost enough to keep you in lobster for each of your nine lives." She started up the stairs, the cat at her feet.

She dressed in a slinky red blouse and a pair of fitted Mario Valentino knickers of soft tweedy fabric. Feeling young and frivolous, she brushed down her Rapunzel hair, fussing with it before finally working it into its familiar braided tail. She secured it with a clip at its tapered end and let it hang free. When she was a girl she had often worn it like this, especially in the summer when she had practically lived in shorts. Her family had liked to tease her about her unconscious habit of tucking the braid into a back pocket to keep it from tickling the backs of her legs.

She kept her lighthearted mood through Anthony's arrival, even when she showed him the distasteful letter from Dick.

"The cheap con-artist," he said, reading the brief paragraph.

They had just sat down to dinner. She'd eaten next to nothing all day long in preparation for what she knew would be a gustatory and calorie laden meal. Her hunger for food, however, was dimmed next to her hunger for Anthony. He looked especially handsome in a lightweight white turtleneck which fit his muscular torso like a coat of fresh paint. A vitality and subdued excitement added to his usual attractiveness. The house seemed electrically charged by his presence. Lauren found it difficult to concentrate on such matters as food, however tasty, and clumsy demands, however distasteful.

He threw her a crooked grin and started on his salad. Nothing dimmed Anthony's appetite. "Don't worry about it. I'll make him an offer he can't refuse." He finished chewing and hummed a bar from *The Godfather*. "I'll tell him to drop it or I'll send Shelly back to him." He lowered his voice conspiratorily. "You not-a worry 'bout a ting, capeesh?"

Lauren laughed, thinking how easily he could fit the dockworker image Lauren suspected Mrs. Hastings of harboring. She could imagine Anthony studying the open sea on a wide-bellied ship, alert for the first silver flash of scales under the water. He had the firm, virile body of a man who worked hard for his living, toiling under a fire-spitting sun, meeting and mastering the elements every day.

In reality, Anthony's people had come to America several generations ago and were as genteel as anyone could imagine. Her smile deepened as she watched Anthony, truly atavistic in his love for any and all fruits of the sea, enthusiastically digging into the excellent *Sole Paradiso*.

"This is great. Eat," he urged, hugely enjoying his filet of sole which was jellyrolled over crabmeat and sprinkled with white grapes and baby shrimp in a light sherry sauce.

All through dinner, she waited for him to tell her his news. But she knew him too well to really expect him to tackle an important subject during a meal. Eating was serious business to Anthony, and when he was really enjoying his food he found little room for conversation beyond matters relating to the food itself. Feeling maternally indulgent, she allowed him to feast in peace. But she couldn't help showing her frustration when he wanted to recover from dinner by watching a movie.

"Oh, let's just talk, Anthony," she protested. "I'm sure you have all sorts of wonderful things to tell me." She linked arms with him as they walked out of the dining room.

"Lauren, do you have any idea how many movies there are up there? All the ones we wanted to see but had to pass on to save a few lousy bucks. Come on, babe, I'm stuffed to the gills. Let's sit back and relax in front of a movie. We'll talk later."

He took her silence for agreement and led the way to the plush entertainment room she'd barely used since moving in. She sat quietly on the couch and watched him put *Only When I Laugh* on the video tape recorder. She didn't understand Anthony's rather too whimsical mood at all. She had expected him to rush right into his good news. Had she been so indifferent to his work these last few weeks that he thought she would be disinterested in his having found what he had looked for so long?

"I love Neil Simon. The man can do no wrong, even though it's basically the same story over and over again." He sat down next to her.

She watched the movie for a few minutes, unable to concentrate. Finally she turned to him while Marsha Mason was swept into James Coco's welcome home embrace. "Damn it, Anthony, you're such a sadist at times. Come on, give."

He raised a questioning eyebrow but kept his attention on the picture.

"I mean it," she prompted. "You've got your new story. I knew it when we talked on the phone last night. I could hear it in your voice. Tell me about it, I can't wait another moment. I was generously going to give you a chance to digest your dinner, but I can't stand it. Tell me." She settled back against his arm, the slippery fabric of her blouse catching slightly on the soft cotton of his shirt.

He rubbed his hand over her shoulder and down her arm in a gesture that merged passion with protective fondness. "Well, you're right." He smiled gently.

She waited.

"It's just what I wanted," he went on when she continued to stare expectantly at him. "Simple, but very touching, ageless and yet contemporary. Something everyone experiences, a sort of identity crisis, but with romance too."

She nodded encouragingly, but he didn't elaborate. "It sounds good. Go on."

"Well, it's set in New York and shouldn't be too difficult to stage. . . ." His voice trailed off.

"But the story, Anthony. What's the story?"

His eyes were back on the screen. "What's her name? The blond playing Mason's friend."

She ignored his question and waited for an answer to her own. "What's it about?"

"No, really, what's her name? It's on the tip of my tongue."

"I don't know. At the moment, I couldn't care less." She eyed him speculatively. It wasn't like Anthony to be so infuriatingly coy about his work. Nor was it his style to let a movie take precedence over a breakthrough on a composition.

She tried again, her excellent mood burning off as she felt herself getting angry with him. "Have you kept that secondary character, the poet? I liked him."

"No." It was a blanket answer. He was seemingly caught up in the movie. "Let's talk later. This is good."

"Anthony." He was being deliberately evasive. "You can see the damn movie any time. You can run it over a dozen times, if you want. Come on, Anthony, tell me about the story." She pulled away from the warm circle of his arm, frowning, but trying to keep her temper in check. She was aware that many creative people were unable to discuss their projects for fear of talking them to death, but Anthony had never felt the need for secrecy before. Especially when something good was going on.

"I just don't feel like talking about it, Lauren, okay?"

He glanced away from her, but not quickly enough to conceal a strange amusement in the depths of his dark eyes.

His attitude might not have affected her so dramatically if she hadn't been feeling so guilty about her recent neglect of him. "Why not?" she asked, greatly injured. "You always want to talk about your work."

He shot her an accusing look but didn't speak. He let his gaze drift back to the movie.

"It's the truth," she said stubbornly. "You usually can't wait to tell me when it's going to hell. And now you don't want to talk about your opera when it's finally coming together?"

He watched Marsha Mason hug Christy McNichols. "Not this time," he said mildly.

She got up, blood rising to her cheeks, her eyes a stormy, cold green. With four giant strides she crossed the room. Without looking at Anthony, she clicked the machine off.

Still calm, he shifted his eyes from the now blank screen to her distinctly agitated face. "Lauren, what are you getting so hot about? I have my reasons for not wanting to tell you about the story yet. Isn't it enough to know the work is going well and I'm feeling better about it? Look, we've both been driving ourselves for weeks, right? You've been pushing to get your act together before the trip, and I've been working like a maniac. Let's just take a little vacation from work tonight, okay? We haven't been together for a while. We've missed each other. I've missed you, anyway. So let's just be together. The hell with everything else for a few hours."

His words sounded reasonable, but Lauren felt childishly shut out. It wasn't like him to need even the briefest of vacations from work. And it wasn't like him not to want to share so important an aspect of his life with her. "I've missed you, too," she said almost mechanically, because it was true. Then she turned to him, taking in the beautifully carved face she loved so much. "I have missed you," she said with a rush of feeling. Whatever it was that was happening to them had to be stopped.

"Do you want to watch the rest of the movie?" He tugged gently on the long braid until she was inches from his face. "Or could I suggest a more interesting form of entertainment?"

She stared at him, torn between conflicting desires. She wanted to confront him about his secretiveness. She needed to talk out her fears that they were growing apart. She wanted to be calm and sensitive, clear the air with a good talk. She also wanted to gloss over the whole thing and let him make violent love to her. The last thing she wanted was to instigate a fight.

For that reason, she was horrified to hear herself say, "You're playing get-back at me, Anthony, aren't you? That's the only possible reason for not wanting to tell me the damn story. I haven't shown enough interest since I got busy with the hotels. Now you want to make me beg my way back into your good graces."

He released the braid and sat back, his eyes narrowing.

"Well, it's true, isn't it?" she persisted. Her stomach tightened and she felt sickened by the look on his face.

He spoke through clenched teeth. "If you think I'm going to dignify such an asinine accusation with a response, you're crazy. Just accept what I said at face value, okay? Damn it, Lauren, is there anything wrong with wanting one night of total relaxation? It wouldn't do you any harm, either." He looked at her carefully. "Or have you already forgotten how to relax? Those big boys, those lions I talked about, they never relax. They're lions twenty-four hours a day. When they talk to you they pace up and back like caged cats."

"All right, Anthony," she said finally, taking pains to keep the hurt from her voice. "We'll put the movie back on and just relax tonight. That's fine with me, if that's what you want."

"Some other time. I'm out of the mood."

"Well, I'm in the mood!" she snapped, getting up to start the movie rolling.

He got up and grabbed her arm. For a moment they faced each other silently, breathing through flared nostrils.

Lauren felt a strange weakness in her knees. His fingers were digging into her arm, hot through the fabric of her blouse. "What are you in the mood for, then?" she whispered.

"This. . . ." With savage need he pulled her against him, bruising her lips with his mouth in a fierce kiss. His arms went around her, moving over her back, drawing her closer until his body seemed to have absorbed her. His tongue probed hers insistently, as if he dared not leave any part of her closed off to him.

Lauren gasped and tried to free herself. They had never tried to solve their difficulties by making love. As much as she wanted him, she twisted her head to escape his lips. "No, Anthony, no," she protested, closing her eyes as his tormenting tongue moved down and over her neck.

Ignoring her resistance, his fingers worked on the buttons of her blouse, then reached around to undo the clasp of her bra with one skillful tug. His lips continued to move over her throat as he pulled away the wispy garments. Naked to the waist, her heaving breasts admitted a truth her protesting whimpers couldn't obscure.

Anthony's strong hands held hers captive while he bent to kiss each extended nipple, scraping the tender flesh with his stubbled skin.

"Damn you, Anthony," she hissed, groaning against her will, knowing pure reason couldn't match this fierce desire.

Lauren pulled free of Anthony's grasp and tangled her fingers in his thick nest of curls, drawing his face savagely against her breasts. "Oh, darling," she cried, her voice husky with an unfamiliar blend of sadness and exultation, "we can't love this away, can we? We should talk. . . ."

He pulled his face away to meet her eyes. "We are talking. In the one language we can . . . If you can't hear how much I love you, feel my love, darling . . ."

She closed her eyes again, her hands caressing his broad shoulders, his wonderful chest, the back of his neck, aware that her prayer for the strength to stop this would go unanswered.

He kissed her with the same burning demand that had begun this spontaneous attack. His hands peeled away her few remaining garments, the stylish knickers, the silken panties. He merely loosened his own clothing, too feverish to wait.

Somehow they were back on the couch and he was covering her body like a clinging sheet. She gasped as he entered her, her senses stunned by the unexpected combination of blood-engorged skin, soft jersey and rough denim rubbing against her hot flesh. A terrible grimace of overwhelming pleasure-almost-pain launched her into another reality and she hugged his body to her, attempting to surround him, enfold him. He was right. She had to admit the rightness of this initially unwanted confrontation of flesh. It was another language, and at last the communication was perfect. The anger was still there; the doubt had not been burned away in the searing heat of this embrace. But they understood each other on the most essential message of all, the power of their undying love.

Chapter Nine

Shelly Noble waited until the movers had set down the last piece of furniture, then sent them away without giving in to her temptation to return the questioning look of invitation in the eyes of the younger of the two delivery men. Over the red company emblem the name Steve was stitched in black thread. He was a gorgeous specimen: Tight clothing emphasized his big muscles. An unbuttoned shirt revealed curling hairs that glinted gold against his suntanned flesh, his arrogant grin said he would be dynamite in bed.

He turned back to give Shelly a last appraising glance as she closed the door behind both men. She grinned after the door was safely locked, rather pleased with herself on several counts. It always thrilled her to know that a good-looking younger man found her sexy. But Shelly was most pleased that, in spite of his obvious interest, he had treated her with careful respect, as if he dared not even hope that she might want him back.

The last was a novelty, a reaction Shelly knew was un-mistakable proof of her new position in life. The delivery man had seen her as a luscious but untouchable creature. The Beverly Hills apartment, the expensive furniture and the classy clothing had told him she might be a successful female executive or perhaps the widow or divorced wife of a wealthy man. But not a kept woman or a high-class prostitute—one session within the gilded interior of Helena Rubinstein's famed salon had taught her the wisdom of exchanging a facade of glib and easy sexuality for an aura of sumptuous sophistication.

Shelly turned her back to the door and studied her new apartment with great pleasure. It was everything she had ever wanted, new and glamorous, furnished with the help of the store's own interior decorator. The building was within walking distance of Rodeo Drive, had a doorman and an impressive security system. From her bedroom window, she could see the stately tower of the Beverly Hills Regis-Royale, where her stepsister was probably hard at work.

She felt a warm glow at the thought of Lauren. If the sky was going to split open and dump gold on anyone other than herself, Shelly was delighted it had fallen on Lauren. She was even able to admit that she was glad fate had pointed its finger at her sister rather than at her. She wouldn't have known what to do if she had been the chosen one. There were too many decisions that had to be made. It made her head spin to even think of what Lauren was doing. Not that she agreed with her choice—Shelly would never have considered involving herself with the business end of her pot of gold. She'd have dedicated her life to pleasure.

On her way to her bedroom, Shelly glanced into the small kitchen, which held only the necessities. She didn't like to cook, probably a reaction to her father, who acted as if food were the most important thing in the world. She took most of her meals out, and when she had to eat in, she made do with anything that could be thrown together with a minimum of fuss. When Brian was home from school for occasional weekends or holidays, she avoided having to cook by taking him out for meals whenever possible, or letting Parker have them over for his special feasts. He adored his handsome grandson and openly disapproved of Shelly for sending him away to school. She cut off thoughts of her father and his critical attitude by moving away from the kitchen.

Shelly's bedroom was large and had its own little balcony. She was proud that she had decorated the appealingly feminine room herself. She smiled a little at the thought that if the kitchen was Parker's room, hers was the bedroom. She felt most comfortable there and was amused by the implications of this admission.

Why not? She was good in bed; what of it? She might not be as talented as Lauren, but the truth was the truth, and Shelly knew that in spite of Lauren's more beautiful face, hers was the better body of the two. Her skin had a warm golden sheen, her limbs were prettily rounded, her torso was tight and beautifully tapered, her bottom could do justice to the most poorly designed trousers.

And if she wasn't as uniquely pretty as Lauren, she was more than acceptable. Her eyes were a dark blue, her mouth was full and provocative and she had a good chin. Lauren was unusual, arresting, with clean and direct features that defied easy classification. But she had never put the kind of energy into her looks that Shelly would have gladly exerted. Shelly had often thought that if she were Lauren, she would have done more with herself. If she had been born with Lauren's assets, she would have become the wife of some great man, or a movie star, or at least a highly paid model.

Shelly sighed and walked over to the all-in-one stereo unit she had taken from Dick's apartment. She knew he was furious with her for taking it, but she deserved something from him. She had taken too much abuse and had endured his drunken, totally selfish lovemaking too often to walk away without anything for herself.

She fiddled with the dial on the FM band and found the rock station she liked best. Rod Stewart was grinding out a hot song in his gravelpit voice. Rod Stewart turned her on. He might look like a scarecrow, but his voice had a way of igniting her blood. She threw herself on her new round waterbed with its cut velvet black and gold spread, deliberately encouraging the great mass of warmed water under her back to roll with the sway of her hips. She loved a waterbed, especially for making love.

Shelly floated on the big bed. She had absolutely nothing to do all day long, and she wanted to bask in the pleasure of being completely free of responsibility. She had known many empty days, since she had worked only rarely, taking jobs as a cocktail waitress when she was desperate for money and afraid to go to Lauren still another time so soon after the last. But this was different. Now she was free to really enjoy herself without tension or pressure. The rent was paid. There was money for food. Nobody was breathing down her back.

Never again would she have to take up with some sexy bum because she couldn't stand her squalid surroundings. She never would have moved in with Dick if she could have afforded to live better. Dick's apartment had been a palace compared to her one-room dump. But it thrilled Shelly that next to this Beverly Hills apartment, Dick's place in West Hollywood was little more than a well dressed tenement.

While Shelly understood that Lauren paid her rent to keep her out of another disastrous living arrangement, Shelly could not help feeling a twinge of resentment mixed in with the gratitude. Lauren could afford to be generous, and not just with her money. She had Anthony. He wasn't rich, but even Shelly knew he was special. He had talent. Other people she talked to had heard of him. She had read newspaper articles raving about his compositions. When had Lauren ever known what it was to be desperate for the arms of even a stranger? When your life was empty and you didn't know how to cope, a solitary bed was torture.

She had been a lonely, unsuccessful child. Her earliest memories were frightening. Her father had been a ghost, there to give her lavish hugs and kisses and then to disappear to make a living. She'd been passed from one relative to another too often. It hurt too much to miss people.

Even when her father had married again, Shelly had felt confused. He was there in the same house, but she had to share him with Barbara and Lauren. She had hated this younger sister and would fall asleep at night playing games of vengeance, imagining Lauren hurt or even dying.

But this new sister seemed intent on liking her, no matter what she tried to do. Lauren was quick-minded and calm; she played easily with other children and was generous about including Shelly in their games. Before long, Shelly found it easier and safer to give up her pointless battle against an opponent who seemed unwilling to fight back. Instead, she let Lauren make life easier for her. In time she had come to love Lauren, just as she had eventually accepted Barbara's unfailing kindness. And she came to trust that, unlike her real mother, Barbara would stay with them. It was far more pleasant to let herself be won over than to keep herself miserably outside the family.

Early in her life, Shelly had accepted a larger truth. Some people came into this world with their feet solidly on the ground. Others, like herself, wobbled and had to hang on to the stronger ones for support. She had settled for hanging on as best she could, to the family, to Lauren especially, and eventually to the men she met. However weak they were, they were still more firmly rooted than she.

Shelly yawned and sat up. She stretched, then got off the comfortable waterbed. Having nothing to do could be soporific. She smoothed down the expensive bedspread. Life was going to be wonderful now, but she was feeling a little at loose ends. Not bored, really, but edgy because she was alone and not doing anything. She wasn't used to being alone and not having something going with some man. She was going to change her entire lifestyle, of that she was sure. No more leaning on men. No more being misused. Still, that didn't mean she had to turn into a man-

hater. Lauren didn't expect her to live like a nun. Shelly
was sure that Anthony gave her plenty of hot action. Anthony, with those smoky dark eyes, that sexy body . . .

No, all Lauren expected was that Shelly stay out of trouble. She grinned. Her body felt ripe. It was the best part
of her, and since her last, imperfect session with Dick, it
had been shamefully ignored.

She turned down the stereo and sat gingerly on the padded
wooden frame of her elaborate waterbed, pulling the small
princess phone to her lap. She tapped out a number quickly
and lit a cigarette while the phone on the other end rang.

"Hello?" It was a drawn out question, followed by a
girlish yawn.

"Cindy? Hi, this is Shelly."

A second yawn. "Oh, hi. What time is it?"

"Time for you to be out of the sack. Unless you have
some good reason for being there." She reached over for
an ashtray, catching the phone before it fell but losing the
long ash of her cigarette.

"No such luck. I'm still sleeping because I work nights
at some sleaz-o coffee shop now. I hear you're in hog
heaven, though. Your sister got dumped on by the bird of
paradise, huh? She must be taking care of you, huh?"

Shelly smiled. "My sister always takes care of me. We're
super close, you know," she said truthfully but smugly.
Immediately she felt ashamed of cheapening her relationship
and Lauren's generosity this way. She changed the subject
quickly. "Listen, I'm in the mood for drinking my lunch
in some elegant bar. You know, dressing like visiting royalty
and who knows, maybe meeting some rich and wonderful
studs who could appreciate two jewels like us. How about
it? My treat."

Instead of matching the lightness in Shelly's voice, Cindy
was hesitant. "I don't know, Shelly. Wouldn't you rather
go to the VIP?"

Shelly understood where the other woman was coming
from. Cindy was a very cute woman with a surprisingly

good body for a mother of three, none of whom were currently living with her. She had natural red hair, an up personality, and she attracted men by the scores, although she had fared as poorly as Shelly in her choice of mates. But she had waited tables most of her adult life, and the idea of entering foreign territory as alien as Beverly Hills intimidated her.

For once, Shelly could take the upper hand. "You know what drudges of humanity hang out at the VIP. I was laying around in my apartment—wait till you see my new apartment—and I was thinking that what we need is to go places where we'd meet some classy guys. Come on, Cindy. It'll be fun. Wear that cute beige dress, the one with the cap sleeves. You look real sexy in it. These Beverly Hills ladies won't stand a chance. How about it? We'll have a good time, and for once in my life, I can afford it." She laughed. "Let's celebrate. You're my best friend." Shelly wondered if her impulsive statement was true. Was Cindy her best friend? If so, it was sad, because they had only one thing in common, a grim talent for picking losers.

Well, she was determined to change all that for herself, thanks to Lauren's generosity and good example. Maybe all good things do come to good little girls who wait patiently. She'd give it a try, but in her own way. And it would help to elevate Cindy, too. "Come on, this is going to be fun, you'll see."

"What the hell. Give me your address. I'll be over as soon as I shower and dress. I'll drink my breakfast while you're drinking your lunch. Oh, boy, will I thank the gods that I'm off tonight!"

She gave directions to Cindy, thinking that her friend's envy of the apartment would be soothed by their having to bar hop in the old Toyota Lauren had given her. Shelly wondered if there was any way she could hint about a new car in the near future. After all, the Toyota looked ridiculous in the subterranean garage parked between a sleek Seville and a Mercedes sportscar.

"Got it? Okay, see you soon." She hung up, brightening at the thought of leaving the Toyota in the garage and taking a cab instead. She could afford it. She still had lots of money left. Getting credit on furniture and clothing had been a snap. Everyone had heard of Lauren Wells. Beverly Hills was buzzing with her name. And everyone was tripping over their own feet for a chance to have contact with the new hotel heiress, even through a close relative.

Shelly got up to shower and change. She wondered if it would be just as easy to get credit on a new car. Lauren wouldn't mind. If her sister had said it once, she'd said it a hundred times: "All I want is for you to be happy, Shelly."

Well, Lauren would get her wish, because she was going to be happy.

Chapter Ten

Anthony's fingers lightly caressed the piano's keyboard, paused, played the few bars over again. His brow was furrowed in concentration as he tried the notes a third time.

Satisfied, he turned to his notes and scratched a few words. Reading them aloud, he played the bars one last time. "Okay!"

Absently jabbing the pencil behind an ear, he got up from the bench and stretched. His body felt stiff all over, like the tin man after a cloudburst. Still reading his notes, he flexed his muscles and walked through his apartment.

It was a mess. Chairs were laden with clothing, dust stood tall on tabletops and his kitchen garbage container was nearly full of empty quick-dinner wrappings.

Anthony looked around in disgust, as if he was seeing the clutter for the first time. He'd hardly stopped working long enough in the past weeks to notice how things were piling up. It was barely seven in the evening and he was satisfied with his day's work. There was no need to go back to the piano until morning. The first draft was completed.

He liked it. He was still at the bottom of a mountain, but at last he had found his mountain.

Filled with energy despite the cramped muscles, he considered calling Lauren before doing something about dinner. She would be home by now, had probably already had her dinner. He tried to conjure up an image of her seated alone at that massive dining room table, served by Valerie while she leafed through reports. But the picture blurred. It was infinitely easier to see her picking at a salad or biting into an organically grown pear at her little table in Silverlake, dreamily looking out at her tiny patio.

He walked over to the phone, unconsciously sighing aloud as he admitted that she seemed to be adjusting to the change in her life better than he was. Every time he came to that house in Holmby Hills, he felt like they were trespassing in someone else's Eden. That Lauren was beginning to take it all in stride both delighted and bothered him. He was proud of her. He was also furious with her. He knew that she'd made the right choice by taking the job and he had faith in her ability to perform well. So why did a part of him still want her to admit that she had taken on too much and renounce the work that kept her from him? So that he could have all of her attention? So that she, his marvelous, talented, capable love, would have plenty of time to wait on him hand and foot?

In disgust, he turned away from the phone without lifting the receiver. Starting with the kitchen, which wasn't too bad since he'd done almost no real cooking, Anthony began to attack the apartment. He worked quickly but methodically, insisting on perfection in performing even the most menial chore. It took him almost two hours to scour the four small rooms, but when he was done the apartment gleamed. Better still, his tight muscles were stretched and the soreness was fading from his lower back.

It was almost a quarter to nine. Again he looked over at the phone. He'd talked to Lauren early that morning, more or less promising to get back to her later in the day.

Since she rarely went to bed before eleven or even mid-night, Anthony decided he would put off the call until he'd eaten. But he wasn't really hungry yet, and besides, there was no food in the kitchen. He would have to go out, which meant changing from his old bathing trunks and tee-shirt, his standard warm weather outfit, to something more suit-able for dining even at a neighborhood bistro. Since he was sweaty and already dressed for a dip, Anthony dug a folded towel out of his linen closet and headed for the pool.

Two of his neighbors, a widow and her twentyish daugh-ter, were stretched out on lounge chairs by the water. He knew them by sight and nodded politely as he walked past them to the other, dimmer side of the deck. He threw his towel over a deck chair, skinned out of his shirt, tossed it next to the towel and dived off the side of the pool into the refreshingly cold blue water.

He swam a few laps, then stretched out and floated lazily on his back. He especially liked to swim at night when he could see the stars. The water was comfortably warm now and he felt as if he could drift here forever, basking in this all-too-rare feeling of contentment.

A shriek followed by a loud splash disturbed his reverie. But it was only the younger of the two women, braving the water.

"Come on in," she called to her mother from the other end. "It's not too cold."

"You young people have thicker skins," the plump lady answered, heaving herself out of the lounge and gathering her paraphernalia. "I'm going in to watch TV."

Anthony swam over to the ladder, aware that he should dry off, call Lauren and then catch a bite, perhaps at Vince's Italian restaurant over on Sunset, right off Hobart. He hadn't been there for a while, but he felt in the mood, as much for the homey atmosphere as the delicious food. It was always like visiting his less Americanized relatives and gave him an opportunity to use his rusty Italian. The lasagna was excellent and served in big, moist slabs dripping with sauce and three kinds of cheese. The wine was also good, and, best of all, Vince kept late hours.

Thinking of food made him realize it had been seven hours since wolfing down a sandwich at his desk. He put one foot on the ladder and started to get out of the pool. The air felt chilly where his flesh was wet and exposed.

"Oh, don't go yet. Please."

Startled, Anthony turned to find his neighbor treading water next to him. Her long brown hair was dripping and her eye makeup was a little blurred, but he could see that she was quite pretty.

"I hate to swim alone." She dimpled becomingly. "Oh, I know I'm only a scream away from help, but I feel much safer if someone is nearby."

Realizing he was glad to have an excuse to stay in the now warm water a little longer, he pushed back from the ladder. "I'm going to do a few more laps before I get out."

"Great!" She swam past him awkwardly, reaching out to grasp the ladder. "I'm Stephanie Fredricks from 310." She extended her fingertips, still holding tight to the stainless steel railing with her other hand.

"Hi, Stephanie. I'm . . ."

"Oh, I know who you are, Anthony DeGiacomo, the composer. From apartment 105."

He showed his surprise. She was, he could see from this new angle, a very pretty woman. Not beautiful like Lauren. Not strong-featured and clear-eyed, but rather on the fragile side, with dainty features and soft doelike eyes that stared at him boldly. Her shoulders were very smooth and her breasts, floating buoyantly on the water, were appealing. Ripe fruits, offered proudly. Anthony was startled to find it difficult to ignore their juicy invitation.

"How did you know my name? And what I do?" She didn't look like a classical music buff.

"I have my ways." She giggled and scissored her legs, rippling the water.

He was uncomfortably aware of the whiteness of her thighs, the snug cut of her bikini. "No, really," he insisted, not giving a damn how she knew him, only passing the time until he could make an exit. It was not like him to be aroused by a strange young woman who had the purring sensuality of a street cat.

Another giggle. "I asked about you," she admitted in a whisper. "You're famous, almost. I knew there was something special about you."

"Why?" One flex of the muscles in his arms, a kick of his legs, and he'd be at a safe distance from this girl. He didn't move but didn't know why.

She took a stroke toward him but stopped just before their bodies touched. "I just knew," she said, running a very pink tongue over a pouty bottom lip. "I can always tell when there's something special, dangerous about a man."

"Dangerous?"

Her eyes had a needling smile in them. "Dangerous. The kind of a man I tell myself I have to stay away from. Dangerous. Hot. One touch and you burn."

Anthony wanted to laugh. Did these cheap theatrics actually work on most men? He didn't mind being seduced by an attractive woman—that is, he hadn't before he met Lauren—but his intellect was offended by such obvious oiling. Why, then, was he so unaccountably aware of those bobbing breasts?

"I think you must have some other guy in mind. I haven't set any fires since I was six."

"There are fires, and then there are fires," she came back at him undaunted. "I even find myself fascinated by men who only want to blow off a little steam."

The kidding had gone as far as it could go. He felt embarrassed and very old. "Stephanie, you're one pretty lady, and if I had the steam, I might take you up on it." He refused to take a last glance at her lush body although the temptation was strong.

He pulled himself out of the water, threw the towel around his neck, grabbed up his shirt, and walked purposefully back to his apartment.

Hair still wet, dressed in clean jeans and an open-necked shirt, Anthony arrived at Vince's restaurant in time to witness the arrival of the owner's distant relatives from Italy. He drank some chianti and watched the fuss made over the newcomers. A wave of loneliness hit him hard, even though he knew he was alone by choice. He had a wonderful, beautiful woman who would love to be at his side. Lauren would have joined him for dinner if he'd asked. And if he had been able to throw aside his reservations, they could have been married by now and, in all likelihood, expecting their first child.

Anthony had already given his waitress his order and was on his third glass of wine when Vince separated himself from his company long enough to greet him. After inquiring about Anthony's health, wealth and happiness, he urged a variety of food on him and then hurried back to his kitchen.

"You look like the morning after, and the night hasn't even begun yet." Teri, one of the regular waitresses, bent low over the table. For the second time that night, Anthony was given a bird's-eye view of tawny-fleshed cleavage.

He forced a smile for the blond girl. "All you see are the ravages of hard work. Something you know all about." Anthony had great respect for waitresses, particularly those like Teri. She was a hard-working girl who supported an ailing mother and still managed to be putting herself through school.

"How's it going?"

"Really well, thanks. Why don't you sit down? Do you have a minute?"

She looked around the restaurant, saw that she had no immediate chores. "Isn't Lauren with you?"

"Not tonight."

She sat down on the chair facing his and moaned. "My

160

poor feet. I'd better not sit for long. My feet will go on strike."

"How's school?"

"Not bad. Good, actually." Her pretty face brightened. "I've got this archaeology class that's really exciting. Maybe I should major . . ."

"Here we go again!" Anthony laughed. "Last semester it was sociology."

Teri wriggled her nose disdainfully. "You don't take me seriously, that's all. I can see me now, out there on a dig, working out a grid, making some great find. . . ." She gave up the fantasy with a sigh. "Where's Lauren? We don't see much of her since she became rich and famous." She said it very sweetly, as if she sensed she might be treading on shaky ground.

He shrugged. "Busy as hell." He shifted in his seat. "She's going to Europe soon. For a business trip."

"Europe! Aren't you going with her?"

His waitress appeared with antipasto and more wine.

Anthony reached out and touched Teri's hand before she could get up. "Don't go yet. Have you eaten? Aren't you about done for the night? Have dinner with me."

She scanned the room again. "Oh, I try not to eat after six or so. Especially in this place. The food's so good I can't stop once I start." She grinned. "I have an Italian heart in an Irish/English body."

"Well, keep me company, anyway, okay? I don't feel like being alone." He was surprised that he made such an admission.

She looked at him speculatively. "Just my luck. Here's a handsome hunk of man, loaded with talent and charm, and he's pining away for another woman."

"Hey, I said I was lonely, not rejected. Lauren's up to her ears in work. I'm really working hard on my opera, racing against a deadline, so we aren't able to spend so much time together." He was aware of the defensive edge

161

that had crept into his voice. "Oh, hell, Teri, don't mind me. My work's going fine at last, it's been a great day, and I'm bummed out because I can't have it all. I think I'm resenting Lauren when I should be wildly ecstatic for her." He looked at the blond girl thoughtfully. "How about it, Teri, what do you think? What would you have done if you were Lauren?"

"Go ahead, eat." She gestured at his salad. "I won't stay if you don't eat."

Obediently he speared a ripe olive and a sliver of salami, glistening with oil and vinegar. "Yes, mother." He realized he was enjoying being fussed over. "Would you have taken on such an enormous job, Teri, or would you have grabbed the cash and run off with a struggling composer, preferably to some sunny desert island?"

She cocked her head to one side, brushed some imaginary lint off her Italian peasant-girl blouse, and laughed. "That's a loaded question, Anthony. It assumes that said composer was up for running away to said island, and it implies that the two lovers would have spent the rest of their lives basking in the sun and throwing money around at will. If you're the composer in question, honey, fat chance that you'd have been so quick to run, no matter how much money you had in your hot little hand. I don't mean to be flip or anything." She reached out and patted his arm. "Go ahead. Eat. I'll shut up if you want."

He sank his fork into some lettuce and a bit of juicy tomato. "No, that's okay. You're right. I wouldn't have gone anywhere. Not until I had finished the opera. And yes, you guessed it, I'm not going to Europe with Lauren. I've got my work."

"And now she's got hers, and you don't much like it, is that it?"

Vince looked out over the counter that separated the kitchen from the restaurant. His hand was poised over the call bell next to a steaming plate of pasta.

"Whoops, gotta go. Be right back." She got up and

162

gracefully skirted a maze of empty tables to the counter.

He watched her shapely legs under the shortish black uniform skirt. She had very good legs. For some reason, he was acutely conscious of legs and breasts tonight.

His waitress brought his lasagna. The spicy aroma made his mouth water. He busied himself with sprinkling parmesean cheese and flecks of dried hot peppers on the lasagna. Mouth full, he buttered a chunk of good Italian bread and was about to attack it when Teri returned.

"Want to eat in peace?" she asked before taking her seat.

Now that he had started his meal, he wanted nothing to distract him from his food. But he indicated that she should rejoin him. "Want some? This is even better than usual."

She patted her rounded tummy. "If I don't get my degree and find some safe job in an office somewhere, I'm going to end up looking like somebody's fat Italian momma. No, I'll get my kicks watching you eat. I'm not like your Lauren. The long and slender type that can eat anything."

"Don't you believe it." He mopped up some of the succulent sauce with a crust of bread. "She eats alfalfa sprouts most of the time. I don't understand women. They starve trying to look good for some guy, then he works all his life trying to put food on her table."

"Well, you won't have that problem, will you? Now that Lauren's so rich."

"Isn't that the truth." He cut into his lasagna and watched the creamy ricotta ooze out. He understood that Teri was trying to be a good friend, but he was starting to feel morose and self-conscious. "Tell me what's so exciting about this class you're taking?"

She took the hint and chatted about school for a few minutes longer. Then she got up to bus her tables. "Hey, Anthony?" She bent over toward him again, once more allowing him a fine view of her breasts. "I don't know what's wrong, but if you need someone to talk to, you know where to find me."

"Thanks, Teri. I'll remember."

She took a deep breath and said what was on her mind. "Anthony . . . If things don't work out with you and Lauren . . . Well, don't forget about me, will you?"

He heard what she was asking, and he felt sad and flattered and a little empty inside. "Thanks again. I needed that," he said. Kindly, letting her know that a lovely, sensitive girl like her couldn't really expect much from a tired composer who was very much involved with a very special woman.

Teri was wise enough to understand and to let it go.

Anthony finished his dinner, got his chance to use his meager Italian during his introduction to Vince's relatives, paid his check and drove back to his apartment.

It was just after midnight when he let himself in. Too late to call Lauren. Because he knew he had set up his evening to reach this precise point, Anthony sat backwards on a kitchen chair, lit a cigarette, and started to think.

The clock in the kitchen had a disturbingly loud tick. The cigarette tasted vile and his throat felt scratchy. He was tired, but knew he could not sleep. He had something he had to do, something he had avoided even thinking about.

It was the most painful thing he had ever asked of himself, and yet he knew it had to be done. It would have taken just a few minutes. All he'd had to do was lift the phone and utter a few direct statements. What would he say?

"Lauren. I've thought it over, and I want you to be completely free while you're in Europe. I think you need some time to think about our relationship. You're moving in one direction now, and I'm moving in another. I don't want to lose you, but I don't want to keep you by keeping you from a life you might ultimately prefer."

It sounded like something out of a soap opera. Even worse, he meant every word. It had been between them from the minute she had been told of her inheritance. He knew now that not only did he not want to follow her in her new world, but he was fearful of her growing fondness for such rich fare. In his mind he had imagined a different scenario . . . his opera a grand success, he and Lauren returning to their comfortable home to plan the nursery they would soon be filling. Throw in Lauren's cat and possibly a hound for him, some slippers and a pipe and it was a perfect picture.

In disgust, Anthony knew this moment of truth had been delayed for too long. Yes, he was learning many things about himself. He had been drawn to Lauren in part because she was not the sort of woman who could live just to serve any man. But he had never expected to have to compete with a career that was so public or fabulous. Though it was difficult to admit, he could easily see why Lauren was excited about what she was doing, why she had jumped at the chance to chair the Regis-Royale board and especially why she had elected to delay their marriage. He understood that part most of all, better, perhaps, than she did herself.

He ground out his cigarette and immediately lit another. Then he got up and fixed himself a cup of strong instant coffee. Back to his chair. Back to his bitter thoughts. The coffee was too hot and burned his tongue. He welcomed the quick tears that sprung to his eyes.

Why wouldn't she be excited? Her job was glamorous, demanding. And she had thrown herself into it with more enthusiasm than he could ever have mustered. She deserved all that was coming to her. And she deserved someone who could share the rewards with genuine enthusiasm. He was a thorn in her side, forever popping her bubbles, dulling the fine edge of her excitement. She didn't deserve that. When had she ever done that to him? She had been unfailingly, unselfishly devoted to his work, even when it took him away from her.

He drank more of the coffee and listened to the ticking of the clock.

Lauren was almost ready to leave for Europe, and the issue had to be confronted. Somewhere, buried deep, was a shadow where once there had been only sunlight. Lauren thought she still wanted to marry him. He had no doubt that most of her was eager for their union. But there was that shadow.

What would her new world offer? What kind of men might there be for her now? Was she making a mistake, tying herself to Anthony when there might be rich, talented, successful men right around the corner? Already she must have met men who spoke her new language.

It had a lot of power, that shadow. It could grow and grow, and no amount of loving reassurances from him or from Lauren herself would be able to sweep it away. Anthony would never allow himself to be the ball and chain that kept the woman he loved from reaching the stars, if she wanted to fly.

He had a shadow of his own, too, formed of doubts and insecurities. His manhood had been wounded in some indefinable way. He had only to consider his evening—Stephanie in the pool, Teri at the restaurant. He'd keenly desired both of them. This might have no significance in the lives of other men. For Anthony, it was a disturbing revelation. It simply wasn't his way to be drawn to other women when he was involved with someone. He was a one-woman man, even in his fantasies. Why, then, had his eyes tracked Stephanie's nearly naked breasts, his hands itched to touch her white thighs, his lips burned to taste her mouth? And why had Teri, whom he'd known for almost a year, felt free to suggest she was available to him? He'd dined alone at Vince's more than once, had even shared a bottle of wine with the pretty waitress. Why had he been so aware of her youthful appeal only tonight?

The answer was obvious and disheartening. He was lonely. He had begun to doubt his masculinity, his ability to satisfy the woman he loved. He didn't want to lose Lauren, but he didn't want her to stay with him out of obligation. He knew he could keep her with him by holding on tight. But that was like closing off the air supply—he would have Lauren, but she would be stifled, half alive.

Now it was time to set her free. Only then could he be sure of her love—and of his love for her.

Telling her would be the hardest part. He hoped she would understand when he suggested that they regard themselves as free agents until her return from Europe.

It was almost one thirty. She had to be at work early the next morning. Didn't have to be. Wanted to be.

Still, he didn't have it in him to wake her out of a sound sleep, one she undoubtedly needed and had earned. It could keep for one more night.

He got up, stretched his cramped muscles and went to his piano. He fingered but did not depress the keys, mindful of the sleepers around him and longing for the day when he would be in a house of his own, far enough from sleepers to play day or night. He looked over his notes, justifiably satisfied with his recent efforts. It was going to be good. It was going to be very good.

He felt no pleasure at all.

Chapter Eleven

"This is sinful! This is like eating a whole box of Godiva chocolates and not gaining an ounce! Whoever said happiness can't be bought had an empty pocketbook! Oh, I love this!"

Chris laughed and gave Lauren's arm a little hug. "Yes, it isn't a half bad way to spend an afternoon, is it? I do enjoy taking orders from you, boss."

Lauren returned the squeeze and led the way across the wide street to still another boutique, this one just off Santa Monica Boulevard, a well-known shop that specialized in custom-made leather wear. Chris had called ahead for appointments to be fitted for coats.

"I'm exhausted. This is harder than working," Lauren whispered as they entered the shop. "But I love it!"

At Lauren's insistence, they had taken the afternoon off to shop for their trip.

"This takes me back to my childhood," Chris said softly as they were ushered into private fitting rooms. "Going out with my mother, picking and choosing and never having to think about the cost of anything."

"I should have had such a childhood." Lauren grinned,

pleased to be able to do something fun with Chris after they had worked so hard for the past few months.

After their fittings they went to a shop that specialized in good knits where they both bought dresses, and then on to a leather goods boutique. By the time they had finished buying Lauren a complete set of beautiful and wildly extravagant personalized luggage, they were ready for a break.

"Want to go eat somewhere?" Chris suggested.

"Are you free?" Lauren knew that Chris had been spending most of her dinner hours with David and his little daughter lately. "How about David?"

Chris shrugged with elaborate casualness. Then she sagged, looking suddenly more fragile than ever, rather like a carefully dressed doll in her rust colored harem pants and creamy beige silk blouse. "Save me from another night with those two, Lauren. I hate myself, but the closer we get to leaving, the more I seem to want to be with them. Let's go somewhere together."

They reached Lauren's Mercedes. There had been no need to pull the car from the garage of the hotel to drive the three or so blocks to the main shopping area of Beverly Hills, but by doing so, both women acknowledged a reluctance to return to work after their spree. "Why don't you stop fighting it and admit you're crazy for the guy. And be glad it's obviously mutual and that he's not Jack the Ripper."

Chris waited while Lauren unlocked the passenger door. She drew herself up to her not quite five foot five and tightened her jaw. "Ridiculous. I'm just keeping in shape for Mr. Wonderful. A girl has to practice, you know. Even a little jewel like me."

Lauren put the key in the ignition and started the car. "I'll bet."

"Believe what you will. Just because you're content with the tried and true doesn't mean we *femmes fatales* aren't prepared to give the rest of the population a break. By the way, are you aware that Jim Reardon is going to meet us in Europe?"

"Oh?" Lauren pulled into the stream of traffic and only then realized she didn't know where she was going. "That's nice," she said indifferently, wondering if it was. She couldn't help still hoping for a miracle, that Anthony would tell her at any moment that he'd decided to come along. "Where am I going, Chris? I know I can afford the gas, but . . ."

"Are you free tonight? Want a night out with the girls? Make that singular." Chris leaned back, digging her spine into the comfortable leather seat. "I want to eat a huge meal somewhere relaxing."

Lauren hesitated. She had more or less promised to see Anthony later. Normally she was thrilled at the prospect of seeing him for even minutes, but something in his tone had put her off. He had sounded down, even though he had insisted his work was going well. Just his gloomy streak coming out, she thought. But she didn't feel like dealing with that side of him right now. She was too hyped up about the trip, in too lighthearted a mood after her shopping orgy. It had been enormous fun. Lauren suspected it had been quite a while since Chris had been able to go on a spree like today's. It was more of that Midas touch Lauren had come to adore having. One scratch of her checkbook and she could bring a smile to any face. No matter how heavily or often she tapped it, there was always more. Only Anthony had escaped her magic touch. He had solidly refused to accept anything from her, even the modest gift of carte blanche to the little music store where they had met.

"Sure," she said finally. "Let's go eat." Something in Anthony's voice had made her dread seeing him. She'd call him from the restaurant and make it for the next night. Friday night would be better for her. She and Chris had elected to take this weekend off—she wanted to spend some time with Shelly and Parker, and she still had things to do before leaving.

Maybe Anthony would be free to stay over and visit with her family Saturday. She was still nervous about the trip, despite her thorough preparations. She needed to be with Anthony—he'd help her regain her perspective.

"What are you in the mood for?"

"Don't ask," Chris sighed complacently.

"Food, I mean."

"Oh, food. Lots of it. Nothing too elegant, if you please. Something substantial, though. We could always go over to Pink's and order a case of chili dogs."

Lauren laughed. "How about Mexican?" She thought warmly of a popular place on Beverly that was a favorite of hers and Anthony's. "El Coyote? The best margaritas in town, lots of great food. Cheap, too. We'll economize. I keep thinking if I don't stop spending money as if there's no tomorrow, I'll anger some great gods who will then feel obligated to dump on me." She turned right on Wilshire, realized her error, and U-turned almost directly in front of the Beverly-Regis Hotel.

Chris sank down into her seat. "Great. I can see us now, busted in front of the hotel." She looked around and frowned. "Talk about the gods. Try that maneauver in an old Dodge sometime. There's no justice in Beverly Hills."

Chris meant only to amuse, but Lauren felt a cold little chill. She was flying high these days. But the higher she soared, the more she had come to dread a fall.

El Coyote was busy as usual, with people waiting for tables streaming out the narrow entrance-way steps.

"Two on the patio," Lauren requested, hesitating before giving Chris's name to the hostess who was dressed in a white blouse and full, colorful floor-length Mexican skirt.

"Afraid of being recognized?" Chris teased, following Lauren into the bar to wait in relative comfort for their table.

They squeezed into a little booth in a corner. "I suppose I am. Isn't that funny? Everywhere I go, people recognize me. I'm starting to get used to it."

"I kind of like it. Happening to you, that is. I only hate it when we're out to eat. I'm sure that one of these mornings I'm going to read about us in the around-town section of the paper. 'Lauren Wells, new princess of the Regis-Royale kingdom, seen at popular eatery with face-stuffing assistant.'"

"We're safe here, kid. Eat away. No reporters in sight. I'll have a strawberry margarita," she said to the waitress as she approached.

"Not me. I'm a purist. A regular margarita, please." Chris began to collect her purse and noticed Lauren was doing the same. "I was going to make a call. To cancel my date with David. You, too? Anthony?"

Lauren smiled ruefully. "You first. What a pair we are. Hiding out from reporters and from men. Such glamour."

Chris returned quickly and Lauren excused herself, fully expecting as effortless a trip to the phone booth as Chris had obviously had.

But Anthony's reaction was surprisingly agitated. "Can't you make it tomorrow night, Anthony? We have all weekend, darling. I'm not working Saturday. Can you stay?"

"Lauren, I really have to see you tonight. I don't care when. Can you come over after you drop Chris off? Do you have to take her all the way to the beach, or just to her car at the hotel?"

"Just to her car. But I don't want to rush, Anthony. I'm beat. We were thinking of having a leisurely dinner and going to see *Evita*. Chris hasn't seen it. It's the last week before it goes on tour. . . ."

"Damn it, Lauren, I want to talk to you."

His voice sounded weary and a little desperate, as if he hadn't slept all night and was going on sheer will. She stared down into the black mouthpiece of the telephone as if she might see him through the pin holes. "Anthony? Is something wrong?"

"I can't talk on the phone, for Christ's sake! No, nothing's wrong. I just wanted to talk about us."

She turned her back against the door of the booth, as if she unconsciously sensed she would need privacy. "Well, talk. You're alone in your apartment, aren't you?"

"Of course I'm alone," he snapped irritatedly.

"Please don't bark at me, Anthony. Can't you talk to me now?"

"On the phone?" He sighed. "Oh, the hell with it, it'll keep another day. Forget it, I'll see you tomorrow."

"No, wait, Anthony. I can't hang up like this. I don't have the faintest idea what you're upset about. I can't very well walk out of the restaurant and leave Chris sitting there. And I have no desire to go try to have dinner knowing you're so upset and not knowing why. Damn it, Anthony, will you please just tell me what's wrong?"

"It isn't something we can get into over the phone," he repeated doggedly.

She was angry now, and resenting him for making her angry without any provocation on her part. "It looks like it's something we have to get into over the phone, doesn't it? Don't do this to me, Anthony. Don't ruin my evening, fill me with . . . with apprehension and then leave me hanging."

He sighed. "All right. I didn't want it this way. Look, Lauren, I'm tired. I haven't slept since the night before last. This isn't right. It'll keep another day."

"Now, Anthony." Her voice was harsh and grating. She closed her eyes to better visualize his face. "Will you please spit it out?" She had no intention of returning to Chris with her stomach tied in knots. Whatever it was, they could take ten minutes to talk it out.

"Okay. Look. Since you insist, what I wanted to say, is . . . I think we'd better call off our relationship until you get back to California. While you're gone, I think the wise thing to do is to be free agents."

She opened her eyes, blinked. It was dim in the restaurant, dimmer in the booth. But bright Christmas lights were strung on one wall as part of the colorful decor, and they hurt her eyes. "What? Is this a joke?"

Again the deep sigh. "No. Now do you see why we can't discuss this over the—"

173

"What are you talking about? You want to call off our
. . . our . . ." She didn't know what to term their relationship. They weren't formally engaged, not in the sense
of rings and public announcements, but they intended to
marry—at least she did.

"Not forever, babe," he said softly, coaxingly. "At least
I hope not forever. That's up to you. Look, Lauren, listen
to me a minute. Damn it," he exploded, "can't this wait?
No, I suppose it can't." He paused. "In view of everything
that's happened, neither of us should have to limit our op-
portunities by a prior commitment. I want you to go to
Europe free and unencumbered. If, when you return, you
still feel we belong together, I'll be waiting. It'll give me
some time, too. To think."

"Is there someone else?" she asked tightly. It was hot
in the booth now. Her hands felt slippery. She held the
phone away from her ear as if it were a loathsome creature.

"No. Of course not. Is that what you think? Lauren,
listen. Try to understand. I need some time to absorb what
the change in your life will mean for us. I know I'll get a
handle on it, but I'm not there yet. You're going away on
this trip, and neither of us knows what it'll do to you. I just
want to give you the space to find out. Listen, I know I'm
botching this up. That's why I wanted to see you. I want
you to go away feeling like you have all your options open.
By the time you come back, you'll have a better idea if
you're going to be content with me . . . or if your palate's
been spoiled by richer tastes. No, I take that back. It's
manipulative and judgmental. . . ."

She listened, still holding the phone at a distance. The
red and green and blue Christmas lights were blurred now.
She squinted and a tear rolled down one cheek. She swallowed and didn't speak until she was certain her voice was
under control. Her free hand patted lightly at her braid, the
way her mother used to. Now she had only herself for
comfort. "I see."

"No. You don't see. I can tell. Look, we need to meet and talk. I should never have said a word on the phone."

"No, that won't be necessary, Anthony. You think we need a chance to see if we're what the other still wants, now that my life has changed so radically." She was amazed by the calm, unemotional tone of her own voice. She almost sounded as if she were reading from a pamphlet. Inside other things were going on. Inside she was freezing up like a machine gone out of whack. The muscles in her throat hurt. Her nostrils felt as if she had sucked sand into them. Somewhere in the area of her heart there was a dull pain. "I can't say I see the necessity for this . . . dissolution of our relationship, Anthony. But if you feel it's best . . ."

"Just like that?" He sounded forlorn, empty.

She welcomed the absurd question. It allowed her to replace her grief with quick anger. How dare he do this and then feel badly about her accepting his decree. "Just like that," she answered crisply, barely moving her lips.

The moment of confused silence was broken at last. "Will you call me from Europe? Write to me?"

"I don't know," she said with a minimum of malice. "I expect to be very busy. Besides, asking me to call or write is putting strings on us, isn't it?" She tried to enjoy her petty victory to the fullest. "I think I'd better wait until I return."

His voice was gruff. "Yes, I suppose." Then he exploded. "Damn it, Lauren, let me meet you later, okay? This isn't what I'd intended to say at all. It came out all wrong. I want you to understand—"

She cut him off coldly. "But I do. Really I do. More than you realize. A trial separation, let's call it. A month or so of freedom. Then we'll see."

"Lauren, I'll be at your house by ten. Will you be back by then? Are you still going to *Evita?* I'll make it midnight."

"Don't, Anthony. Please. Really. Let's leave it this way, okay? I . . . I'll call you when I return." The anger was

175

dissolving too quickly. She was on the verge of tears. She was like a wounded animal. She had to be alone. "Goodby, Anthony."

Lauren hung up and folded her hands together tightly, shutting her eyes and bowing her head. She really did understand. For all his liberated speeches, he couldn't bear a wife who was in a position to compete with him. No, that wasn't all. It couldn't be all. He really did want to be sure she would want him even after she gave herself a chance to meet other men on this trip.

Instead of consoling her, the thought was infuriating. How dare he patronize her? How dare he assume that she would be so overwhelmed with all that money could buy and fame could bring that she would be dazzled by the men she met. Just how well did they truly know each other?

She was also not completely convinced that he hadn't met someone new, some pretty little thing content to worship at his feet?

Lauren reminded herself that she didn't have to sit back and let him run the show. She gulped back an anguished cry, stiffened her spine, thrust her strong chin forward. She could go to his apartment, tell him how ridiculous he was being. But how could she?

Knowing she was far too proud for any such act, she told herself that perhaps Anthony had made a point worth considering. How could she be absolutely certain that Anthony really was the only man for her? The world had opened up. There might be any number of interesting, attractive, talented men out there who could make her happier than Anthony could.

She would fill her month with excitement.

Let him sit at home and fill his with dread.

Carefully, Lauren walked out of the booth and back to Chris and her waiting drink.

She needed both.

Chapter Twelve

London was fabulous, and the London Regis-Royale a palace that rivaled the only slightly more famous Palace farther down the lane. The city was like a postcard come to life. Stately English taxicabs and bright red buses scurried briskly on the wrong side of the streets, flourishing window boxes spilled multicolored flowers over soot-blackened buildings, and elegant bobbies directed traffic with a style all their own. There was an air of happy lunacy that destroyed Lauren's prior assumptions about stuffy, drab old England.

Getting there had been a different story. The private jet was designed to be as comfortable as possible and the flight crew as thoughtful and sensitive as any entrusted with the care of distinguished and demanding passengers, but it still had been a long and tiring trip.

Lauren's giddy expectation of all that was before her vied with her dulled sorrow over Anthony. She coped with the sadness as best she could, deciding with an astonishing degree of resolve to put Anthony out of her mind during this adventure. She had work to do. She would do it well.

She was embarking on a thrilling journey. She was going to have the best time of her life. No matter what.

Dressed to the teeth, Lauren arrived at the airport in a company limousine. Her soft blue Oscar de la Renta light-weight knit two-piece outfit accentuated her slender waist and shapely calves. A very fine silver thread ran through the knit. It picked up the silver in her plaited hair and in the braid around her Pancaldi shoes. On her shopping sprees with Chris, she had bought some stunning silver jewelry, and she wore every bit of it. Patiently, she posed for photographers before boarding the plane.

Once on board, with the plane to themselves except for the crew, she and Chris immediately changed into jeans and casual tops, creamed off their makeup and toed into sandals, aware that before reaching their destination they'd have to dress all over again.

They had breakfast. Chris brought out a stack of files and reports and Lauren worked. Still, time barely passed. They flew over the ocean for so long that Lauren began to have the fantasy that the earth had disappeared, washed off in a great tidal flood. Chris, who had flown to Europe as a girl, was as unruffled as ever—or at least seemed so on the surface.

Eventually Lauren dozed off, right in the middle of a page of notes she was reading. She abruptly awakened, alarmed by something in her dream, but the thought was gone immediately. "Chris," she said finally, interrupting the other woman's reading, "what do you expect most out of this trip?"

The dark-haired assistant smiled brightly. "Romance. Excitement. Finding the man of my dreams."

Lauren wondered if Chris heard the desperation in her own voice.

They lunched, watched a movie, played *Othello* a few times, had dinner. It got dark much sooner than it should have, and that led to a fascinating discussion about time. Which, unfortunately, took a very short time to exhaust.

"See, if you'd taken my advice," Chris stated complacently, "we'd have left in the late afternoon like civilized folk, slept, and arrived in London at eleven or so, refreshed and alert, ready to tackle the first day. Now we'll get there in the middle of their night, our bodies feeling like it's early evening. We'll be so jacked-up we won't know what to do with ourselves, and by the time we fizzle out, it'll be time to start the day."

"Yes, mother." She'd been adamant about leaving in the morning, looking forward to fully enjoying the flight itself. But she was bored with the view from the jet and tired from the effort of working when her mind refused to behave. She settled deeply into the comfortable lounge chair and allowed her thoughts to drift until they came to Chris's too-bright statement about finding love in Europe. What would happen if Anthony was right, if she did meet some wonderful man? She tried to imagine a face that would thrill her more than his, a body that felt better against her own. Someone a bit older, perhaps, sophisticated, secure in his successes with business and women. A man who, in Anthony's shoes, would never have permitted her to leave him on one continent while she dashed off to another.

She conjured up a longish face, nicely crinkled around the eyes, creased at the jaw. Strips of grey at temple and sideburn, salt and pepper goatee neatly clipped . . .

She met Tommy at the high tea held in her honor the day she arrived in London.

He hadn't been introduced as Tommy, and his hair was all of one color, a tawny gold, worn a little long. He was also clean shaven, too youthful to be considered mature, and Tommy suited him far better than Sir Thomas Montrose Tollby III.

"I look rather a boy, don't you think? At my ripe old age I should look like a Sir Thomas. Tommy it is, though, if you don't mind." He struck an amusing pose. "I shouldn't mind in the least—one ages so rapidly—but nothing's sacred any more. I'd be a man of mystery if I could get away with it. No family name, no age, nothing. But what use is pretending? Everything is written down. Not only the statistics. Every last dreary detail is all there, somewhere, all neatly printed in black and white." He had studied her with his penetrating blue eyes. "Privacy is a luxury of the poor, don't you think? Not only in England. Everywhere." He steered her gently but firmly to the far side of the room where it was less noisy. "You are an excellent example. We have never met before, and yet I know a frightful lot about you already." He inclined his head to study her more closely, an ironic smile on his nicely featured face. "But not nearly as much as I find I want to know about you. . . ."

It had been a frantic, unnerving morning and day. Chris had been correct in her summary of events to be. They arrived in London at two in the morning, were met at the airport by a hotel limousine with a sleepy Regis-Royale hotel manager in attendance, were then quickly driven to the London hotel. Refusing a meal, tea or a drink, eager to let the poor executive get his sleep, Lauren and Chris asked to be taken to their suite at once.

Their quarters were lavishly bedecked with flowers. On a table next to the settee, there was a silver bowl with an artistic arrangement of fresh fruits, each piece so highly polished and plump it seemed to be carved of wax. Because this was—had been—Alexandra's private suite, it contained rare works of art, a complete set of Agatha Christie's works bound in Morocco leather, antiques, trinkets, china, all gathered or ordered by the previous hotel head to insure her comfort while in London.

Although it was only eight o'clock California time, Chris took a sleeping pill and advised Lauren to do the same. After she had retired, Lauren went from window to window, absorbing as much as she could of the sight and feel of London. She was too excited to sleep. Finally, she had made herself undress and go to bed. She took one of the Christie novels with her, pleased to see she and her benefactress shared a taste for the works of the great storyteller. It was the perfect book to read on her first night in England, but she couldn't concentrate on the story. She wanted to be out there, roaming the streets, peeking into alleys, exploring to her heart's content. She finally slept in the pearly twilight of early morning, awakening two hours later, surprisingly refreshed and eager to begin her day.

But by the time she met Tommy she was exhausted. There had been two major meetings that day, the first with the executive heads of all the Great Britain Regis-Royales, the second with the board that met quarterly to prepare reports and present a financial analysis of the country's branches of the conglomerate.

At the first meeting Lauren was so distracted by her efforts to appear knowledgeable that it took her a while to realize she was knowledgeable. She understood perfectly the issues under discussion. She telegraphed her pleasure to Chris, who caught and comprehended Lauren's expression, grinning back a teasingly smug *I told you so*.

Confidence bolstered, Lauren participated boldly at the second meeting, willing to risk a possibly naive question or two in order to gather needed information. It delighted her to find that her questions were answered seriously, and in one case, debated at length and a change in policy was agreed upon. It dealt with a standard telephone surcharge the Great Britain hotels imposed routinely on their guests, a practice being dropped by competing hotels. Lauren had read an article on the issue while flying to England and at the termination of the meeting, several members of the board commented favorably about her raising the point.

Despite the fatigue of jet lag and their hard day's work, both women made a fine impression at the special high tea held at the royal blue and gold Century Room of the hotel. Chris looked far too gorgeous in a finely tailored Chanel suit of the softest of greys, her dark hair sleek and glowing, to be easily dismissed as a mere employee. Lauren, stunning in a Halston dress, a subdued rainbow of blues, her braided coronet adorned with tiny blue pearl clips, was beautiful enough to elicit an audible hum of appreciation from the local luminaries assembled to welcome her to London.

During the introductions, even while her lips formed the right responses and she managed to appear relaxed and calm, Lauren kept up a running internal dialogue with herself. Her senses felt heightened. She was living out a fantasy, and for a moment it rocked her deeply, this tremendous change in her life, this dreamlike existence that had come to her almost as easily as leaving one movie theater and walking into another. What had she paid? Had Anthony been her admission price? Was that really how life worked? She had always heard that everything had a price. Was her precious Anthony the cost of this spectacular lifestyle? She could see herself at this moment as clearly as if she were watching a movie on a wide screen, floating easily through this glittering mob, a woman of importance, of wealth and power. She had been a woman like any other, with expectations and dreams, when she had been magically transported to this place where the air was sweet and intoxicating.

If Anthony was the price, could she really pay it?

If she did, would capricious fate offer a consolation prize?

At that moment, she was introduced to Tommy.

"I mean it," he said, staring down into her eyes, "I want to know everything about you. Where shall we start?"

She had to laugh at his aggressiveness. "I thought that British men were cautious and reserved. You're destroying my illusions."

"Our press has been somewhat misleading, I suppose. I'd be quite delighted to present a more accurate view of British men by offering myself as tour guide." His eyes needled hers. "Shall we start tonight? A bit of supper?"

She was finding herself very conscious of his nearness. Tommy couldn't have been more different than Anthony if they had been a separate species. This eager foreigner was a sun to Anthony's moon. Tommy was light and airy, radiating heat, the flash of passion. Anthony was moody and intense, heavy with purpose, and his passion was ageless and inscrutable.

But Anthony was gone.

"I'm dead on my feet," she said, needing to be coaxed.

"You look very much alive," he prompted, his eyes trailing over her like a caress. "And you will need dinner, won't you?"

Lauren smiled at Tommy. She'd be a fool to return home without using the freedom Anthony had foisted on her. Tommy was amusing. He was charming. She could feel her womanly self responding to him. With very little effort she could imagine herself in his arms, his lips on hers.

"I suppose I will."

They agreed to meet at eight, and he reluctantly gave her back to the others. For the next hour their eyes met across the large and crowded room, a secret amusement in his that provoked and excited her.

"Do you need me for dinner?" Chris asked sleepily before going to her room for a much needed nap after the tea.

"Why? Got a heavy date?"

Chris flashed that familiar mischievous grin. "As a matter of fact, yes. With a dashing old boy with a perfectly marvelous moustache."

Lauren gave her a quick hug. "Go for it."

"And you? Or are you planning on a gala evening in bed, catching up on your sleep?"

"Eventually." She laughed and told Chris about Tommy. "Sort of a handsome Prince Charles, don't you think?"

"Okay, Di, have a ripping old time." She glanced at the clock, yawned, and headed for her bed.

Smiling, Lauren undressed and wriggled under the blankets. She had left word to be awakened in time to dress for the evening. A nap would get her through. But she didn't fall asleep immediately. It had been a wonderful day. She had been successful and dynamic. She was in Europe, in her own suite, in her own hotel. She had been feted and admired. And tonight she would be going out with a titled Englishman, who clearly found her fascinating.

She slept lightly but comfortably, awakening to the call she'd ordered with eagerness.

Tommy took her to a terribly chic supper club. All through cocktails he talked about London and the current social season, relating amusing little incidents with wit and sophistication. "Well, you've certainly changed my mind about the staid English," she commented after laughing over the undeniably unrestrained antics of a well-known London playboy.

"I'd rather hoped to alter your perceptions in a somewhat more personal way, Lauren." He shook his handsome head sadly. The light of the candles turned his beautifully cut hair to gold. "Must you really leave so soon? Will you be back?"

"Of course I'll be back. I love what I've seen so far, and I haven't seen nearly enough."

His eyes had a delicious sparkle. "Of London, or me?"

She pretended to deliberate. "Perhaps both," she finally answered. He *was* attractive and she hadn't remembered ever being with a man who made her laugh as much.

He wasn't laughing now. "I hope so. Really, I do. I know it's a bit premature, Lauren, but I don't want to lose you. I want to find out who you are, ask you all sorts of impertinent questions. I want a chance to become important to you." He said the last with surprising humility. "Come on, let's get out of here. Are you really leaving London tomorrow?"

She took his hand and got up. His palm was warm and dry. "I must. I'm on a tight schedule this trip." They walked out into a damp English night.

"It's terribly ironic. I leave for Los Angeles at the end of the week on business. Do you think we can manage to be in the same city at the same time in the future? For more than a few hours, that is?"

She waited until Tommy had tipped the parking attendant

and ushered her into the warm leathery interior of his sleek Jaguar sedan. "That would be nice." She thought of Anthony with confusion. What if Tommy meant what he was saying? She suspected he did. How would Anthony react if parts of her European adventure followed her home? Or was he secretly hoping such a thing would happen, so that he could end a relationship that had become excessively complicated?

Tommy let the engine purr as he stared at Lauren in the near darkness. Without his faintly mocking expression, his long, pale face was extraordinarily handsome, almost angelic. Intuitively, Lauren sensed that some of Tommy's banter was a cover-up for a deep loneliness.

"Are you terribly tired? You are, of course, but I can't imagine letting you go just yet."

"I am tired. . . ." She didn't want to say goodby so quickly, either. "But I did sneak a little nap."

"What would you say to a drive, then? To give you an idea what you'll be leaving behind. Other than myself, of course."

They drove for hours. He was a perfect tour guide, bringing London to life for her with wonderful stories that revealed London's long and proud history. Parker had told her about Times Square many times with the fondness of a displaced New Yorker, but Picadilly Circus had to rival it for activity and excitement. The traffic was dense and noisy, with everyone going, for Lauren, the wrong way with careless abandon. Tommy whipped through the streets, pointing out various spots of interest, lacing his stories with personal history. Except for his school years and time spent at his family's manor in the country, he had lived his entire life in London and, for all his traveling, found it second to no city. "The only truly civilized spot in the world. At least here one can live with a modicum of comfort and grace."

Lauren wasn't so sure. She saw the splendor, the graciousness, the timeless beauty. But she also noticed the slums, the desperate-eyed people who dwelled in them, shuffling through shabby streets without enough clothing on their backs to protect them from the cold, damp night. On one corner a half-dozen men huddled around a makeshift fire, a silent rebuke to the Jag and its two comfortable riders. Tommy seemed not to notice them at all. Lauren wondered if it were possible that for him, such unfortunates simply did not exist. It made her realize how very far apart they were, she and this attractive aristocrat. A sharp longing for Anthony induced anger. He should have been with her, seeing the disparity between the two Londons. He would understand how she felt in a way that Tommy, who had never wanted for anything, couldn't possibly fathom. In turn, like a circle closing, her anger toward Anthony for not being there induced a renewed warmth for Tommy, who was. She forgave him his blindness—probably, he had never been taught to see. "What was it like, growing up here, Tommy? What was your childhood like?"

"Oh, the sort of stuff of any childhood, I suppose," he answered offhandedly, staring into the night as he drove. "Growing up is tiresome. It takes far too long to become one's own person, don't you think?"

"No, I don't. Come on, Tommy. What was it like? Do you have brothers and sisters? Tell me about your parents."

She drew him out, fascinated by his recitation of a boyhood in a socially and emotionally stable family. The settings were equally enviable—the big old house in the country, the faithful servants, the proper but affectionate parents, a predictable picture with shaggy sheepdogs, fine horses, boxwood hedges and distinguished ancestors. It was impossible not to imagine herself safely esconced in such a sturdy scene, married to this man, bearing his children who would, some day, be as unconsciously blind to human deprivation as he. "You make me think of my favorite childhood story, *The Happy Prince,*" she said thoughtfully. "Living in splendor all your life, protected from the grimness of other people's lives . . ." It was an unfinished analogy, and she wasn't prepared for his disturbed reaction.

"I know that story quite well, as it happens. And the point is supposed to be, I trust, that to have been fortunate is to have been unfortunate—deprived of a knowledge of human suffering and squalor. Everyone experiences loss and pain. Who is to say my suffering is less intense than that of those poor men standing by the fire back there? It just comes from different lacks. . . ."

"I wondered if you'd seen them," she admitted.

"Of course I saw them. But what's to be done for them? What can either of us do to alter that hideous reality? Yes, certainly, we can feed them for a day. For a week, perhaps, speaking collectively of the poor in this city. And then? Don't deceive yourself, my dear. Don't fall into the trap of taking responsibility for a world not of your making. Enjoy what you have. This life is not without its own misery. That, I fear, you will discover before too long."

She watched his pensive face, chilled by his words. "I'm sure you're right." She felt a sudden desire to see that faintly derisive grin on his face again. "So tell me about how you've managed to resist aging. Won't you ever look like a Sir Thomas Montrose Tollby III?"

His smile, like the sun obscured by a cloud, was eager to reappear. "Sir Thomas is safely hidden away in a closet, aging more gracefully but out of public view." He threw her a shrewd glance. "Oscar Wilde had stories for adults, too, remember."

She laughed. "Truce?" As they were idling at a traffic light, she extended her hand.

He took it and brought it to his lips. Then he turned it over and kissed her open palm. "What is there to do? I'm afraid I'm going to be putty in your lovely hands."

He returned her to her hotel. Both were silent. Lauren knew he wanted to be asked to her suite. She was amazed and faintly alarmed by the strong surge of desire she felt for him. His boyish charm hid little of his decidedly masculine nature. Lauren felt a fierce longing to be tightly

187

pressed to him, to abandon all thought for a few hours of intimacy. It had been so long since she'd been with Anthony.

The thought was sobering. She was instantly ashamed of herself. She had no right to think of using this nice, caring man as a substitute for the man she really wanted. *Damn Anthony!* she thought. But her anger wasn't enough to enable her to keep the truth from herself.

"Lauren, my dear! I don't know how to say goodby." His eyes focused without blinking on her face. "It's been so very long since I've felt this way about a woman. You will come back? You will let me see you if I come to Los Angeles?"

She didn't know what to say. Mercifully, her exhaustion caught up with her, numbing her mind and body. "I don't know, Tommy. I . . . there is someone else. In Los Angeles. I don't know what I'll find when I get back."

He was silent for a moment. Then he sighed and dredged up the mocking grin. "I don't give up very easily. May I call?"

Instead of answering, she leaned over to kiss him good night. His response was immediate and hungry. His strong arms folded around her; his mouth was hot and seeking.

Startled by his intensity, Lauren had no defenses against her own leaping desire. Gasping, her lips parted, her tongue meeting his in a passionate embrace. Quickly—but not as quickly as she wished—she flattened her palms against his chest and pulled back.

His arms still held her. "There's still tonight. Let me stay the night, Lauren. Please."

She gently, firmly, released herself from his grasp. "Don't think I'm not a little bit tempted," she admitted with a shaky smile. "But I'm not very good at using one man as a means of forgetting another."

"It's not the worst way to go about it." He lifted a pale eyebrow. "I'm at your service at any time. You will keep me in mind?"

She gestured for him to remain seated while a doorman opened her door and stood by to help her out of the Jaguar. "I give you my word, Sir Thomas."

Her mind was buzzing with thoughts as she bathed and slipped into a nightgown. But as soon as her head touched the pillow, she was sound asleep.

Chapter Thirteen

"Don't kid a kidder, Shelly, my love." Randy polished the bar with professional swipes of his cloth, coaxing a shine from the battered wood. "There you are in paradise and you're not happy. What's bugging you?"

She watched the cloth spin by dangerously close to her rum and cola, then turned her back to the bartender and gazed at the sparse mid afternoon crowd. The VIP was an evening bar, coming to life only after dark, when lonely singles needed to escape from their close-walled apartments. "What could be bugging me?" She spun around on the stool to face Randy. "It *is* paradise over there. They don't even allow dives like this in Beverly Hills."

"Don't blame them." He grinned goodnaturedly. "I have no illusions about the VIP, even if I do own half of it." Randy watched Shelly fumble for a match and pulled out a white plastic lighter, bringing the flame to her cigarette. "So why are you here instead of over there?"

"Trying to get rid of me?" She said it gruffly, but she wasn't really annoyed. Randy was an old friend. They had even been lovers once.

Shelly looked up at him appraisingly. He had really liked her. They had been good in bed together. He was big and blond, rough on the outside but a basically kind and gentle man. He swore and drank a little too much, and he might not have been the most faithful of husbands. But he was a nice guy, and he'd wanted a real relationship with her. So why hadn't she stuck with him? Because he wasn't a bastard, like Dick, or her husband, or any of the other dregs of humanity she had found irresistible?

It was all irrelevant now. Randy had married his boss's daughter more than a year ago, had been made a partner, and in a month or so would be a father. She tried to imagine herself as his wife, pregnant, secure. It wasn't an exciting image. Not all the logic in the world could make it exciting.

"Come on, honey, give," he pushed, ignoring her question. "Lauren cut your allowance?"

She laughed shortly, then grew serious. "I don't know what's bothering me, Randy. Everything is great. I'm seeing a couple of classy guys, I'm crazy about my place. . . ." She thought about inviting him over. Knowing where that would lead, she bit back the suggestion. "I don't know."

Randy acknowledged a gesture from a man at the end of the bar and reached for a bottle of gin. He poured tonic and gin with a graceful twist of the wrists, served the drink and returned. "You just need to lighten up a little. Why don't you call Cindy and go out on the town? She was in here last night and mentioned she hadn't seen you for a while. She really dug your apartment. She's a good kid. Why don't you two party a little? That'll chase away the blues. I think she's off tonight."

Shelly was grateful that a party of four at a rear table called Randy away. She didn't want to see Cindy. She was still embarrassed by her last outing with the waitress. Instead of taking her advice, Cindy had shown up looking like a cheap hooker, wearing obscenely tight pants, a sweater cut almost to her nipples, and enough makeup for the entire cast of a Broadway show. They had created a stir at the very nice bar off Rodeo Drive all right, but not the kind Shelly had wanted. On reflection, it was amazing how much she had already learned from living in Beverly Hills. Lauren had opened a door to a beautiful world. She desperately wanted to be a part of it. This was her first visit back to the VIP, and she realized it was a mistake. She needed a better class of friends, new interests. It wasn't enough, just to be on the fringes. She had met some men in the watering holes of Beverly Hills and nearby Brentwood. But Richard was a schemer, and she suspected that he owned little more than the flashy T-bird he drove and the fine clothing on his back. And Wayne wasn't so different from Dick. Only Wayne was sharper. He always had a trick up his sleeve. Currently, he was peddling a screenplay. Shelly had read the play. It wasn't much, but Wayne had a way of presenting the tired old story with so much energy that he'd been bilking would-be investors out of money for over a year with it. He'd already asked her to move in with him, but her apartment was twice as nice as his, and as long as Lauren was willing to foot the bill for it, Shelly had no intention of leaving.

"A little partying is good for the soul," Randy said, pausing near her on his return to the bar. "Wish I could join you, but Iris would frown on that."

"You've got a good wife. Don't blow it," she warned absently. Randy had no idea how much partying she'd done lately. She really didn't have much else to do. Both Richard and Wayne partied almost every night. They managed to be on the list for most of the Beverly Hills happenings. She had met scores of movie stars already, people in every phase of the entertainment world, socialites, business people. But no one really paid much attention to her—unless they knew she was Lauren's sister. And even then they were only interested in hearing about Lauren.

Shelly began to smile. "You know something? I think a party might not be such a bad idea, Randy," she said more to herself than to him. It was one thing to go to parties—

it was another to give one! She would be center stage all the way, instead of being just another unnoticed guest. She was Lauren Wells' sister. People would come. Wayne would help her throw an unforgettable party. He would know just who she should invite. Hadn't she already met enough important people to light up a party?

Shelly took a last sip of her rum and cola, and stood up. The floor felt wobbly under her feet. She had better watch her drinking. If she wasn't careful, she'd end up like her father, cuddling a bottle in bed instead of something better. Giggling, she waved a farewell to Randy and weaved her way out of the dark bar into the busy, bright afternoon streets of Hollywood.

Chapter Fourteen

The vineyard stretched out beyond the veranda in every direction.

Even in the darkness, Chris could see the neat rows of vines. Little did the precisely placed plants realize they had paid for the magnificent house in which she stood, or that they had lifted a once impoverished merchant to great wealth, had established his reputation as a major producer of Bordeaux wines.

"It's wonderful, René. No wonder you love it here." She turned to the elegantly dressed man, not really surprised to find that he had silently moved right behind her. René's face was bathed in the silver light of the full moon. He was terribly attractive, Chris thought not for the first time.

They had met the night before last. René was one of the directors of the French branch of the Regis-Royale corporation, and meetings, as well as personal attraction, had kept them together for most of that time.

It wasn't so much his carved features, or the pale eyes with their heavy lashes, or the fine cut of his brown hair.

It was his energy, his positive approach to life and his unstinting pursuit of his goals that made him so appealing. René Raison insisted on winning whatever he considered worth having.

And, from the way he was looking at her, Chris knew that she fell into that category, at least for now.

"I thought you would like it here, Chris." The moonlight struck his eyes directly, showing their steely intelligence. "The setting is perfect for you. Perhaps I decorated the veranda with you in mind." His speech was only slightly accented, the result of a childhood largely spent in San Francisco. Even now, he kept a home in the Bay area, perhaps to counteract those early years of deprivation.

"You knew I'd pop into your life someday?" She heard the playfulness in her voice, not at all pleased with the kittenish tone.

"To be sure. I also read minds."

She hesitated, knowing exactly what she was expected to say. Although she had enjoyed being with René for the better part of two days now, a part of her was distant from him and coldly analytical. Was it, she wondered, because René was so obviously *the* man about whom she had always dreamed? Tucking the question away, she teasingly responded to his statement. "Really? And what am I thinking now?"

"That I'm about to kiss you. And wondering if you will enjoy it."

Instead of laughing, making some sort of provocative reply, or simply lifting her face toward his, Chris considered what he had said. "Yes, I was thinking that you would kiss me. But no, I have no doubt that I would enjoy it very much." Her voice was serious and she looked at him probingly. "I suspect that you kiss very nicely, that you're an experienced, thoughtful lover. I think you do everything well, René." Then she did allow herself a small smile. "I think you might be nearly perfect."

He lifted an eyebrow questioningly. "Perfect? I would

hardly go that far. But I do know about perfection. For example, you are perfectly beautiful. This night—for me—is sheer perfection." His voice deepened. "And I am perfectly serious about finding you so very perfectly desirable. . . ."

She watched him move still closer, felt his arms gently enfold her. His lips touched so softly to hers that she scarcely felt the warmth of them. Then he ran his long lean fingers up her spine, urging her closer against his strong body, and his mouth began to move in earnest over her lips.

Her response was genuine and immediate; her body followed its desires, the complex debate in her mind forgotten.

René ended their kiss abruptly and stared down into her face. "Chris. Is there any way I can persuade you to stay in France longer? This is insane, meeting like this and having to let you go away."

She was startled by his sudden intensity. "I can't stay, René. My job . . ." She was aware of the rapid beating of her heart. This was so much like a dream—the anguish in his voice, the moonlight playing over his handsome face, his enormous wealth. And, like a dream, they knew nothing about each other.

"Then let me give you a job. Here."

She smiled, a little amused, flattered, confused. "I . . . I couldn't, René. I . . . we hardly know each other."

"That is what we must correct, Chris. We must have the chance to know one another." He took her hands. "Or perhaps that is not essential. Do people ever really know one another? I once loved a woman, some years ago. We were to be married, but she insisted we know each other very well before such a commitment. We got to know one another so much that by the time we were about to wed, the excitement was gone. We lost it in a maze of fact finding. Do you understand? Since, I have vowed that if I ever again found a woman I thought I could love, I would marry her first and discover her taste in food, art and literature afterwards." He laughed, but even his laughter had a keen edge to it.

Chris looked at him doubtfully. She wanted to challenge what he had said, but the honey blood of kindled passion had mellowed the bite of her intellect.

"I know what you must think," he said after a pause. "That after the excitement died down, I would regret such a marriage." He shook his head firmly. "When I marry, it is for a lifetime. My parents were of the old school. They reasoned that two people did not marry because they loved one another, whatever they believed their feelings to be. Love, they said, came as a result of their joint efforts to steer their family through the difficulties of life. True love came later, a result of sharing experiences. I would love my wife and I would see to it that she loved me."

They stared at each other, Chris wondering with a shock if he were about to propose.

Undaunted by her silence, René continued. "I have much to offer a woman, Chris. More than the comfort and protection of wealth." He released her hands to stroke her hair and shoulders.

"What *are* you saying?" she asked when she found her voice.

He looked at her thoughtfully. "I'm not entirely sure. Except that I want you to stay. Very possibly forever." He lifted her chin.

But what of David? The question surfaced unexpectedly. David? What did he have to do with this? With her? What was the matter with her? René Raison was everything she'd ever dreamed about. He was the perfection she'd never really expected to find. She hadn't even known what perfection was until tonight. Unconsciously, he'd sensed her deepest fear, her greatest dread—of someday being abandoned, as she and her mother had been when Adair had arrived on the scene. René would marry and stay married forever. No burst of passion, no mid-life crisis, no yearning for a lost youth would make him forget his marriage vows. And he was rich, successful, handsome, sexy and intelligent. He had it all, and he was offering it to her.

How could she be thinking of David now? That moderately attractive, unestablished lawyer with a bad marriage behind him and a small daughter to occupy a good deal of his attention. A sweet-faced, bright button of a little daughter who wanted Chris to teach her how to make cookies.

René kissed her again, and she was grateful for the surge of desire that blotted thoughts of David and Nipper from her traitorous mind. She wound her arms around René's neck, steadying herself by holding on to him as his tongue slowly invaded her mouth. It had been a long time since she had been with a man. It amazed her to realize how long. She had managed to keep David at arm's length for many months, and during that time she hadn't even wanted to find a man for release. It wasn't natural, normal. The way René's tongue made her feel more than proved that; her flesh felt as if it were softening, expanding. Flowerlike, she was opening herself to him in every cell of her body. Who was this David, this nobody lawyer with a complicated past and an uninspiring future to make her defend her emotions so masterfully that she forgot she was a woman?

She would change all that. Here. Tonight. On a splendid country estate in France, to which she had flown with René in his own small plane. She wouldn't rush anything, make any binding commitments, but she could and would take a step toward her own ultimate happiness, the fulfillment of a lifetime of dreams.

Her speech was slurred, husky with desire. "I don't know about forever. Not yet. But I could stay for tonight. . . ."

His groan was answer enough. "We start with tonight, Chris. But it is only a start for us."

Then she felt herself being lifted, carried like a child across the veranda, into the house. Furniture looked funny at this tilted angle. The walls seemed to be moving while she remained at one place. Bubbling laughter spilled from her throat. "Like the movies," she said, giggling. "I love it!"

He smiled down at her, obviously enjoying the romantic gesture at least as much as Chris. He rested his cheek against her hair, cradling her as he moved easily through the house to his bedroom.

She felt the weight of his head on hers, relaxed into the firm strength of his arms, feather light and girlish and free of any responsibility now that she had committed herself to their night together. She told herself she was happy, happier than she'd ever been before. A woman had to feel happy when her dreams were starting to come true. The only thing that marred this happiness was the lingering thought of David—who had no place here, in this dream-come-true.

She was being carried through a doorway. Tightening her hold on René's neck, Chris tucked in her legs to avoid the edge of an exquisitely carved eighteenth century French armoire. Then a massive, towering four-poster bed with matching carved wood sideboards came into view. A satin spread came up at her like a pale peach wave. She tumbled onto it, giggling at its slick coolness. But the laughter died as she looked up at René, his hair tousled, his eyes bright, bringing the light of the moon into the room. She was acutely conscious of herself in her sea green silk dress, its skirt fanning the bed, her hair, loose for once, haloing her face. She appreciated the compliment in his eyes, as well as his sensitivity in giving her a moment to subdue her giggles and resume the sensual mood that had prompted her offer to spend the night with him.

Loosening his tie, René sat down on the bed by her and smiled. He touched the fine line of her jaw, lightly traced her neck, reached lower and palmed her breasts through the dress. Then he kissed her, his lips starting at the corner of her mouth and working toward the center, short little kisses that teased and tested, inflaming her while requesting permission to go on.

Chris reached out and slipped her arms around his neck, needing to feel him close to her. She was aware of a strange mixture of emotions. For all the desire she felt, she was oddly sad. Perhaps it was a certain degree of anticlimactic reaction—she had lived in hope of such a night, and now the dreaming was over. The reality would follow a set course. She and René would be wonderful in bed. He was already impressed with her quick thinking, her sense of humor, delighted to have met a woman who understood business and yet retained her femininity. At somewhere in his early forties, he would want a woman old enough to view life in a mature fashion, but young enough to bear him children. It all added up. She would spend the night, he would want her to stay. He would want her to marry him. She was sure of it.

So why the sadness? she asked herself, enjoying his touch and the fluttery little kisses that had reached the other corner of her mouth. Her body was growing impatient with her mind. It wanted nothing more than to relax into lovemaking. She turned her face to meet his lips and kissed him crushingly. *Goodbye, David,* she thought, telling herself she was doing the right thing, that a lifetime of planning and waiting was bearing the most rewarding of all fruit, happiness.

The sadness lingered as René's fingers began to loosen her clothing. To dispell the unwanted feeling, Chris put her lips near his ear. She would promise to stay here in France with him. Now. Before she lost her nerve. Lauren would be fine without her. There was no reason not to stay with René. What would she be leaving behind? Much as she loved her rooftop apartment, any one room in this estate was more magnificent.

The dress was open now and his strong arms were lifting her so that the silk garment fell away from her body. She moaned, kissed him just below his ear. *Say it,* she commanded of herself. *Say you'll stay!* She knew it would please René and settle something in her own mind.

But then René's lips had recaptured her mouth and she

was drowning in sensation. She could tell him afterward. What did it really matter? She had come to a decision, hadn't she?

She closed her eyes and returned his kiss ardently. But just off to one side, at the very edge of her consciousness, was a crazy, tree-shrouded dome, like a soap bubble in the sky.

Chapter Fifteen

In his fury, Chef Raymond was punctuating each word with a fine spray of saliva. "I quit! I . . . quit! Now! Right this minute!"

Parker was having a difficult time rousing himself enough to figure out if the temperamental chef was merely having a fit about something or was really about to walk off the job just before the mayor's lunch party was due to arrive.

"What . . . seems to be the trouble?" Parker asked, taking great pains to keep his words from slurring. The kitchen seemed to dip and blur as he tried to focus his distorted vision on the sputtering man.

While the chef shouted at him, Parker tried to decide if he were angry at the explosive man or merely amused by his passionate fury. Chef Raymond really did look funny. His immaculate whites and traditional hat seemed to be doing a little dance. The big man was prancing around as he accused Parker of sundry misdeeds. He looked like a cartoon chef, waxed moustache bobbing, fleshy cheeks a bright red. Parker almost laughed, but he was angry, too.

It had taken the better part of the fifth of scotch hidden in his desk to reach a tranquil state this morning.

"Listen, keep it quiet there, huh?" Parker tried to get up, felt the floor tremble under his feet and decided to stay seated. "Not to worry, hear? You get excited too easily, old man." He dimly noticed that most of the kitchen staff were finding reason to wander closer to his desk.

"Excited? Never, never in my career have I had to suffer such impossible conditions! It's over! I'm leaving. Never have I walked out in the middle of . . ." He looked beyond Parker to Jerome Abrams, Earl Regis's assistant. "I quit! This . . . man can tell you why, if it is still possible for him to speak coherently." He turned on his heel and marched away.

The next five minutes were confusing and noisy. Parker was very sleepy now and unable to keep his words from tumbling together. He didn't really understand why everyone was so upset. He had forgotten to order some things, line up some equipment. . . . It was all too disorienting. They didn't realize what it was like, trying to organize an operation like this. He had run kitchens all his life, but this was a three-ring circus, Times Square and Disneyland all heaped together. He was doing the best he could, didn't they realize?

Abrams sighed. "I wish the hell Earl was here, but he's gone for the day." The two assistant chefs who had arrived on the scene as soon as Abrams put in an appearance exchanged glances. Earl was next to useless.

Parker shrugged, wishing they would all go away, get Raymond mollified and back on the job, and allow him to sit in peace.

"Mr. Fields, you've got to apologize to Chef Raymond. Beg him to stay. The mayor's party is just about to arrive."

Parker stiffened. "Beg that son-of-a-bitch?" He snapped his head around. "What's the panic? Hell, I can finish up myself, if I have to." He forced himself to his feet, swaying dangerously. "Everything's ready, isn't it? So we don't have the right kind of whatever it is. You should have seen the parties we threw together in the Navy. Out of nothing."

Grimacing, Abrams stepped out of harm's way. "This is not the Navy." His face made it clear that if anyone was walking off the job, it should be Parker. "I'll talk to Chef Raymond. I'd advise you go home and sleep it off, Mr. Fields."

Parker was insulted. "You think I can't handle this? Why don't you fire me? Can't, can you? My little girl owns this dump. Don't you forget it!" Satisfied, he slumped back into his chair. He wanted some peace and quiet. And a drink. He thought of the nice little restaurants he had owned. How easy they were. What was he doing here, anyway?

Abrams had left. He had caught Chef Raymond and was speaking quietly but earnestly to him, reminding him that walking off his post at a time like this would follow him wherever he went, regardless of the provocation.

Parker watched Abrams deal with the irate chef, not especially caring how it turned out. He wanted to get home. Turn on the stereo. Listen to a little Thelonious Monk, maybe have a drink or two to the deceased musician's memory. He got to his feet, stumbled.

With a gesture, Abrams sent two sturdy kitchen employees to his side. Between them, he shambled out of the kitchen, his head held high. He was untouchable. He couldn't be fired.

He wished he felt more grateful about that.

Chapter Sixteen

It was glorious to have an afternoon completely free for once, to be absolutely alone in what had to be the most perfect city in the world. Paris! And all hers, at least for a little while.

Lauren walked along the Rue du Faubourg–St. Honore, relishing the few hours she had left before meeting Claude for dinner. Unfortunately, there was no time for a visit to the Louvre, the Arc de Triomphe, the Sorbonne, Notre Dame or any of the other must-see tourist attractions.

She had lunch on the second level of the Eiffel Tower, with all of Paris at her feet in one spectacular slice. Though she was only a few hundred feet from the ground, she felt a million miles in the air, a goddess smiling down on a city ripe with romance.

The next time she came to Europe, she vowed, she would allow herself months to explore and experience all she barely had time to glimpse on this business trip. She sipped her wine and wished for a fleeting moment that she had taken the Regis money and fled. Life was so short. How could she possibly want to waste any of it in offices and board rooms? When she had first envisioned herself at the helm of the hotel conglomerate, hadn't she imagined a highly glamorous career? In reality, it had been hard work so far. Her brain ached with all the facts and figures that had been crammed into it, and even the plushest of executive chairs strained the back when the body bent over paperwork hour after hour. Wouldn't she rather be on a permanent vacation?

But Lauren knew that her griping had the flavor of a mother complaining about the limitations imposed on her by her children, all the while knowing she wouldn't want it any other way. She loved what she was becoming, whatever the cost. This trip, for all she had missed, had given her so much. It had shown her that hard work paid off, that she was capable of learning and understanding this complex business. Everything was falling into place. Already she felt competent enough to make judgements about matters she initially had thought beyond her ken. It was exciting, and incredibly gratifying.

The matter of the merger, for example—once a concept so foreign to Lauren that she wondered if she would ever be capable of making a decision. She had learned enough, seen enough to have an intelligent grasp of the risks and rewards on either side. More, she was secure enough in her knowledge to stand by her decision. She knew she would support Alexandra's position. Not for sentimental reasons, but because she sincerely believed the Regis-Royales would fare better in the long run by retaining their stately image. It was true that some modernizing would have to be done— she had undertaken complete inspection tours of each hotel she visited—but she believed they could sustain the expense without a merger. The motels would certainly bring in a tempting amount of new revenue, but these were uncertain times. People weren't traveling as much. Everyone was cutting back on frills. Motels and drastic modernizations would cheapen their image. So much would be lost in altering the concept of old-world elegance. The idea had become repugnant to Lauren, as it had been to Alexandra. But here, Lauren had a distinct advantage. Alexandra had been too close to the hotels. Her love was too blind. Where Alexandra was adamant about preserving every inch of the hotels, Lauren welcomed realistic change. She would offer a compromise that should win approval, even if some members of the board were reluctant. There would be no quick money to be made from Lauren's proposals. But there would be a steady growth through the next few years, and this would be critical in bringing people around to her point of view. Her way was risk free. With the stock market fluctuating like crazy and the Dow on a plunge, any risk free guarantee would be welcomed. A merger couldn't offer that, especially under the current high interest rates. She would remind the board that the financial picture for the nation had altered considerably since the merger had been proposed.

No, she wasn't sorry that she'd chosen to throw herself into the hotel management position. Look at her—lunching in Paris, dressed in fabulous designer clothing, successful at meetings and lionized socially. And the men—what about the men?

Nibbling on her lovely trout as a steady army of cars weaved through the Arc de Triomphe far below, Lauren allowed herself to think of Anthony calmly for the first time since that terribly painful phone conversation. She had been too angry to think about him clearly. What had he done that was really so terrible? she asked herself. He had given her a reprieve from a commitment that might no longer be in her best interests. And it gave him time to adjust to the fact of Lauren's inheritance.

Far below, two automobiles bumped fenders and traffic was tied into a tight knot. It was like watching a cluster of dancing ants. From her lofty position on the patio of the Eiffel Tower, she felt affectionately removed from traffic jams but not out of touch with humanity. Anthony had a good head on his shoulders. He was not always right, of course, but he was thoughtful and rarely impulsive about important matters. He had made the decision for them— which she still resented—but she bowed to his rationality. And was making the most of this experiment. First she had met Tommy in London. And Jan Brictman in Amsterdam. Now Claude Michel D'Argene, a real live French count, was pursuing her in earnest. Tommy, charting her trip across the continent, filled her rooms with flowers daily and wired amusing little messages to her every few days.

She met Jan, an eminent Dutch psychiatrist with an international reputation, during her four-day stay in Holland. They were introduced at a cocktail party at the Amsterdam Regis-Royale, the newest in the chain and therefore a hotel Lauren especially wanted to inspect. The first Amsterdam Regis-Royale had been the oldest of the overseas hotels, but after a much publicized kitchen fire which had claimed two lives, it had been torn down to be replaced by this one.

There had been a great deal of pressure on Alexandra to build a streamlined, stainless steel hotel. But Alexandra had insisted on building a replica of the original—with modernization where it was least obvious.

Lauren completed her tour, firmly convinced that Alexandra had been a woman of great genius and superior vision. At first glance, it was impossible to believe that the stately hotel was barely six years old. It had the weathered, highly polished look of a landmark, the ambiance of an institution that had catered to the upper classes for a hundred years. But behind the scenes, where the real work of the hotel took place, everything was as modern and contemporary as any hotel anywhere in the world. Again, because she didn't have Alexandra's strong biases, Lauren could see room for a few more changes. There was a great deal of wasted space in the solariums, music rooms, extra lobbies and other little-used areas that could more profitably be utilized as additional suites or bars and cafes.

Weary of all the parties and anxious to consolidate the day's work, Lauren had resolved to spend the least amount of time politely possible at the cocktail party thrown in her honor. But her thoughts of a quick escape were aborted by Jan Brictman. He was tall and fair, with sharp features, piercing eyes and a somewhat contemptuous smile. When they were introduced, Lauren sensed that he, like herself, felt his time could be better spent elsewhere. He was strikingly handsome, mouth and nose cut cleanly, his slender body long and athletic. He had a soft but deep voice with an accent Lauren found charming. He was also the only man in the room who didn't seem to be particularly impressed to meet her.

Lauren knew she was looking exceptionally well. She wore a pale gold linen suit with yellow gold accessories. Around her throat she wore a delicate gold chain with a deeply cut topaz that brought out the subtle smokey threads in the linen. She looked distinguished and elegant, womanly but restrained. It was a look that suited her particularly well. Anthony would have summed it up in one word: classy.

Of course, having the money to invest in her own appearance had helped. Before, she had selected garments from racks, trying them on before cheap mirrors in cramped dressing rooms. Now she went to the best designers who were not only happy to discuss her selections, but insisted on it. They saw that she had the very best in fabrics, the most cunning workmanship, the absolute perfection in accessories. The gold linen heels she wore, for example, had been made to compliment her Chanel suit. The result, in Lauren's case, was to take an already beautiful woman and polish her to a pinnacle of perfection. Looking her best made it child's play to act her best in any situation. She exuded self-confidence, and that made the biggest difference of all.

Jan Brictman appeared indifferent to her at first—not that Lauren had any initial interest in him either. She had enough to handle with Anthony and Tommy without involving herself in any more emotional mazes.

A small incident brought them together. Lauren had

reached over to accept a cocktail from a young and obviously new waiter. In his nervousness, his hand jerked and a few drops fell on Lauren's wrist. Kurt Voight-Neilson, the manager of the Amsterdam hotel, happened to be glancing in their direction at the time. Working with her normal put-it-together-in-a-glance speed, Lauren pointedly apologized to the young waiter, as if the minor mishap had been her doing. She had no desire to see the boy called on the carpet simply because it happened to be her he had been serving, which no doubt contributed to his nervousness.

Three of the people with whom she was chatting seemed oblivious to what had happened, but Jan was smiling. As soon as he decently could, he moved closer to Lauren.

"Do you always go around rescuing people?"

It was a moment before she connected the spilled drink with the question.

"You know, save waiters from irate bosses and such?"

She had been embarrassed. Mildly annoyed as well. With a touch of smiling defiance, she nodded. "I'm afraid I do. It seems to be a bad habit of mine."

"I suspected as much." His smile was friendlier but still faintly cold.

Her annoyance grew. "Oh, yes," she said, staring directly into those icy blue eyes, "you're the psychiatrist." Her tone held a faint contempt for psychiatrists who psychoanalysed people at cocktail parties.

He caught her meaning and laughed. "The postman must have his daily walk." But he was instantly contrite and strived to make amends. "Come now, tell me what you think of Amsterdam."

Lauren was oddly pleased—Jan wasn't even aware that this was a welcoming party to celebrate her first day in the lovely old city. No stargazer he. "I just got here and I don't suppose I'll have the opportunity to see much of anything. What little I've seen is beautiful. I'd like to stay months, but I'm afraid this will be a quick visit. I'm due in Zurich the day after next." She caught a glimpse of Chris, looking in their direction with approval stamped on her smiling face.

They chatted for the next few minutes and then others claimed her attention. But she was only a little surprised when he called her suite later that evening. She was committed for dinner but agreed to see him later that night. The next day, Thursday, was free after a morning meeting. She agreed to explore the city with Jan. He had proven to be excellent, intelligent company the night before. Unlike Tommy, he was serious and thoughtful. But unlike Anthony, he was dispassionate about life, more intellectual than emotional. So much so that when, during dinner at a private club off one of the canals, Jan turned the discussion to personal matters, Lauren was surprised.

He talked softly about himself, his practice, his latest book and, finally, the break-up of his twelve-year marriage. While he spoke, he often looked out the huge window at the brightly lit glass boats that ferried passengers up and down the canal.

Listening to him, Lauren realized that she was with yet another terribly attractive man, but still a different kind of man than any she had known before. Anthony had had good reason to hesitate to lock them into marriage. She was meeting fascinating men with purpose, not unlike Anthony himself. But, unlike Anthony, they were not uncomfortable with the glittering world in which Lauren now lived. She still had a lot of thinking to do and was now glad Anthony had provided her with the opportunity to do it.

When Jan took her back to the hotel, he asked if he might come to see her in Los Angeles soon.

"Call me," she said, still dazzled by a way of life that included a hop across the world to pursue a woman of interest.

"That I will do," he assured her before touching her lips with his own. "And you will come back to Amsterdam. If I have to bring you back personally."

His confident authority thrilled her, and his lips were smooth and warm. She shivered and he felt it, but he didn't press, wouldn't ask, as Tommy had, to spend the night. He seemed to understand that she had complexities of her own to master before being completely available to him.

It was Lauren who solicited a final kiss, leaning into him. He pulled her to him with unexpected passion and kissed her deeply.

After he was gone, she found herself surprisingly shaken.

And then there was Claude Michel D'Argene. He had a permanent suite at the Paris Regis-Royale. She had been introduced to him by Phillipe Marchand, the executive manager of the hotel. Claude was not young, probably in his late fifties, but he was devastatingly attractive and virile in appearance and attitude. He was a widower of almost three years, a man of great fortune and charm.

He had been immediately attracted to her and had pursued her without gentleness or timidity. His attention was overwhelming. His age didn't matter at all—he looked much younger than his years, making it impossible to imagine him old and feeble. He had dark hair with silver streaks, a straight, noble bearing, wonderfully commanding dark eyes and a strong masculine jaw. On meeting him, Lauren thought he looked like Ricardo Montalban playing the part of a French count.

And again, he was different from all the others. Anthony was intense, Tommy highly seductive, Jan brilliant and aloof. Claude was dynamic. It was the only word for him. He was the sort of a man who could rule a country with ease. He was immensely wealthy and powerful, not only in France but throughout Europe as well. He had one daughter who lived in Australia with her husband, but he had told Lauren that since the daughter was unable to have children, he had been thinking of marrying and starting a new family for some time before meeting her.

Once they had been introduced, Claude had seemed to

surround her from all sides. He was simply always there. At first she had been annoyed as well as fascinated, but inside of three days she was finding herself excited by his singleminded attention.

He had tried to seduce her from their first evening together, and he had been rather surprised to find her resisting his advances.

"But why?" he had asked after Lauren had made it clear that much as she enjoyed his kisses, she had no intention of sharing his bed. "We are, after all, not children any more."

Because she knew he sincerely wanted an answer, she told him briefly about Anthony, and the commitment she still felt to him in spite of his releasing her from it.

He seemed pleased that she was a woman who respected commitments, that she was not in the habit of having sex lightly. "I see." He had smiled. "Then I will have to marry you. So be it. It is time."

He had said the words casually, but Lauren knew immediately that he meant what he was saying.

Each time they had seen each other after that, Claude had acted as if matters were settled but for the details. She had tried to put a stop to his plans for a future she had far from agreed to share, but he wasn't put off in the least.

"You won't even give me a chance to breathe, much less think! I have a world of my own, Claude. I'm going back to it shortly, remember? I'm not ready to give it all up, not even to become the wife of the fabulous Count Claude Michel D'Argene."

"I am not a man known for his patience, Lauren. In your case, however, I am prepared to wait. But do not think that by the end of the month, when you plan to leave France, you will be prepared to walk away from me. I will give you reason to forget your composer, your work. You will see."

Thinking of him, warmed by the memories and the wine she had consumed with lunch and not wanting to leave this

213

magnificent vantage point just yet, she ordered a pot of black souchong tea.

"Do you know I've combed Paris for you? Chris said you planned to lunch on the tower, but this is my third tour of this king-sized erector set toy. I was about to give up."

For the briefest of moments, her heart stopped cold in her chest. Her eyes, focused so long at long range, blurred as she stared at the familiar face. "Jim!" she said, disconcerted. She had thought for a moment the voice belonged to Anthony.

"Who would have guessed you would be here. Or are you so enthralled with the view—spectacular as it is—that you haven't noticed how damp and windy it is out here?"

She reached over and took his perfectly manicured hand in both of hers. "Jim! Sit down. What are you doing here?" She laughed, embarrassed, because of course she had known he would be on hand for the important meeting the next day. "I mean here, at the Eiffel Tower, rather than at the hotel."

"I could say that I just couldn't wait to see you again." He smiled shortly, but behind the smile was a note of seriousness.

"I'm flattered," she began, but Jim's smile faded so quickly that Lauren felt a chill of apprehension. "Is anything wrong?"

He attempted to regain the smile. "Look, doesn't a weary man get a moment to compose himself? What are you drinking?"

"Tea, now," she said just as the waiter set down a silver pot.

He ordered coffee and looked around. "The last time I was up here it was raining cats and dogs. I could barely see Paris and I damn near got pneumonia."

"Is everything all right at home?"

He waited until he had his coffee in front of him, and the waiter was gone. "No." He took a quick sip of the steaming coffee and looked directly at her.

She gripped the table edge and Paris swam before her eyes. Anthony was dead. Or he had married while she was away. The absolutely absurd second thought brought her back to her senses. Her lover, dead or married to someone else. Those were the first two images her mind dredged up as soon as she heard there was trouble at home. Then panic took over again. Parker? Shelly? "What is it?" she asked quietly, in control but holding on very tight still to the edge of the reassuringly firm wooden table.

"Norm Lowenthal died, Lauren. Yesterday. His heart finally went."

"Oh." She slumped back in her seat and felt a great sadness. The old attorney had been a good friend. "Had he been hospitalized? I knew his health had worsened in the last few months. . . ."

"No, in fact, he was trying to reach you when he had the attack."

"Me? Why?" She felt chilled and sipped at her tea. Norm had been her only living link to Alexandra. With the old man gone she knew she'd be really alone. She had already told Chris she could stay on in France with René for another few weeks. "Are you sure he was trying to reach me?"

"Yes." Jim looked uncomfortable and drank some of his coffee. "The funeral is in two days. Do you plan to go back for it?"

"Yes," she said unhesitatingly. "Oh, the meeting tomorrow!"

He nodded. "You can fly out directly after the meeting. I've already had Chris alert the pilot to the possibility."

She smiled at him, a sad little smile. She couldn't stop thinking of Norm and wishing she had had a chance to say goodbye. "I suppose Rome and Venice and Madrid and all those other places will still be there when I return some other time."

"It's not imperative that you come back for the funeral, you know." He glanced over the railing at the city below, but his eyes didn't seem to be taking in the glorious view.

215

"Jim, what is it? What else has happened?" She looked at him sharply.

He turned back to her, his face troubled, vaguely defensive, obviously uncomfortable. "Do you want a drink? Why don't you have a drink?"

"What is it that I need a drink before hearing?"

He smiled a little. Shrugged.

"If you need a drink before telling me, go ahead and have one. I'll wait." She spoke calmly, as if to a child.

He sighed. "Forgive me, Lauren. I . . . the truth is, you'd better go home. You're about to be taken to court. Earl Regis is challenging your claim to Alexandra's estate."

"Earl is what?" She couldn't comprehend what he was saying. "Why? On what grounds?" She thought a moment. "Why haven't I been notified?"

"Earl is suing to be named beneficiary of the Regis estate. You haven't been notified because those responsible for the action wanted you to be surprised. You were to know nothing until formal notification went to your lawyers. I didn't agree." He glanced around. The waiter was hovering nearby and tourists were babbling noisily at the next table. "Look, it's cold and windy here. I have a car down below. Let's go where it's quiet and talk, shall we?"

She let him pay the check and escort her down the Tower elevator that rode the metal girders at a slant to the ground.

He led her to a chauffeured limousine and helped her into its roomy, dim back seat. In fluent French, he told the driver to return in fifteen minutes.

She had been thinking furiously since leaving the Tower restaurant. "This isn't Earl's idea. He doesn't have it in him to try this. I take it that some of my . . . friends . . . on the board are behind this?"

Jim's discomfort did more than answer the question she had asked.

"You, too, Jim? Are you a part of this?" Part of her wanted to whine *but I thought you liked me*—like a schoolgirl betrayed by a boy who had seemed quite taken with her only days before.

"It's just business, Lauren. Nothing personal." He spoke softly, earnestly. "It wasn't my idea, but once it gained momentum, I felt I had to involve myself."

"They want to make you chairman of the board. They were going to, until I stepped in." She looked at him, trying not to lash out at him. After all, he didn't have to be here at all. "But you won't get away with it. Alexandra had the right to leave her holdings to anyone she wished. Just because Earl . . ."

"The suit is more complex than the issue of blood relationship to the family." He faced her squarely and his voice was not unkind. "The suit contends that Alexandra was not competent when she made her final will. It also claims that you are citably incapable of heading the hotel chain properly."

She didn't allow her feelings to distract her. "How can Alexandra's competence be proven one way or the other? Why didn't this come up before?"

"Mainly because Earl didn't contest the will before. He is the only one with authority to do so. Not only is he a blood relative, but he is also the most logical choice to head the conglomerate."

Lauren looked at him disbelievingly. "How can you, of all people, say that? If it wasn't for his family tie and his talent for picking competent assistants, Earl would have been out in the streets long ago. Everyone knows that. Earl even knows!" She looked at him shrewdly. "Do you think what you're doing is right, Jim?"

He stared at her silently in the dim recess of the car's plush interior. "I have no desire to hurt you, Lauren. In fact, I feel certain that if I were to return to Beverly Hills and tell the board that you've reconsidered and wish to resign from the board, the suit would be dropped. No one begrudges you the fortune Alexandra wished you to have.

But exercising your option to control the hotels is not in the best interests of the business. Do you understand?"

"Perfectly, Jim," she said without any real bitterness. Now she did understand. She hadn't been crafty enough. Someone must have realized her intention to kill the merger deal. "The investment company must have sweetened the pot considerably to get what they want."

Jim didn't hesitate to admit as much. "The offer is irresistible. You would also benefit from it. Why is this so difficult, Lauren? You would have all the money in the world to do with as you wish. You could have any man . . ." He looked at her longingly. "You are beautiful, exciting. You don't have to waste your life on this."

"Waste?" she challenged. "Is it a waste of your life, too? You want it so much!"

"No! It is my life! I've worked for it." He was facing her now, his voice pitched with emotion.

"Yes, and it fell into my lap! That's what you're thinking. Well, you're right." She settled back against the comfortable cushions and calmed herself. "I did have the world fall into my lap. But what do you know of my life? Or how hard I've worked to get somewhere?"

"Where do you need to be?" He was staring at her, trying to understand.

She smiled at him gently. He was not a monster—he was just an ambitious man. But he didn't understand. Anthony had been right. She was with the lions now. But she felt up to the deadliest of roars. "Right where I am," she answered at last. "At the top of the world. And here I intend to stay."

Jim Reardon's face was a mixture of irritation and admiration. "You haven't a chance, Lauren," he said softly. "Your family has seen to that."

"Jim's right," Chris had said in their suite in Paris after lowering the phone back in its cradle. On hearing the news, she had placed a few calls back home to reliable sources.

218

"Tell me." Lauren sat on the bed with her legs tucked under her. "What have they done?"

"Shelly decided to throw a blockbuster of a party at the hotel last night." She shook her head and sat down next to Lauren. "I don't know what she was thinking, but apparently she invited the who's who of Hollywood. People she couldn't possibly have known. Big name stars, top agents and producers, directors, society types—you name it. Naturally, nobody showed."

Lauren closed her eyes. "And?"

"And she flipped out, of course. Alone, with just a handful of her old pals, she got plastered and threw one hell of a scene. Screamed and yelled, broke things . . . Went out into the lobby and insulted people, even tried to divert guests from another party to hers." Chris patted Lauren's shoulder. "Poor Shelly, she probably was hoping to make the papers with her party. She made them, all right, but not the society pages."

"And Parker?" she pressed, needing to hear it all.

Chris filled her in with a detailed report on the mayor's luncheon, their famous chef, the way the tension in the kitchen was beginning to affect the quality of the food served in the hotel's many restaurants.

"Lauren," Chris had said at the end of the report, "I've never tried to tell you what you should do. I've advised and suggested, right? And I know I have no right to insist on anything. But, you've got to cut these people loose! Immediately. I don't care that they're family and you love them! Earl's lawyers are sure to use Shelly and Parker to prove that you aren't competent to run the hotels. And they're wrong. We both know what you've managed to do in a few short months. But if you're not very careful you'll never get a chance to show that you can take up where Mrs. Regis left off."

"Cut them loose?" Shelly and Parker were her responsibility; they couldn't make it without her.

"I don't mean desert them. Just sever certain ties. Fire

Parker. That has to be done at once. Word is that Chef Raymond will return once Parker is out. If we move swiftly enough."

"How can I fire him? Damn, do you have any idea what he's been through since my mother got sick? Have you ever seen anyone you love go downhill fast?"

"Yes," Chris had answered softly. "It's painful as hell to sit by and let it happen. But . . ."

Lauren had set her jaw and stared at her tightly clenched hands. "I can't do it. I won't. Besides, firing him now would only serve to help me in court. I'd be doing it for me, not him. I'll see that Parker doesn't drink on the job. We can offer Chef Raymond more money."

"He doesn't need the money! It's a matter of principle now. He won't come back unless Parker's fired."

"Then let him go! He isn't the only chef in the world. We can find ten excellent ones to take his place!" She was angry. Why couldn't Chris understand her feelings? "And what am I supposed to do about my sister?"

Chris had seemed about to crumble, but she steeled her back and met Lauren's angry gaze. "Go on taking care of her, if you must. Oh, Lauren, didn't it ever occur to you that Shelly might start taking care of herself if you weren't there to do it for her?"

"I asked what I was supposed to do about Shelly in regard to this party mess," she retorted coldly.

Chris sighed. "Get her out of town. Lauren, Shelly can't help being an . . . embarrassment to you. I suspect she always was, but before, it didn't matter so much. Damn it, Lauren, you can't make life good for these people, just because you want it so much for them. Don't you see that?"

Lauren saw only that she was standing before a road divided many times, each lane going in a different direction. She sent Chris off to say goodbye to René—her devoted assistant now refused to stay in France with so much trouble brewing at home—and thought hard about the paths before her.

Jim had helped put her head in a noose, but he had offered a juicy bone. She could meekly bow out of the business, allow him to fill her chair and ascend to the presidency, in which case there would be no court battle, no humiliating scandal to fill the newspapers. She would have all the money she and her family could ever want. All that would be lost was a great deal of work and trouble. She could travel. She could do whatever she pleased. Even business would not be denied to her. She could open a restaurant if she wished. A chain of them, probably. There was money enough.

But she knew it wasn't what she wanted. No one, not even Chris, knew how strongly she felt about fulfilling Alexandra Regis's deathbed wish. But it went deeper than that. Lauren believed that everyone had just one true destiny, and fate had moved mountains for hers. She was precisely where she was supposed to be. A woman she had never met had contrived to bring her to this lofty eagle's nest of power. And, once here, she had worked hard to be worthy of this miracle. She would be good for the Regis-Royale chain. The compromise she had devised on the merger issue proved that. She had to stay where she was.

But could she? Would it be possible to prove that Alexandra had been sane when she drew the final will? There were many who believed leaving everything to a total stranger was an act of madness. What if she fought for what she had and lost? That could mean losing everything. How could she risk that? How could she endure going back to where she had been before, working for someone else, dragging herself back to some cramped apartment at night, wondering if she and Anthony would ever be able to get married. Or had she blown that too? Would Anthony still want her? Even if he did, what kind of a life could they make together, after what they'd been through? Wouldn't there always be a trace of recrimination in his eyes, knowing that but for her ambition, they could be happily enjoying a life of luxury that would allow him the leisure to compose his beautiful music?

It didn't stop there, the many roads, the terrible questions. There was no doubt that Tommy and Jan were greatly interested in her. Win or lose, she might become the wife of an English nobleman. Or the wife, perhaps, of a famed Dutch psychiatrist.

There was Claude, too. He had been deeply distressed when she called to say she would be returning to America the next day.

She finally gave in to his insistence that they meet in her suite for a few minutes.

"I can't accept this," she whispered, looking down at the ring nestled in the little black velvet box.

It was breathtaking. The square-cut diamond was huge but so delicately cut that it looked fragile in spite of its massive size. A triangular emerald graced either side of the diamond.

"I couldn't possibly," she insisted.

They did not quarrel. She simply explained that the death of a close friend and mentor coupled with business problems required her immediate presence in California. Claude remained charming and reasonable. He did not press to accompany her to Los Angeles but informed her that he would join her as soon as possible.

It had been an uncomfortable parting, because Lauren had come to like him enormously. She might even come to love this man in time, if she had to. But it was the thought of seeing Anthony again sooner than expected that filled her with excitement and dread. She felt as if she had lived several lifetimes in the few weeks she'd been away.

She had left angry and betrayed, had not heard from or about him since that phone call. She had no idea where they stood, and yet she knew now that he had left an indelible mark on her soul. She could not even consider the possibility that she might return to find their love a thing of the past.

Could she face losing Anthony as well as all the hard work she had done to prove herself worthy of her inheritance? If the waiting were not so difficult, Lauren would have put off finding the answers to these questions forever.

She climbed in between the cold sheets. The loneliness of her bed mocked her.

Chapter Seventeen

"God, I'm sorry, baby. You know I didn't mean it! I just had a little too much to drink."

Shelly tried to shake off Wayne's hand on her arm, but her own muscles were too weak. She felt the tears slide down her face, felt the heat in her cheek and knew that the flesh would be red with the print of his hand. His slap hadn't really hurt her; she was more startled than injured. What had they been arguing about, anyway?

"Ah, come on, honey, I said I was sorry. I didn't hurt you, did I?" He moved closer to her on the bed and attempted to take her in his arms. He was naked and warm-fleshed and his breath smelled of scotch.

"Sure, you hurt me," she said, not exactly resisting his embrace but not making it easy for him. "Go home, Wayne. Get out of here. I don't let guys hit me and then make love to them." It wasn't true, but she wished it were. And she wished that Wayne's hairy chest didn't feel so good through the thin black gown she was wearing.

"Ah, come on, you don't really want me to leave, do

you? I'm here so much lately, I don't know why I don't just move in. Since you don't want to come stay with me." His big hands were stroking her back.

Shelly knew she should sit up and demand that Wayne leave immediately. What she should really do is never see the bum again. If she acted like a woman who wouldn't stand for being slapped around, no matter what, he'd think twice in the future. "I want you to leave, Wayne, I mean it." But her voice lacked the proper tone. Even in her own ears it didn't sound convincing. His hands were moving all over her now, distracting her. He had that certain way with women. . . .

"You don't want me to go, baby, now do you? Let me make it up to you, okay?" He tried to kiss her but she turned her head away. Grinning, he cupped her chin and turned her back to face him.

"Wayne. Quit it. . . ."

"Come on, sweetie, you know you don't want to be alone. I'll never do it again, honest. I'm a little drunk, you know?"

"You don't understand. . . ." He didn't. She wasn't sure she understood, either. It was hard to keep feeling indignant. She could no longer feel the slap and it was so easy to pretend it hadn't really happened. He was right. She didn't want to be alone. Wayne had stayed with her since the disaster at the Regis-Royale. She hadn't been able to face any of her other friends. At least Lauren was still in Europe. "I know what it is to be a little drunk," she said. She'd been very damn drunk—she hardly remembered going into the hotel lobby and accusing the manager of preventing her guests from showing up.

"I was, but I'm not now. Drunk, I mean. You sure feel good, Shelly. It's hard to believe you had a kid." He rubbed her silky leg, inching the nightgown toward her thigh.

"What day is this? Is it the weekend?"

He laughed and kissed her bare shoulder. "We already had the weekend, baby. It was a real lost one."

Shelly closed her eyes, remembering she'd half promised to bring Brian home for the weekend. It was just as well. Then she'd have had to face her father. She wondered why he hadn't been around, furious with her for embarrassing Lauren.

She felt a tug of resentment. It wasn't fair that Parker was always looking out for Lauren. She should have come first. She was his natural daughter.

"Should we make it a lost week while we're at it, baby? I got a meeting with this possible investor couple of days down the line, but nothing pressing right now." He had a satanic laugh. "Other than the obvious."

Feeling guilty about thinking unkindly of Lauren, Shelly struggled as Wayne's mouth pressed down on hers. But he knew how to kiss, how to set off all the right firecrackers and it took all her strength to avert her lips long enough for one more plea. "Promise you'll never hit me again, Wayne?"

"On my sainted mother's grave, baby. Hey, I really love you, don't you know? I want you to come live with me. We could maybe even get it made legal, if you want. You know, when I sell the script."

The words were so familiar to her. She'd heard similar ones so many times. "Whose script is it, anyway?" she asked thickly. He was a warm blanket over her, protecting her from the world, at least for this moment.

"What does it matter? I won it in a crap game. That makes it mine. . . ."

What did it matter? Really? She turned back to meet his demanding lips.

Chapter Eighteen

It was a weepy, rainy day. Perfect for a funeral, as if the sky were shedding tears in farewell to Norm Lowenthal.

Lauren stood alone in the chapel after the service. It had been a simple, dignified affair, attended by the lawyer's many friends and business associates. There were still knots of mourners outside, lingering on the ornate porch of the funeral home, but Lauren was reluctant to leave the protection of the chapel.

She walked closer to the casket, glad it was covered but feeling a need to be physically close to the old man one last time.

If ever she had needed him, it was now. She looked down at the casket and said softly, "Old friend, thank you. You'll be missed." Feeling utterly alone and very young, she turned from the casket.

She was not alone, though. Anthony was coming down the aisle toward her.

"Anthony!"

"Hello, Lauren."

She felt strangely shy, hesitant. Why were they standing there, grinning awkwardly at each other? Didn't he know she had missed him, wanted desperately to be in the safe harbor of his arms?

He pulled her close then, but it was a little too late, and she was being released a moment too quickly.

"How did you know I'd be here?" Instantly she regretted the words.

He looked at her with a trace of reproof. "Shouldn't I know you well enough to know that you'd return for the funeral?"

"You're late," she said softly. "The funeral. It's over." Had he deliberately tried to avoid seeing her and still pay his respects to Norm Lowenthal?

"I know. The damn car wouldn't start. I had to get a new battery."

Agonized, she looked at him. Where were the words of joy they should both be proclaiming? "How's the opera going?"

His smile was full and real. "Good."

She waited for him to say more but he remained silent. Stifling her resentment, she turned to the casket. "I've returned to find myself in some hot water." Suddenly, she had to talk about it.

Fixing her eyes on the spray of yellow roses over the casket, Lauren told Anthony the whole story. When she was through, he led her over to the chairs. "Sit down."

She did and waited until he was seated next to her.

"I suppose you've considered the alternatives?"

She nodded.

"And I suppose you don't want to step down and keep the money? You plan to fight?" He was watching her intently.

She nodded, well aware that Anthony, more than anyone, would want her to give up without a fight and come out of the whole thing a very rich woman of leisure. But old habits were hard to break. She was used to trusting Anthony completely, certain he would want only the best for her. "I don't want to lose what I have, Anthony. I've worked hard. I know now what I'm doing. I'm right for this job, Anthony. Oh, I don't have to devote my life to a desk. I don't have to be Alexandra Regis all over again. I just want to do a good job. Mrs. Regis didn't want these men to get controlling interest, so she gave it to me! I can't just sit back and let them take it away!"

His eyes never left her face. "Then there are certain steps you must take."

She looked away from his steady brown stare. "Fire Parker, you mean? And . . . disown Shelly? Boot her out of Beverly Hills because she's embarrassed me? Don't you think both of them have been kicked around enough already?"

Anthony sighed. The rain was only a light drizzle outside now, and the clusters of mourners were dispersing, some of them glancing through the oval windows for a last glimpse at the casket. They didn't notice the couple seated in the corner, but Anthony waited until it was again quiet.

"You can't be mother to the world, Lauren," he said softly. "Parker and Shelly are responsible for their own actions. You've convinced yourself that you're responsible for everything they do. It isn't fair to them, and it isn't fair to yourself. It might not even be fair to Alexandra Regis, who certainly went out on a limb naming you in that final will. Maybe the board is right; maybe you don't have the guts to do the dirty work your job sometimes demands."

Bright spots of red dotted Lauren's cheeks. She looked at him angrily.

But before she could speak, he continued. "You've always tried to help your family. Maybe you've always tried a little too hard. And when you got the inheritance, you got a touch of Midas fever, I think. All of a sudden you had the power to make everyone happy. Have you made them happy? Is Parker happy, knowing he's doing a lousy job? How do you suppose Shelly feels, in that fancy apartment she knows she doesn't deserve? A wasted life is a wasted life, Lauren, even in paradise."

"I can't give them the axe just to save my own skin! Don't ask me to do that," she said emotionally.

He looked at her with considerable surprise. "I'm the last guy in the world to ask you for anything, Lauren. I don't ask. I just wait." He smiled his familiar smile and put his arm around her shoulder. "I'm getting good at waiting."

She looked at him, but he had turned his attention toward the casket, the smile replaced by an expression of respectful contemplation.

She wanted to stay angry at Anthony. For what was he waiting? For her world to crumble around her so that he could claim what was left of her? Did she even want such a man?

Or was he waiting for her to say the words that would assure him that she had found nothing in Europe to replace him in her heart?

Had she?

Tommy would come if she called. Jan would be happy to fly to her side. And Claude—in his heart he had already laid claim to her future.

What then did she want with this man from her past, this man who dared rebuke her for what she had done for her own family in the name of love?

Too tired to think more, sure only that having Anthony next to her on whatever terms felt better than being near anyone else, Lauren leaned back comfortably against his steadying arm.

Together and yet apart, they bid a silent farewell to Norm Lowenthal.

Chapter Nineteen

Chris watched Earl Regis stir martinis in a glass shaker and felt two distinctly conflicting emotions: contempt for him and amusement at being in his "secret" apartment in west Hollywood.

She had known about the apartment, because she had been the one to rent it for him. At the time, she'd thought little about it. Even though he could have stayed overnight at the hotel whenever he wished, after meeting Earl's plump little wife, Chris had understood why he might want a little hideaway all to himself elsewhere.

What Chris hadn't realized then was that Regis had wanted the apartment for her. "Pick anything you think is nice. But be sure it's private."

Things got a little messy when Chris discovered that she was the bird intended to occupy this gilded cage. But Earl was too weak and ineffectual to push the issue. Much as he desired her, he would not risk provoking Chris to leave her job.

"I wasn't sure you had kept this place, Earl," Chris teased, perfectly aware that he had. Her remark was intended to remind him of his once frantic sexual interest in her.

Earl had been stunned to see her near Lauren's office earlier that day, thinking her still in Paris with her boss. It was the trapped, frightened look in his eyes that had given Earl away. He had looked away from her, furtively trying to leave the area without being observed.

Chris was more certain than ever before that Earl had not instituted the legal action against Lauren on his own. Alden Chambers, S. D. Hollenbeck and Jim Reardon had pumped him full of hope juice, promising him money and prestige. And Earl had taken the bait, even though he already had more of both than he could handle by himself.

He was nothing more than an oversized infant, still yearning for comfort from an oversized breast. He would always reach out for the single ripe fruit rather than tend the sapling that would someday produce bushels of fruit. It was his nature to seek immediate and easy gratification, and he lacked not only the discipline but also the desire to change.

All of these thoughts came to Chris at once as she watched Earl Regis sidle away from her. With the realization came the solution as well.

Without Earl to front the legal attack against Lauren, the action would fall apart. While it was feasible that the claim of Alexandra Regis' incompetency could be pursued, there was a danger that other heirs could pose a greater threat than Lauren already did. For all anyone knew, distant relatives would crawl out of the woodwork. Earl was safe— he could be easily controlled.

Chris had smiled to herself as she played with the obvious answer. She knew one sure way to remove Earl's name from that suit and torpedo the entire action against Lauren.

She could make Earl a better offer.

She could make him an offer he couldn't refuse.

She could offer him . . . herself.

232

Why not? What better use could she have for a body that had betrayed her?

Not for the first time, she sent René Raison a silent apology. And a final farewell. Chris accepted the humiliation of her failure to fall in love with her perfect man and hoped she had spared René an ultimately larger pain by saying goodbye to him forever before she left France.

He hadn't understood, could see no reason why she had to leave with Lauren instead of staying on with him, as she had promised.

"You won't need the job," he had reminded her. As René's wife, Chris would never have had to work again. "We are so perfect together."

Unwittingly, he had used the one word that could act as a knife in the raw wound of her disappointment. René was perfect. Too perfect to saddle with a marriage that would only fulfil her own childish dreams. Her perfect man. She had found him at last. In bed, at the time when two people should be fused with that magical blend of love and passion, Chris had found herself acting out the role of lover, faking emotions she could not feel, trying to force a fairy tale to come true.

Even now she couldn't understand what had happened to her in René's bed. It was nothing he had done. He was kind and gentle, loving and passionate. He had technique and tenderness, and his intention was to please as much as to be pleased.

Yet she hadn't been able to respond. He had kindled a flame at first and her body had done its best to blot out her thoughts. But as he continued to caress and kiss her, her mind had struggled out of the honey haze of frantic passion.

Why? she had asked herself, naked in his embrace, eyes slitted but carefully studying the man making ardent love to her. *What's wrong?* For an entire lifetime she had waited for someone like René, someone who could give her a beautiful life, be a faithful husband, never betray their children. And yes, she wanted the frills, too. All the luxuries she'd had in her early childhood. Was that so wrong? She would hurt no one. She would strive to bring happiness to such a man. And now here he was, willing to love her.

And she was cold in his arms.

Most shamefully, the realization came too late, when she had no choice but to simulate a passion she did not feel. Humiliated, determined to spare René, she let the play go on, relieved when, at last, he moaned in ecstasy and was still.

She'd never felt intense remorse over past sexual encounters that had been little more than a release from tension. She was living at a time in history when women were free to demand gratification on all levels.

But it had been different with René. Because this time she had expected more than release. She had wanted love and permanence, and had ended up with nothing but sorrow.

She had returned to Los Angeles feeling tired and washed out. She was afraid, too. Just as her dream of the perfect man had been destroyed, so her dream of reaching the top of the ladder in business was also jeopardized. If Lauren lost her control of the Regis fortune, where would that put her? Back in Earl's office, playing lackey to him? Or back on the street, looking for a job in a depressed economy?

Then she had seen the ferret-like expression on Earl's face and everything fell into place. She would offer him a trade. He would drop his suit against Lauren, and she would consent to become his mistress. She had pretended a fine passion with René—Earl wasn't subtle or sensitive enough to demand even that much. He would only care that she was there when he wanted her, accepting his predictable lust. She wouldn't even have to soil her own bed.

What would it take from her, really? Who would know? Earl would refuse to take part in the suit, the legal action would fall apart, and at least half of her life would remain as it had been.

Chris hashed it all over again as Earl made and brought the martinis to the couch.

"I won't even ask who you've been bringing here," she said coquettishly, positive that he knew why she was here at last. She could almost see the furious activity going on in his brain. He was weighing his choices and the dues he would have to pay on any decision he might make. He was not so stupid as to believe having Chris wouldn't cost him a considerable price.

Chris felt supremely confident. She knew Earl would need some help in explaining his decision. He couldn't very well admit he was acting out of lust. She was used to doing his thinking for him. She could feed him the right words, even manage to make him sound wise and honor bound to the Regis family when he announced his change of heart. The other men would be suspicious. They might even guess his true motives since his desire for Chris was not much of a secret. Revenge on her for leaving him for Lauren had in all likelihood been used to spur him to sue in the first place.

But Chris would see that Earl stood firm this time. And that was all that mattered.

"The question should be . . . why you're here, Chris," he said, tasting his drink.

"Are you sorry I'm here?" She pouted prettily and crossed her legs. They were encased in the sheerest of nylon. She watched his eyes go to them before she demurely pressed the full skirt of her shamelessly frilly Kappi silk dress back around her golden knees. It was a soft rose silk, accentuating the lotus flower delicacy of her exotic beauty. She had dressed for this meeting to entice Earl but not overpower him. Even her choice of perfume was light and flowery. She intended to make Earl want her more than he'd ever wanted anyone or anything. Perhaps, she thought grimly, she had chosen the wrong line of work.

He wet his lower lip, a broad slab of loose flesh the color

of raw veal, with a disturbingly pink tongue. "Sorry? Come on, Chris, you know I put all this together just for you."

She smiled her encouragement and felt a trace of pity for him along with her contempt. Earl had to be close to sixty. He was too old to come unglued because a good-looking woman was about to offer her body in sacrifice.

The phone rang shrilly. Earl jerked his head toward it nervously.

Lauren suspected this private number was only known to his new assistant and Abrams, the assistant manager of the hotel. "Go ahead, answer it," she said reassuringly. "I won't run away. Got to powder my nose, anyway."

"Promise?" He set down his drink and caught the receiver between rings. "Yes? Oh. Well, what is it? Couldn't you take care of it . . ."

Chris escaped into the large bathroom, equal in size to the bedroom.

It was an interior bath, with artificial lighting that had a variety of functions. From a gleaming mosaic of frosted glass panels in the ceiling one could be bathed in light bright enough to apply stage makeup, or dim enough to prevent a night mishap without fully awakening a sleepwalker.

Chris touched the wrong switch and the room was flooded with a soft pink glow. The night light. Well, it was light enough for her. In the wall-to-wall mirror she was all-over rosy pink, except for her shining dark hair loose around her shoulders. Her face stared back at her, dull-eyed, hard, hurt. She looked ravishingly beautiful but queerly pathetic, a doll caught outside the dollhouse.

For a moment she couldn't imagine why she was standing there. In the inner sanctum of Earl Regis's tawdry little love nest. About to auction herself off for a price that wasn't even going into her own pocket.

Chris touched a hand to her face and found her cheek unnaturally warm. She was a little dizzy. Still operating on European time, she probably needed to collapse into a deep sleep before doing another thing. She had come from the airport to her office and then to this apartment, stopping at home only to change. She was disoriented, suddenly unsure of the day or time. Everything had been out of focus since leaving Paris.

Lauren had been justifiably withdrawn on the long flight home. Chris's silences hadn't been as obvious. When they arrived at LAX, Chris had found herself straining her eyes for a glimpse of David. She hadn't realized she was doing it until a dark-haired man with a little girl came by and her heart skipped a beat or two. It was absurd. Why should she think David would be at the airport? He had no idea she had returned. She'd had no contact with him since she'd left. She had sent a few postcards, mainly to Nipper, knowing the little girl would be thrilled.

The face in the mirror was frowning, and Chris forced her brow to smooth itself. What was the matter with her? Why was she thinking of David, of all people? He was the last person in the whole world she wanted to see her now. She could imagine the shock, the disappointment, the sadness in his face if he were to know.

Not that his opinion mattered. She was doing what she wanted to do, what had to be done. If Lauren couldn't get herself out of the trouble she was in, even if some of it was of Lauren's own making, Chris could and would save the day.

She was tired and confused. She knew it, because a little dust storm was flaring up in her brain, like a warning bell urging her to pay attention to its silvery ring. She had a feeling she'd heard it before but couldn't remember just where.

If she weren't so exhausted, surely she'd know why she was feeling this odd sensation. She kept staring at her face in the mirror. Something was wrong. Very wrong. Despite careful logic, her equation didn't seem to add up right.

"Chris? Are you all right?"

Earl's whining voice was muffled by the closed door.

"Yes. I'll be out in a few minutes." Even his voice

annoyed her. And yet she was willing to go to bed with him?

Why?

Oh, yes, to save Lauren. And, incidentally, herself.

Okay, let's think about this. Starting with myself. Since when do I have to sleep with anyone to get, keep or improve a job? She'd never needed a job that badly. *And what's this about saving Lauren?*

The face in the mirror began to smile. That warning in her mind was sounding off like a rattler giving alarm before the strike.

No wonder she'd felt that sense of déja vu! Hadn't she been telling Lauren how wrong it was to try to step in and correct the mistakes other people made? She'd begged Lauren to allow her stepfather and stepsister to live their own lives, make their own decisions and reap the rewards or disappointments of their own acts. Now here she was, doing the same thing on Lauren's behalf, offering herself as a sacrificial lamb to Earl to buy Lauren out of a situation the other woman had helped create.

She almost laughed out loud. The pieces of her bizarre scheme came together all at once. Her feverishly denied feelings for David. The bitter disappointment with René. Her ridiculous attempt to become Earl's mistress.

Grimly, she faced her moment of truth. *There's a part of me that actually wants the escape of a fruitless union with a man I couldn't possibly love!* Her generosity, she now understood, had frightening undertones.

All these years of searching for a perfect love! It was all a lie! No wonder I felt nothing when I met René—I never wanted a real relationship at all! Prince Charming was only a device, a way of keeping myself from allowing love into my life. Love. It's always seemed too frightening, too risky. If I loved, I might lose, just as my mother and I lost. Why did I never realize how I felt?

By keeping a dream alive, she could avoid the real thing. Then fate had brought her René, who challenged that dream.

And she couldn't open her heart to him because, much as she'd denied it to herself, she was already in love.

Chris turned on the tap, ran cool water over her fingers, patted her face. She knew she'd go on helping Lauren protect her holdings, but not this way. Lauren had a duty to fight for what she wanted. But so did she.

It was David she would fight for now. She was ready to take her chances in a world that offered no guarantees. A risky world.

But a real one.

She left the rosy isolation of the bathroom and smiled at Earl Regis, who uncertainly returned the bright, artificial smile. Then she took one small sip of the martini. "Earl, I have to leave."

"Leave? Now? I don't understand."

She laughed. "It doesn't matter. As long as one of us does." She barely noticed the bewildered expression on his face. Her mind was too busy thinking of soap bubbles in the sky, specifically one she was suddenly very sure would never pop.

Chapter Twenty

"Chris! You came back! Daddy, Chris is home!" Nipper's little face was ecstatic. "Daddy!" She gripped the woman around the hips as if she were afraid to let her go.

"Well, sure, pumpkin. Did you get my cards?" Chris kneeled to give the girl a hug.

"Hey, Nip, you going to keep Chris out there all night?" David's voice held a gentle reprimand as he came to the door.

Then she was in his arms. "When did you get back? We've missed you."

"Today. I'm dead on my feet, but I wanted to see you. Should I have called first?" With a rush of panic it struck her that David might be entertaining. Here she was, all wrapped up in her own feelings, never once thinking that David might even now be seeing another woman.

He kissed her cheek. "Of course not. You know you're always welcome."

"I'm glad." She regretted the cheek kiss, ruefully aware

that she was the one who had set the rules for their contact with each other. Were they so established as friends that they could no longer become lovers? It was a disturbing thought. *Careful what you wish for lest you get it.*

Nipper's excitement to have her back shut out her other thoughts. Patiently, Chris listened to the little girl's stories about school and solemnly met a rag doll who had become the newest addition to Nipper's growing family.

Finally, Nipper settled down in front of the television to watch a cartoon special and Chris and David could talk together in peace.

"You weren't due back for another ten days. What happened?"

She brewed coffee and told David the whole story about Lauren. He interrupted often with questions. The lawyer in him struggled with the problem in an unemotional fashion.

"Something's bothering me about this," he said finally, getting up and pacing the small area of his den. "I know something . . . Norman Lowenthal . . . Lowenthal . . . Something about him . . ."

"Perhaps you heard about his death." She drank her coffee and watched him pace, wondering why she'd ever thought him only moderately attractive. He looked beautiful to her now.

"Yes, but something else. Something pertinent."

Watching him, she noticed the intelligence in his eyes, the selfless energy he was expending on a problem that wasn't his. Without giving herself a chance to think about and then possibly reconsider her actions, she put the coffee cup down, stood up, and walked up to him.

"I'm so glad to see you again, David. I missed you." She very simply put her arms around his neck and kissed him on the lips.

His surprise gave way to pleasure. "I missed you, too, Chris. More than you could guess." He wound his arms around her slender waist, inhaled the flowery perfume, crushed the frilly Kappi pink dress against him and kissed

241

her again. "They say absence makes the heart grow fonder," he said thickly, wonderingly.

"Did it?" she asked, scarcely breathing at all.

He looked at her tenderly. "In my case, it couldn't."

"David. . . ." She rocked against him.

All of a sudden, he released her. "Damn!" He snapped his fingers. "Now I remember!"

She looked at him in surprise.

"Norm Lowenthal! Of course! Now I remember!" He gave her a quick kiss, rather as if their relationship was so secure that there was no need for constant reaffirmations.

"What is it?"

"I don't want to get your hopes up, but let me check something out. Wait a second." He crossed to the phone on his desk. He punched out a number, shifted his weight impatiently and winked at her. "Nate? David here. . . . Fine." He turned to Chris. "How about getting us some hot coffee?"

Chris took the cups and stopped on the way to the kitchen to see how Nipper was doing. She was wrapped up in her TV special, but happy to take a moment to return Chris's kiss.

"Want some hot chocolate, honey? With a marshmallow?"

"Goody!"

Chris ruffled her hair and went into the kitchen. She felt pleasantly housewifely. She boiled water and warmed the coffee, found a mug and the bag of marshmallows she'd spied while brewing coffee earlier. It occurred to her then that only with David, of all the men she'd ever known, had she felt completely secure, able to be herself. No kittenish manipulations, no artificial teasing seductiveness. She realized theirs would be a sweatshirt-and-jeans kind of marriage, without much of the glamour she'd thought she would have to have.

Marriage? Wasn't she jumping the gun a little? She hadn't even proposed to him yet!

She gave Nipper her chocolate with lots of paper napkins and strict warnings about burning herself. Then she brought the fresh coffee to David.

He was still on the phone. "Thanks, Nate, I really appreciate this. You're sure you don't mind? If it's too late, it could wait until morning. . . . Fine. See you in a bit." He hung up, took a cup of coffee, sipped at it, put it down and hugged Chris.

"Look, I've got to go somewhere, check something out. Can you stay here with Nipper? I'll be gone maybe two hours. I know you're wiped out, but can you do it? I think it'll be worth the effort."

She was confused but instantly nodded. "Is it about the will?"

He looked excited. "Yes, indeed!" He kissed her again. "I'll be back as soon as I can. With good news, I hope."

He left after kissing Nipper and telling her she had to go to bed as soon as the TV show was over.

Chris sat on the big old couch and finished her coffee. During one of the many commercials, Nipper came over to the couch and sat down next to her. A moment later, she was curled up on the couch, her head on Chris's lap. A full day at nursery school and the excitement of seeing Chris again had taken its toll on the little girl; she wouldn't make it to the end of her show.

Chris knew she should hurry Nipper to her bed, but instead she cuddled the pajama and red robe clad child to her. As she stroked the silky soft dark hair, she realized that there was more than one way to become a mother. Perhaps love was the best way of all.

Finally, she lifted the sleeping child carefully in her arms and put her into bed, leaving the robe on but removing her slippers. She tucked the covers snugly around the tiny body and lightly kissed the velvety cheek.

Unbearably content, she washed the few dishes, tidied up the apartment and, without the slightest bit of indecision, showered and slipped naked into David's big bed.

Whatever news he had could wait until morning.

She hadn't realized she'd dozed off until David's voice roused her. "Chris?"

She sat up against the pillows and yawned, holding the covers to her chin. "What's that?" He was holding something that looked like a video cassette.

"What?" Oblivious to anything other than the fact of Chris in his bed, David stared down at her.

"In your hand, David." She giggled.

"Oh! Yes, this. It's the end of Regis' law suit. It's irrefutable proof that the old girl was very much aware of what she was doing when she made that will. When you mentioned Norm Lowenthal, I remembered a conversation I'd once had with my friend Nate Beglau. He's a junior partner at Lowenthal, Biggs and Clark. He'd mentioned something about Lowenthal getting into video taping complex wills as a hedge against just this sort of thing." He held up the boxed tape. "Presto."

Chris smiled. Somehow she wasn't very surprised. It seemed so very right that David would pull them out of this mess so neatly. Her Lancelot. It pleased her that she still believed in fairy tales, deep down.

He dropped the tape on the night table, still unable to take his eyes from her. As if she might vanish if he looked away. "I'm sure you want to see this. . . ." It sounded like a question.

"I'm sure it can wait until morning." She let the blanket slide down over her perfumed body. Her breasts, full and tense-nippled, came proudly into view. "Can't it?"

Without a word, David began to undress.

Chapter Twenty-one

Lauren slept for ten hours straight after Anthony brought her home from the cemetery, and still she was exhausted. It had taken all of her remaining strength to put in a second call to Lowenthal, Biggs and Clark. Norm's partners had been at the funeral, of course, but she'd felt it inappropriate to approach them there.

All she got was a receptionist eager to close the office for the night. "Your call was returned earlier, Miss Wells. I believe we tried to reach you in Paris this morning, as well. I'm sure someone will try again tomorrow."

Unable to touch dinner, she had excused herself to lie down for a few minutes before joining Anthony for a drink and, hopefully, a good, long talk.

But when she awakened, it was morning and she was still fully dressed. Someone had covered her while she slept and put Tuxedo on the bed with her. He stretched his furry body in greeting to the new day, but Lauren felt as if she'd hardly rested at all. She wanted to pull the covers up over her head and pretend it was still the middle of the night.

The last thing she wanted to do today was go to the hotel. There would be embarrassed silences everywhere she went. Instead of being glad to see her, her staff might shun her, not wanting to be seen with her now that her position was in question.

Lauren forced herself into the shower, shampooed, dried and braided her Godiva hair and pinned it into its usual coronet around her head. Looking neat and in control again, she dressed in a businesslike brown dress and applied a bit of blush to her cheeks and gloss to her lips. If she was stepping into hell, she didn't want the devil himself to suspect that she was upset.

She was surprised to find Anthony at the table, eating breakfast. "Did you just get here?"

He poured her coffee. "Uh-uh. I camped out all night on the couch in your bedroom alcove. I wasn't sure if you'd passed out from exhaustion or what, so I thought it would be a good idea to hang around."

She felt comforted by his concern and worried by it, as well. He was proving his willingness to stand by her through her difficulties, but there was no indication of his deepest motives. Were they to continue as lovers, or was friendship all he was offering?

Lauren watched him eat and wished there was some way to tell him that she wanted and needed his passionate embrace. Already it was becoming difficult to remember how it felt to be with him, to feel him naked beside her, crushingly close, so much a part of her that she wasn't sure where she left off and he began. The room still felt supercharged with excitement merely because he was in it—her lips still ached because his were near. As hard as she tried to comfort herself with thoughts of the men she had met in Europe, the more distant and trivial they seemed.

And the more Anthony kept her at arm's length, the more sure she was that only he could make her feel alive again. Was it too late for them? Had she gone a little crazy when she came into the inheritance? Why had she thought that

Anthony had to change his image to participate in her new life? Just because he was a little intimidated by her office? Well, she had been intimidated, too.

What was keeping her from putting down her cup of cooling coffee and telling him exactly how she felt? They were not strangers. They had been as intimate as two people could be with each other. Was it pride? She couldn't afford pride. Not if it meant that he spent the night on her couch rather than in her bed.

Before she could act on her intense feelings, Valerie came into the room.

"A Dr. Brictman is on the telephone, Ms. Wells. Calling from Amsterdam."

"Oh!" Lauren got up and excused herself, unable to fully meet Anthony's eyes. "I'll only be a moment."

Cursing the timing, Lauren went into the office to take the call.

"Darling, I just heard about your trouble. Is there anything I can do?"

"Thank you, Jan, no, but it's nice of you to call. How are you? How's Amsterdam?"

In the brief lull between her voice and his, the gap caused by the enormous distance between them, Lauren realized that she really had very little to say to Jan.

"Amsterdam is lonely without you."

"Jan, I'm afraid you've caught me at a terrible time. I have so much . . ." She felt ashamed of herself. There was no need to make weak excuses. He deserved honesty from her. "I'm trying to work things out with Anthony," she said softly. "I'm sorry."

"Don't be," he said after the pause. "Just keep my number, won't you?"

She smiled sadly into the phone. "I will. And thank you."

A carefully disinterested expression on his handsome face, Anthony barely looked up when Lauren returned to the table. "Oh, I almost forgot. A Sir Thomas Tollby called while you were asleep. I took the call."

"From England?"

"San Francisco." He reached into his pants pocket. "Here. He left his number. He seemed a little put off when I took the call. Said you should return his call. If you cared to, that is."

Lauren would have smiled, if she dared. In Anthony's great show of indifference was all the pent-up jealousy of an uncertain youth. She looked down at the hand holding out the folded bit of note paper. She shook her head. "I won't be needing that, Anthony. Thank you anyway."

He grinned, crumpled the paper to a tiny ball and crammed it back into his pocket.

Lauren smiled back, praying the phone wouldn't ring again.

"Okay, team, what's the game plan for today?" He pushed away his plate and started on a fresh cup of coffee.

Knowing that her moment for putting her feelings on the table was gone, she considered his question, her spirits taking a nose dive as she contemplated what was before her. "I thought I'd better go to the hotel today, same as usual."

"Are you sure that's necessary?" he asked gently.

She shrugged. "I think it is. I'm still chairing the board and I have work to finish. There will be time later to prepare for my big day in court. The wisest course seems to be business as usual."

"It might be unpleasant down there today. The papers are making a big thing out of this suit, Lauren. Do you want to see the *Times?*"

She shook her head. "It's funny, isn't it? One minute they're pushing you up to the top and the next, they're clawing you down again. Just like you said. Remember?"

"I remember. But Lauren, you know you don't have to do any of this. You don't have to get involved in a court action. You don't ever have to step foot in a Regis-Royale again, unless you want to."

"I intend to fight them, Anthony. Chambers, Hollenbeck,

Jim Reardon, all of them. I want to prove that I can do the job Alexandra Regis entrusted to me."

"Have you made a decision then about Parker and Shelly?" He reached over and took her hand. "I came down on you hard about them. I had to. But I do know what you're going through."

She was grateful. Of course he was right. Any fight for her inheritance would be considerably weakened if she didn't make some firm effort to correct her mistakes. Parker had to be fired before the hearing, and Shelly had to be censured. What Chris and Anthony failed to understand was that it was unbearable for her to take those steps simply in order to better her own position in court. Oh, yes, Tommy had been right—this life was not without its pain, either.

"Dealing with Parker and Shelly is the hardest part," she answered Anthony at last, her eyes glazed with unshed tears. "I'm either good for the hotels, or good to my family. It seems I can't be both."

He looked as if he was about to argue, but with a shrug, he held his peace. "Are you sure you don't want to just stay home and rest a day or two? The world won't fall apart in a couple of days."

She shook her head. "No, I've got to face this. I'll probably only want to stay a few hours. We'll see. Are you going home to work?"

Again he smiled that secretive little smile he'd flashed the last time she'd mentioned his work. "No," he answered without elaborating. "I'll take you to work and stop back in a couple of hours."

It was even worse than she'd expected. Anthony insisted on driving her to the hotel in his old car. She wanted her entrance to be as unobtrusive as possible. He dropped her off and she walked through the hotel and rode the elevator without coming face to face with anyone other than the elevator operator, who merely nodded. But she had the impression that they couldn't reach the top floor quickly enough to suit him. Lauren felt much as she had the first few times she had taken this now familiar route—very naked, covertly observed. Only this time the eyes were not merely curious. They were searching for signs of weakness, of fear. *Lions*, she thought, again appreciating Anthony's words. *Lions looking for easy game*. It was the human condition, to fatten and then to drain, to take as much as had been given. She found she was actually grateful for all she had learned. This, at least, no one could ever take from her. Knowledge was a prize that could never be lost.

Chris wasn't in the office, and she didn't answer her phone at home. Surely the newspapers weren't keeping her away. Chris would hold her head up high if tied to the stake. But perhaps she was wiser than Lauren. Perhaps she knew it was time to quit.

Both her desk and Chris's were piled high with messages. Ignoring them, sure that at least Earl wouldn't be stopping by as usual with a dozen problems he could easily have handled if he were at all competent, Lauren got to work, drafting a report on her European trip.

Before Anthony returned, she had done all she could and considered taking her usual tour of the Regis-Royale. But that would mean having to see Parker, and she wasn't up to that quite yet. She still didn't know what to do about him. Luckily, he hadn't called her yet. Nor had Shelly. Very likely neither of them knew she was back from Europe, but they would before the day was out. Many of the messages on her desk were from the media. If they knew she was back, the world would know it by the morning paper at the latest.

Anthony arrived moments after Lauren decided against taking the tour. He gave her a hug.

"Bad?"

"Not wonderful." She sighed. "But I did get a lot of work done. Come on, let's get out of here. I think I could stand a little nap." She looked up at him with a heavy-lidded stare, hoping he would see her need for him. "How about you?"

In answer, he kissed the tip of her nose with infuriating lightness.

There was a message from Chris waiting for her at home. "Chris and David will be over at four," she said with surprise. Had Chris been with the young attorney all day? Lauren hoped she had found the explanation for Chris's absence.

It was almost three by the time they sat down to a bracing and calorie-laden lunch of creamed chicken and fresh hot rolls. Lauren didn't have much of an appetite—she worried about her figure just as much during times of disaster as other times.

She watched Anthony eat in that food-is-serious-business way of his, still uncertain as to why he was solidly by her side but pleased that he was. As much as she wanted to see Chris and David, she was sorry they were arriving so soon. The thought of taking a nap with Anthony, if he were open to her earlier suggestion, was very enticing. In each other's arms, all doubt would be gone. One way or the other.

It's no big thing, she told herself. *If he still wants me, I will marry him immediately if not sooner. If he doesn't, I'll simply slit my throat!*

In spite of her gory promise, she was beginning to feel like her old self again.

Chapter Twenty-two

Valerie brought a tray of *tapas* and sherry while David and Anthony fiddled with the video tape recorder in the entertainment room. They had hit it off immediately, talking as they rewound the video tape David had brought, giving Chris and Lauren a moment to talk privately.

"I don't know what happened, Chris, but just looking at you gives me a big hint."

"It shows, huh?" She grinned.

"Let's just say that anyone who looks as radiant as you do in an old pair of jeans and a tee-shirt must be in love."

"Miss Marple, I do think you've hit the nail on the 'ead, old girl."

Lauren gave her a quick hug. "I'm glad, Chris. A little jealous, but glad."

"Why jealous? That isn't chopped liver you've got over there, you know."

Before Lauren could comment on that, Chris began talking again. "Oh, Lauren, David did it. He really did it! I haven't seen the tape yet myself, but he told me about it! Earl Regis, eat your heart out! Listen, if you don't hire David as your personal attorney after this, you . . ."

"I hope you won't mind, Lauren," David began as if he had heard their conversation, "but I had to say I was your new attorney in order to get this copy. I figured it would save time all around." He straightened up.

"But I still don't understand. If it isn't the will, what is it?"

"Call it the pot of gold at the end of the rainbow," Chris answered happily. Excited, flushed from a night of love-making, her hair loose around her china-doll face, she looked like a carefree teenager. "Or the axe that gave the Regis clan its forty whacks."

Anthony grinned. "Sit down, honey. I think it'll explain itself, from what David tells me. Come on, show time. I'll get the lights."

He darkened the room and sat down next to her, giving her a quick kiss. "Oh, well, what the hell. I've just about accepted the terrible fate of having a rich wife, anyway. We can't all be lucky enough to marry paupers."

Bewildered, plunged into a sudden bath of warmth at Anthony's words, Lauren watched uncomprehendingly. "What . . . ?"

"Shh," said Chris, who was seated on the edge of her chair devouring *tapas*, her eyes glued to the screen while David rubbed her back with understated possessiveness.

"Let's see now . . ." the thickened voice of an old woman began, "It's Thursday, March the 26th, 1981. Four o'clock by this bedside clock, so that makes it three fifty-five in the afternoon for the rest of Los Angeles. Don't laugh—I've always managed to stay a little ahead of my time."

As the wrinkled, sallow-faced woman on the screen smiled with considerable effort, Lauren sat bolt upright on the couch. "That's Alexandra Regis! I didn't recognize her at first because she's so sick here!"

"Shh, now, just watch." Anthony pulled her back into the warm circle of his arm.

". . . is Alexandra DuPar Regis, my address is . . ."

Lauren listened in a haze of excitement, at last catching on. Norm Lowenthal, that wily old fox, had suspected that there might be bitter fighting for Alexandra's empire. He—or perhaps Alexandra herself—had made a video tape to prove that the old woman was in sound mind when she wrote the will that left everything to Lauren.

". . . and my age should be recorded in Ripley's next effort. . . ."

"She's marvelous, isn't she?" Chris asked. "I wish I'd had a chance to know her better when she was alive. But Earl wouldn't let me within two rooms of his aunt. He was afraid I'd give him away."

A man appeared on the screen with her. It was the old woman's doctor. He was asking Alexandra something, but Lauren had been listening to Chris.

"When I was young, I made my mistakes, as we all do," Alexandra was looking directly into the camera. She seemed to be in pain, but there was no mistaking the eagle-like sharpness in those tired eyes. "I kept on making them, too, but that's a different story. Well, if not for Barbara Madison, my roommate at college, I might not have lived to go on making them. Mistakes, and a fair amount of money as well. My debt of gratitude to Barbara was never paid. In recognition of that debt, I have decided to leave the bulk of my estate to her only daughter, Lauren Wells."

Lauren felt a distinct thrill at hearing her name directly from the old woman's lips, and the tribute to her mother brought quick tears to her eyes. Understanding, Anthony hugged her tightly.

"It is also my wish—not my command, and as everyone knows, I'm damned good at issuing commands—that Ms. Wells replace me as chairperson of the Regis-Royale board of directors, as well as president of the company.

"I make this request for several reasons. For one, it's my

belief that none of the present members of the board is fit to fill my chair. Certainly not my nephew, Earl Regis." The tired eyes twinkled mischievously. "Earl has only one talent . . . well, two, really. First, he was born into the right family, and second, he has a good eye for picking able secretaries and assistants, like the young woman he has doing all his work for him now."

Chris jumped to her feet and took a quick bow. Her face, however, was flushed with real pleasure.

Lauren listened attentively as Mrs. Regis carefully named the other members of the board, listing their assets and liabilities to the company. She was fair and impartial, but always humorous in her comments.

"Most of all," she said in summation, "the company needs new blood. I expect Ms. Wells will make her mistakes. We all do. But a study of her background has convinced me that she'll learn from our organization. I wish her my best, whatever her decision. It is my hope the others will prove me wrong, that they won't let greed override their senses and attempt to deprive Ms. Wells of her rightful inheritance, one I bequeath to her in full possession of my mind and what is left of my body." Alexandra Regis paused and turned a canny eye to the camera. "In which case, this video tape will never be seen. I sincerely hope that is the case. I sneaked a quick look at myself in the mirror this morning. Loni Anderson I'm not."

There was a little more to the tape: the doctor asking questions about the weather, politics and various charities she had named in her will, all designed to convince the most wary viewer that the old woman was alert and acting on her own convictions.

"Well, that sums it all up, I think," David said, turning off the recorder. "I don't think you'll have to bother with that day in court after all, Lauren."

Chris switched on the lights. She came over to Lauren, obviously very moved. "I guess we're still in business, boss. Oh, and that means you don't have to do anything about

Shelly and Parker, if you'd rather not. There are other chefs. You are the boss." She grinned. "The boss does get special privileges, and I guess that extends to her family, as well." She couldn't seem to stop smiling.

"We're still in business, all right. And it looks like we've got a new attorney. David?"

He shook his head. "It's a tempting offer, Lauren. And I really appreciate it. But I enjoy the kind of law I practice—helping people in trouble. I have the feeling this is the only trouble you're going to be in for a long time." David grinned. "But listen, you do need a new attorney, and I know just the man. His name is Nate Beglau, and he's an old college friend of mine. He's the one who found this tape. He's a junior partner at Lowenthal, Biggs and Clark, and being your attorney would cinch that promotion he's been wanting. He's a little fond of the soft life, but he's a damn good lawyer."

"Ask him to drop by my office on Monday, okay? Have him call Chris for an appointment."

"Oh, well. There goes my hope for snaring a rich lawyer for a husband," Chris complained happily, hugging David's arm.

"And Chris . . . about Shelly and Parker . . ." She felt strong and sad. But she knew what she had to do. "You're right. The boss does have special privileges. Not necessarily pleasant ones, either. Talk to Abrams in the morning, will you please?" She smiled tiredly. "Ask him to tell Chef Raymond he's back on his terms. I'll tell my dad myself."

Anthony came to Lauren's side. "I'll help, if you want."

"Does it help to know you're doing the right thing? For them, as much as for anyone?" Chris asked softly.

Lauren shook her head. "No, not very much. It hurts to hurt the people you love. For whatever reason. Even for their own good. But I can't go on wanting their happiness more than they do. It's got to be up to them now." She sagged against Anthony. "Okay, you guys, go on home now," she said gruffly to David and Chris. "You two are making me ill with all this togetherness. I'm too tired out for so much romance. Bah! Humbug! Go home and stop wasting this lovely night."

She kissed each of them, and they all went downstairs together. As they neared the door, Lauren took Anthony's hand. As soon as Chris and David were gone, she turned to him.

"I want you to go home tonight, too. I have some thinking to do, and then I want to see Parker."

"Tonight, Lauren? Why don't you get some sleep? It'll keep until the morning, won't it?"

"Maybe, but I've been putting it off long enough."

Anthony looked at her curiously. "Why, babe? Why are you doing this when you no longer have to? That tape cinches things. You can do what you want. If it makes you feel better to have Parker and Shelly where you can keep an eye on them, why are you doing this?"

"Because I was wrong. And now I can correct my mistakes precisely because I know I'll be doing it for their sakes, and not just to save my own skin." She bit at her bottom lip, terribly close to tears. "And because, damn it, Alexandra Regis was right. I do . . . damn, double damn . . . learn from my mistakes. Eventually."

He put his arms around her. "Okay, tiger. But do I have to go? I kind of hoped . . ."

She buried her face against his chest. "Soon. But double, triple damn . . . not tonight."

He gently pushed her away so he could look at her face. "Lauren . . . one thing. Did you find . . . what you were looking for in Europe?"

She looked at him with feigned injured innocence. "Why would I look for what I already have?"

He kissed her then, his lips warm, seeking. Her arms tightened around his neck, their bodies pressed against each other.

"Do you realize," she said huskily when the kiss finally ended, "that this is the first time you've really kissed me since I came home?"

"This is the first time you've let me know I should."

"Anthony?" she said as he was leaving. "You'll be back?"

He laughed. "Try to keep me away."

As soon as he was gone, not giving herself a chance to reconsider, Lauren went to the phone and punched out Parker's number on the lighted discs.

It rang and rang. Finally she hung up.

After a moment's hesitation, she tried Shelly's house. There was no answer there, either.

Frustrated, Lauren considered asking Anthony to come back.

Smiling to herself, she instead went upstairs to bed.

Chapter Twenty-three

Lauren was afraid to wait until after Parker had finished his shift to talk to him. Gossip had it that Parker was finished long before his shift these days.

She caught him before he started, as soon as he was about to enter the hotel.

It was a full minute before he noticed her sitting in the Mercedes by the side entrance he always used. She was shocked at his appearance. When had he grown so old? A dozen images of him passed before her eyes. The surprise birthday party he had thrown for her when she was nine. The first time he, not her mother, had come to hold her when she had a nightmare. The way he had acted out a movie she had had to miss because she was sick, playing every part. That terrible night when they had held each other, both of them crying—the night her mother had died.

For a moment she was very tempted to drive on. Perhaps she shouldn't have given him the job in the first place. But she had—the best, most important job of his life. How could she take it away from him?

She took a deep breath and got out of the car, reaching him just as he got to the door. "Dad!"

He blinked at her uncertainly. Then his face lit with the old familiar smile. "Lauren! Honey!" He put his arms around her in his old bearish way but there was no strength in his embrace. He smelled of gin and sorrow.

Sorrow. Did it have a smell, like the stench of fear? What was it she had perceived? The fetid aroma of defeat? The effluvium of failure? Her heart ached for him. "What do you say, Sam?" she quipped, not knowing how to play it straight when she was on the verge of hurting him badly.

"I heard you got back." He let go of her. "Couldn't be soon enough for me. They been giving your old man a hard time, honey." He gestured toward the hotel. "It's dog eat dog in there."

She took his hand. "Come on, Dad. Let's go somewhere quiet. Let's talk."

"I got to get to work, remember?" He looked at her with hangdog anxiety.

"I'm the boss, remember?" How long had they been playing these skits with each other? When had they last talked straight, without hiding behind routines? After the first time she had had to put him to bed because he was so drunk he couldn't take care of himself? "I get to call the shots, right?"

Hand in hand they walked to the car.

She drove him home. On the way, she said, "You don't look so good, Dad. Want to talk about it?"

He was angry, but he tried not to show it. He stared through the windshield as she stopped for a light. "Have they been telling you the old man is drinking too much? Listen, I got a lot of enemies in that place. So do you, from what I hear. We can't let them push us around, right?"

"Dad. It isn't even nine in the morning yet, and already you're half crocked," she said softly. "Isn't that something to talk about?"

He didn't answer. In silence, she found a parking spot and walked with him to his apartment.

"Want some coffee? Hell, how about a drink, kid? Don't

harp about the time. I always take a drink with bad news."

She looked around the apartment. It was shabbier than ever. He'd done nothing to improve his living conditions in spite of his enormous salary. The sobering fact strengthened her resolve. "What makes you think I've brought bad news, Dad? Actually, it's good news." She kissed him softly on the cheek and said tenderly, "You don't have to go back there any more, Dad. That lousy job. It's all over. How you must have hated it."

He turned his back on her, walked over to the makeshift bar and poured a shot of gin. "Now that's a new approach to firing a man." His voice was flat.

His eyes were wet. She blinked, bit down on her lower lip until it hurt and she could go on. "Dad. . . ."

"I let you down, Lauren," he said brokenly. "I failed you. I made an ass out of myself. . . ."

"No, please. You don't understand. . . ."

"Yes. Yes, I do. Yes. I really do. I put the heat on you. Me and Shelly. Mostly me. I got that high mucky-muck cook to walk out, and because of me, they're going to take away your inheritance."

"Dad." She held both of his arms as if he were a child. Realizing what she was doing, she let him go. How long had she been doing this, treating the father like the daughter, the sister like an infant? "Dad, that's not an issue any longer. The suit isn't going to work. I'm not letting you go because I want to protect my position. Not any more. I'm letting you go because you're the wrong man for the job. It never was your kind of work." She smiled faintly. "You need to get behind the grill and cook wonderful food. You need to joke with customers, not direct traffic backstage and cater to temperamental chefs. You're temperamental enough yourself."

His mouth twitched slightly. "Maybe a little."

"Look, Dad, try to understand. I wanted you to be happy, only I didn't bother to ask you what would make you happy. I decided that myself. I thought you needed a job. So I got you the best job I could find. It was an inappropriate job. I acted inappropriately. Anthony said I got the Midas touch when I struck it rich. I thought that anything I touched would turn to gold. I guess I forgot the rest of that myth. So look, Pop, you tell me what you want. You do the talking. Tell me *if* you need help, and how you want me to help. Like two adults who respect and trust each other, okay?"

He looked at her. "It's a long time since you called me 'pop.' Not since you were a little girl and needed me."

"I'll always need you." She let her head fall against his chest.

He patted her back awkwardly. "Don't cry. Hey, don't cry." He held her at arm's length and thrust out his jaw the way he used to when he was about to say something really important.

"Lauren."

"Yes, Pop?"

"You really want to do something for me?"

"Yes, I do."

He took a deep breath. "Okay. Help me get a little place of my own. Nothing much. A little coffee shop, a cafe. Maybe a truck stop out of the city. A little place I can throw together my way, fix up. Something I can do myself, cook my kind of food, kid the customers, all the stuff I know I can do, you understand? Listen, those kinds of places are still making money. Only it has to be a loan, a real one. Not like the kind of loans you make to Shelly. I'd have to look at the books and watch them move out of the red and into the black. Otherwise, it's worth nothing to me."

"That sounds good, Pop. You'll have to find the place yourself, though. I'm going to be busy."

He grinned. "That's the way I want it. But there's more."

"Shoot the moon." She grinned. Before her eyes he was turning into himself again, the old Parker Fields. Filled with optimism and unashamed ego.

"If Shelly doesn't want to or can't be a mother to Brian,

get her to let me take the boy. I don't want my grandson growing up in a boarding school. He might as well be locked up. He hardly knows he has a family, you understand? I'll see that he goes to school. Then he'll give me a hand in the restaurant. Shelly can come see him when she wants, but meanwhile he'll have a home. What do you think?"

"I think that's a wonderful idea! Why didn't I think of that?"

He slapped her playfully on the arm. "You think you got the only brain in the family? Listen, if Shelly wants out of the mess she's in—you know what I'm talking about, her with those bums—she can come, too. I've sort of let you take care of her all these years. That wasn't fair to either of you. Or to me. I didn't start out as much of a father to her. I'd like another stab at it. If she wants."

"I'll do what I can, Pop." She kissed him again. "I'm glad I inherited a few of your brains."

"And Lauren." He stared down at the shot glass on the bar. "There's one more thing."

"Yes?"

He kept his eyes on the drained glass. "Oh, hell. Before any of this happens, I want you to send me to one of those places."

"What places?"

"You know, like they advertise on the tube. Something hills, a hospital . . . a place where an . . . alcoholic can go for a cure." He couldn't bring himself to look at her directly until he had gotten the words out. "I want to dry out, baby. This stuff is killing me. All of a sudden I don't want to die anymore." His eyes met hers. They were bright with tears, but clearer than they had been for a long time.

She had trouble finding her voice. "Shake on it," she managed finally, holding out her hand.

He took it and held tight. "Just don't ask me to drink to it," he wisecracked in his best Brooklynese.

Chapter Twenty-four

"Who is it?"

Shelly roused herself as the knocking continued.

"Get the door, baby. It's the damn door," Wayne grumbled, pulling the pillow over his face.

Shelly sat up and looked groggily around the bedroom. It was a mess. An ashtray had been dumped on its side and foul-smelling butts and grey ashes were all over the table and carpet below. Clothing was everywhere; soiled wrappers from take-out foods littered the floor. "Just a minute!"

Head pounding, Shelly fumbled for a robe, hiked up the strap of her nightgown and left the bedroom, taking care to step on as few things as possible.

The living room was in better shape. Not clean, but not as big a disaster as the bedroom. She and Wayne hadn't spent much time outside of the bedroom.

"Yes?"

"It's Lauren, Shelly! Let me in!"

The voice was like being doused with ice water. "Lauren! Hey, hold on, I'll be right there!" Wide awake now, ignoring the throbbing of her head, Shelly dashed for the bedroom.

264

"Wayne!" she hissed, "Get up! My sister's here! Come on, Wayne, get up! Get some clothes on."

He stirred, then sat up. "Ah, the golden goose. Yeah, sure." He threw back the covers and looked around for his clothing. "Maybe she'd like to invest in a script." He rubbed his head. "Ow. . . ."

"Look, please, Wayne, don't mention the script to her, huh? Not now. Just try to look respectable, okay?"

He made an obscene gesture with his narrow hips but started getting dressed.

Shelly grabbed a brush and pulled it through her blonde hair as she hurried to the door, closing the bedroom door behind her.

"Well, about time!" Lauren smiled and gave her sister a hug.

"Come on in. Sorry, I wasn't quite together. What time is it, anyway?" She felt as if her stomach was tied in knots. It didn't help to look at Lauren, who was immaculate and absolutely stunning in a cool linen pants suit, a bright Yves Saint Laurent scarf at her throat, smelling deliciously of Norell. "When did you get back? Why didn't you call?" She covered but didn't hide a yawn. "How was Europe?"

"Slow down." Lauren took a hasty glance around the apartment. "Looks like you're still partying."

"Oh, that," Shelly said, glancing nervously at Lauren's face. "I'm sorry. I was messed up that night. See, I wanted to give this party and . . . oh, I don't want to talk about it. Are you mad at me?"

"No."

Shelly breathed more easily, because she could see Lauren had told the truth. "I was afraid you might be. That hotel of yours . . . It's kind of stuffy. Not that I didn't blow it, I admit. What I was trying to do . . . oh, I really don't want to talk about it."

"You don't have to. Look, do you want some coffee? I could make some. I wouldn't mind a cup, either."

"Yeah. Let's go into the kitchen and see if I've got any.

265

I don't remember if I remembered to . . ." She glanced up as Wayne came into the room, more or less decently dressed and groomed. At least he'd made an effort, dry shaving and combing his hair. She tried to see him through Lauren's eyes. He was handsome. Not that looks had ever made the same kind of an impression on Lauren as they had on her.

"Lauren, this is Wayne Miller. Wayne, I'd like you to meet my sister, Lauren Wells."

If Lauren was taken by surprise, she didn't show it. Once again Shelly envied her sister her composure. "Hello, Mr. Miller," she said coolly, inclining that regal head of hers.

Wayne came over to take her hand. "Call me Wayne. I'm practically one of the family." He held her hand until she smoothly retrieved it.

"I'm afraid I've come at a bad time. I wanted to talk to Shelly, but I can come back."

Wayne quickly cut her off. "I was just going out to get cigarettes, anyway. Why don't you have your little talk, and maybe later we can all go out for lunch together or a drink or something. Get to know each other better."

"Yes." Then, flushing slightly as if aware that she was being less than gracious, Lauren made an obvious effort to pump some warmth into her goodbye.

"I'll stop by the apartment and see if I've got any mail. Be back in a couple of hours." He kissed Shelly quickly and left.

"I hope I wasn't rude, Shelly. I didn't realize he was here. It's just hard for me not to judge your men—considering the ones that have come before."

Shelly searched the coffee table for a cigarette and found one in a partially crumpled pack. Lauren's apology irritated her. "Oh, hell," she burst out, "don't patronize me. Wayne *is* like the others. So big deal. At least I know what to expect."

"Expect? Or want?" Lauren put a hand on Shelly's robed arm.

"Don't play shrink with me, huh?" Shelly moved out of

266

reach, aware that Lauren's easy dismissal of the hotel party fiasco had made her feel terribly guilty. Guilt never brought out her best side. She stubbed out the barely tasted cigarette. Her throat burned. Too much booze and too many cigarettes. Too much sex and sleep. Her skin was dull and her head ached.

"Perhaps someone should, Shelly. God knows, I'm not even qualified to play Midas."

"What are you talking about?" She turned to her sister and dredged up a smile. "Look, you know what a grouch I am when I wake up. Why don't you sit down a few minutes, give me a chance to grab a shower and dress, and we'll go out and have some coffee and breakfast, okay? You can tell me all about Europe."

"I'd rather not. I wanted to talk to you privately. Want to see if you have any coffee?"

The thought of actually putting anything in her stomach made Shelly gag. "Not unless you want some."

"No. Look, let's sit down, okay?" Lauren pushed aside a few of Wayne's shirts and cleared two seats on the couch.

Shelly sat down and stared at the shirts. "Wayne really isn't so bad. At least he loves me. He wants us to get married."

Lauren sighed. "We're supposed to learn from history, not repeat it," she commented shortly. "Why would you marry him? What kind of a father would he make for Brian? Or did you even think about that?"

Shelly relit the cigarette. "Brian's better off where he is."

"Is he? Shelly, do you know about what's going on with Parker? Or about what the papers are saying about me?"

"What? Is Pop okay? He's been hitting the bottle pretty hard, huh? I haven't been seeing much of him. I've kind of been avoiding him since that party thing. I figured he would give me a hard time." The smoke was rough going down, but it seemed to steady her nerves. "I haven't been reading the papers, either. Not lately."

Briefly Lauren told her about the Regis suit.

"God, I'm sorry, Lauren. I didn't mean to make it bad for you."

"Bad for me . . . that's not exactly how I'd put it." Lauren's face was filled with pain.

"I said I was sorry!" She laughed nervously. "What are you going to do, dock my allowance?" She asked the question with a teasing voice, but inside she was starting to feel really sick. She was nearly out of money and almost a week behind in the rent. She'd already decided that if Lauren didn't return soon or send money, she might have to take Wayne up on his offer to her to move in with him.

"Dock it, no," Lauren said very softly. "Stop it, yes."

Shelly couldn't believe what she was hearing. "Because of the party? Because you have to cut me off to get yourself out of trouble?" Anger stained her milk-white cheeks a dangerous red. "That's great! Thanks. Man, money sure has changed you! You'd throw your own sister to the dogs, just to save your own lousy neck."

"No, Shelly, you're wrong. My 'neck' has already been saved. They won't be able to attack Mrs. Regis's will." She turned her sister so she could look her in the face. "Shelly, honey, don't you realize that you're perfectly capable of taking care of yourself? Of making a real life for yourself and Brian? I've been holding you up so long you haven't had a chance to find out you can stand on your own. You can work. You're bright, pretty, fun. You like people and they like you, when you give them a chance. I've never given you a real chance to find out what you can be. I was always there, turning on all the lights for you before you even found out if you were afraid of the dark."

"No, Lauren, you're wrong! I am afraid. I can't make it on my own! I never could. I need help. I can't make it alone." Panic forced the words out. The stub of the cigarette was burning her fingers. She twisted away and put it out in an overflowing ashtray, hardly feeling the pain.

"You can, Shelly. How do you know you can't? When

did you ever try? You never needed me. Not in the way I thought you did. I'm more than willing to help you, but this time I can only help you help yourself. I foolishly thought if you had a nice place. . . ." She looked around. "This isn't such a nice place anymore, is it? You knew in your heart you never deserved so much for doing so little, so you've brought this place down to a more tolerable level. Damn it, Shelly! Look around."

"Is that all? I'll clean the apartment, Lauren! I've just been out of it, that's all. Is that what's bothering you?" She laughed a little hysterically. "Two hours, it'll look like it did when I moved in."

Lauren shook her head and passed her hand over her eyes, rubbing the skin on the bridge of her nose. "No. I was just trying to make a point. Shelly, what I'm trying to say is that it's over, no more free rides. I'll always be there to offer you a hand. But I won't pay to let you go on wallowing in the muck. Do you understand?"

"But what about the apartment? I don't have any money. Not even for food. And Brian? What about Brian? Who will pay for his school?" Shelly could still hardly believe this was happening.

"You have a last month's rent paid on the apartment, right? So that gives you a month more to get a job and another place to live, a place you can afford."

"There's no last month here. I . . . never actually said there was," she defended herself, looking down at her clasped hands. The burned spot on her finger was starting to form a white bubble.

Lauren paused. "Okay. I'll write you a check for the rent and food for a month. Then it's up to you. If you haven't found a job, you'll have to make other arrangements on your own."

"And Brian?" Lauren had always been soft about her nephew. Shelly could use her handsome son to put a stop to this madness.

"Parker had a good thought about Brian, Shelly. And it

could be good for you, too. I'm going to help him get a little restaurant somewhere outside the city. Something he can handle himself, with maybe one other person. He wants Brian to come live with him. He could go to a regular school and have a regular home life. He could help in the restaurant. They'd be good for each other, I think. And Shelly, Parker would like you to come, too. You could wait tables for him, you'd be with your father and your son. You'd have a real life, be part of a real family. You could all help each other. You could even have what you used to want so much, your father." She smiled a little. "All to yourself."

"Pop wanted me to come?" She was touched but suspicious. "He said that?"

"Yes. He said he wanted to be a real father to you. He wants one more chance with you. But first . . . he's going away. To a hospital. To dry out."

Shelly looked at her, wide-eyed with disbelief. "Was that your condition for helping him?"

Lauren shook her head. "No. It was his idea. You see, I only thought I knew what was best for him. Deep down he knew what he really needed, no matter what I thought."

Shelly worked Parker's decision over and over in her mind. She felt a grudging respect toward him. "That took guts. I didn't think Pop would ever face the boozing head on."

"Yes, it did take guts. And that's what you've got, too. You're his daughter, you know. Come on, Shelly, if he can do it, so can you. A million times easier. You're younger and stronger. You have Brian. You have a whole life still in front of you."

Shelly, still staring down at her hands, thought hard. Her father wanted her. She could learn how to be a mother to her son. But what would it be like, really? Some small dive of a cafe in some hick town. With what, maybe some nine-to-five guy with no excitement in his life, that would be her future. Sure, she'd like to be starting all over again with

270

her father, but it would be the same old story. Every time
she went out with some guy, Parker would be giving her
that look. And Brian . . . suddenly start to be a mother
when you don't even know who your son is? And what
would her days be like? Waiting tables, getting fat on Parker's cooking, smelling like grease by dinner time. "I don't
know, Lauren. Listen, how about letting me stay on here
a few more months, huh? Until Pop has his place going and
is sure he's going to stay. . . . You've got the money. You
wouldn't miss it."

Lauren, her lips compressed and her eyes wet, shook her
head. "Parker will be out of the hospital in a month. You
could start out together, the three of you. You can't wait
for him to do it all, set it up for you or it'll only be more
of the same. You won't have any real part in it. It won't
be yours, too. Sure, you'll miss the hard work, but you'll
also never know the rewards of that effort."

"I've never been real big on hard work," she said sul-
lenly.

"And you haven't had many rewards, either," Lauren
added. "Look, Shelly dear, this is your chance to get out
of a life-long habit of taking the easy way out. To stop
leaning on me, on men, on everyone but yourself. Support
is fine. You need it, Parker needs it. I need it. The choice
is going to be yours now. The way it should have been from
the beginning. You can start to build something, or you can
go on grasping at straws. You have to decide which way
it's going to be. And you have to make that decision for
Brian, as well. He's your son, not mine."

Shelly knew Lauren was right about that. The kid deserved a home life, family. He would be good for Parker,
and Parker for him. Whatever she decided for herself. Besides, if Lauren wouldn't foot the bill, there was no way
she could keep him in that fancy school. "Brian would like
being with his grandfather. Yes. About Brian. I . . . I have
to think about it for me."

271

After Lauren left, Shelly remained on the couch, the check for fifteen hundred dollars in her hand. It wouldn't go far, not if she paid the already overdue rent.

For a moment she contemplated being with her father and son, working in the restaurant, growing old and dull in some little town somewhere. Maybe she could do it. Maybe hard work did have its rewards. She tenderly touched the blister on her finger.

Wayne walked in. "Hi, baby. Where's the sister?"

"She left." She looked up at him. "She cut me off, Wayne. She's not going to give me any more money. She's sore about that party. It got her in trouble, and she cut me off." There seemed no point in telling him more. "What am I going to do?"

He stood there a moment, his face set in a deep frown. Then he brightened. "So what? Big deal. You've got me, Shelly, baby. I wasn't putting you on. I've really got a big thing for you. What's that in your hand?" He walked over and took the check. "Hey, hey!"

"That's for the rent and a little extra," she said dully. "It's already late."

He laughed. "Great. Listen, here's what we do. We very quickly and quietly blow this dump. I can get this furniture sold and hauled away in a couple of hours. We grab our stuff and move on over to my place tonight. In a fancy set-up like this, they won't know what happened for weeks. They won't be expecting it. With this money and what we get for the furniture, we're in comfort city until I get my next check from the new investor. We'll do great." He sat down next to her and pulled her onto his lap. "Hey, don't look so sad. I said I'd take care of you."

She looked up into his bland, handsome face, felt his strong arms around her. What was it Lauren had said? Something about clinging to the easiest solution to her problems rather than working for a real happy ending?

Wayne kissed her hard. She could feel that old excitement stirring again. She sighed contentedly. Maybe she was doing it again. Tying herself to the same kind of man she'd always settled for in the past. One who would eventually tire of her and leave. Or one who would abuse her so that sooner or later she would leave.

But for the moment, she was safe. Lauren was right. She was an adult. The choice was hers to make.

Chapter Twenty-five

The whole beautiful weekend was theirs, hours and hours to squander however they wished. They planned for it like two children approaching a long-awaited summer vacation.

"We'll go to the beach, of course. And to Lion Country Safari." Anthony screwed up his gorgeous features. "Unless, of course, now that you can afford the real thing you'd rather hop over to Africa."

"This one will be just fine, thank you. Now that I've got you, I don't want to risk losing you to some cannibals." Lauren laughed. "Where else do you want to go?"

He turned the Mercedes toward the beach, taking Sunset Boulevard with its long curves and beautiful homes. "I'll tell you my real fantasies for a beautiful weekend alone with you later. First some sun, then some fun. . . ."

There were some very nice things about being rich, she decided as they sped past Brentwood. They would stop at the first store they passed and buy tanning cream and suits and whatever else they wanted. They could lunch at any restaurant they wanted, or just snack from the hot dog joints on the coast road. They could do anything. It was a nice feeling, but she no longer had the same old illusions. It would be a good life, but they were still the ones who had to make it good. Money alone could never buy happiness, just like the tired but true cliche said. She knew. She had already put it to the test.

"Just one more question, before we forget about work for two blissful days," Anthony said, negotiating a curve with ease. "You know, I'm glad I grew up enough to be willing to take your car and leave mine home when we're together. I hate to admit it, but it handles a whole lot better than mine."

"Good. Your question?"

"Why have you decided to keep quiet about the tape and let Earl Regis have his day in court, after all? The newspapers are really giving you a beating with all those innuendos about firing Parker and axing Shelly to improve your chances at the hearing."

"Chris and I talked it over. I feel it's as good a way as any to flush out spies. The board needs a good shake-up. New blood, Alexandra called it. She's right. I'm going to place Chris on the board. And Nate Beglau is really terrific. With him at my side, it'll be my day in court, not Earl's. It's time he retired, anyway. Poor Abrams has deserved that job for a long time. Alexandra might not be Loni Anderson, but she deserves prime time, don't you think?"

Anthony laughed.

They found a clothing store and a drug store, bought beach towels as well as suits, and located their old favorite spot in Malibu. The sun was just right, good and hot but not too cruel for their first day out. The sand warmed their toes, and the water was cold enough to make them feel fresh and alive.

After a quick lunch, they made the long trek to Laguna Hills and leisurely drove through Lion Country Safari. Both of them loved the unusual zoo that allowed its animals to run free while the people were caged in their cars. They parked in the middle of an elephant herd, watched baby lions tumble, turned off the motor and made faces back at an inquisitive flock of ostriches that were peering through the windshield. Then they bought silly hats and ice cream.

They arrived back at Lauren's house in time for dinner. Tuxedo went to Anthony before greeting his mistress. Lauren pretended to be deeply hurt.

Later, upstairs, they listened to music and took turns showering.

"When are you going to tell me about your opera?" she asked, combing her long hair while he watched, naked but for his jeans, his own hair still damp.

"Later."

"When later? Why later? It's finished, isn't it?"

He smiled his secret smile, but it didn't bother her any more. She knew him too well, trusted him too much to cloud her happiness with senseless doubting.

"The opera?" He laughed. "Yes, it's done."

"Well, tell me about it."

He laughed again and took the brush from her hand. Gently, he pulled her from her chair before the dressing table and into his arms. Her silky white gown was like a thin layer of ice separating the warmth of their bodies. "I will. Before the night is over."

"Isn't it over?"

He brought his lips close. "No. It's just about to begin."

He kissed her then. It was a kiss unlike any she'd ever had from him. It held no question, no restraint. His mouth moved over hers, taking, demanding more, igniting lightning flashes of desire, fire storms of passion. He only stopped kissing her long enough to strip the white gown from her trembling body, kick his way out of his jeans.

Naked, every inch of their flesh embracing, they kissed again. His hands clutched fistfuls of waving oceanic hair, bringing it forward to cover them both, a waterfall of silk, screening them and their magic love from the world.

Somehow, they found their way to the bed. Somehow, the lights were dimmed. And somehow, in the near darkness, in the finite span of one night, they managed to find enough time to die and be reborn over and over again.

Weak and still trembling, they held each other tightly, kissing, touching as if they would never be able to stop.

"So are you going to make an honest woman out of me or what?" she asked, barely able to speak as the dawn filtered through the windows in pale yellow shafts.

"Didn't I tell you?" He kissed her ear. "In the fall."

"The fall?" she complained. She made a feeble attempt to sit up but failed and slumped back against him, laughing. "Can't I be a summer bride?"

"It has to be in the fall. And in London." The secret smile was back. He squinted at the first rays of morning. "And I'd better tell you quick. The night is about over, I guess."

"Your opera!" She twisted so she could see his face better, careful not to move out of the precious shelter of his warm arms.

"It's called *The Princess of Park Avenue*. And it will premiere in London on the tenth of October. I thought that would be a catchy date for our wedding. Besides, it will make remembering anniversaries a snap."

"October 10. Ten/ten. Not bad. Not bad at all." She could see his face very clearly now, even the fine blue stubble on his chin. "It's morning, and you promised. . . ."

He began to stroke her body, but she grabbed his hand.

"No distractions. Not until you're through," she said, holding his palm to her breast.

He sighed and placed his stubbly cheek against her soft hair. "Well, it's a story about a very special woman who inherits a kingdom of limitless splendors—all of Manhattan in the opera. It's a modern day fairy tale, you see. Filled with metaphor and allegory, romance and morals." He looked at her with sheepish amusement.

"And what happens to this . . . woman?" But she was smiling, amused and pleased, already well aware of the identity of Anthony's princess.

"She goes off in search of an even greater treasure, which turns out to be the love she has always had."

Laughing, she snuggled back down in his arms and lifted her lips for his kiss. "I never would have guessed."

She knew she could wait for more details later on. She was already living the "happily ever after" part.

About the Author

Marsha Alexander is a full-time writer who was born in New York but did most of her growing up in Hollywood and the Los Angeles area. Having New York, Hollywood and Beverly Hills as playgrounds was a terrific break for a budding novelist: her classmates were future movie stars and colorful jet-setters. Peter Bogdanovich was her first love (at the age of thirteen), and together they "wrote" and "directed" pictures on the streets of Bayside, Long Island.

More significant, however, was Marsha's chance to observe the dual nature of wealth and fame. Early in life she learned that every Midas must pay a price for that touch of gold, and that when it comes to love, we are all equally required to put in a long apprenticeship.

A widow, she is kept busy with her three daughters— Lauren, twenty; Kimberly, thirteen; and Sage Autumn, four. A dog, a cat, a hamster and four goldfish (Moe, Joe, Bo and Arrow) make up the rest of the household. Together they all continually remind her that in matters of love, she, too, is still serving that apprenticeship.

Enjoy your own special time with Silhouette Romances

Take 4 books FREE!

Silhouette Romances take you into a special world of thrilling drama, tender passion, and romantic love. These are enthralling stories from your favorite romance authors—tales of fascinating men and women, set in exotic locations.

We think you'll want to receive Silhouette Romances regularly. We'll send you six new romances every month to look over for 15 days. If not delighted, return only five and owe nothing. **One book is always yours free.** There's never a charge for postage or handling, and no obligation to buy anything at any time. **Start with your free books.** Mail the coupon today.

Silhouette Romances